YARN AUTHORITY
PRESENTS

We'd like to thank our families for supporting us, all of our local friends, and the beautiful northern Vermont, for providing all of the inspiration necessary to bring this novel to life.

*Murder Mountain* is a work of fiction. While real life people and locations have inspired our words and illustrations, everything herein is fictitious and any uncanny resemblance to reality is coincidental.

# MURDER MOUNTAIN

## A ROSEFIELD SERIES NOVEL

WRITTEN BY

**OWEN CURVELO**

ILLUSTRATED BY

**KATYA STRASBURGER**

**ROSEFIELD**
*Mountain Resort*

**TRAIL**

**GUIDE**

# ROSEFIELD
## Mountain Resort
### BRING YOUR BUDS

**TRAIL GUIDE**

Easy Way Around ◼

Elvis Chute ◆

RUSCH CHUTE

◆ Boulder C

Sc

◆ The Foot

THE HITCH

THE FISHBOWL

Le Jardinet ○

◼ Upper Parade

◼ Mule Run

◼ Ma Biche

Easy Way Around ○

◆ W

THE KITCHEN

The Barge

Whittle Path ○

◼ Squirrel Run

◼ Open Glade

◼ Lower Parade

Greenh

WE

Meet Rosefield's Patrol Dog:
12 year old Boomer.
We've asked him to retire. He
says next season.

🅿

🅿 PARK & GRILL

🅿

○ Beginner
◼ Intermidiate
◆ Advanced

**UPHILL TRAVEL POLICY:** You must purchase an Uphill Travel Pass at Customer
Service. DO NOT snowshoe, hike, or skin without first purchasing an Uphill Travel
Pass. We don't care that your cousin's best friend works in the rental shop.

**SUMMIT ELEVATION:** 3,342 ft.

**VERTICAL DROP:** 1,267 ft.

**ANNUAL SNOWFALL:** 583 cm.

**SKI AREA BOUNDARY POLICY:** If you leave the ski area, you're on your own. Just kidding. But seriously, if you get stuck in the Flats, it's a long hike out. And Ski Patrol will give you their snowshoes from the '50s.

**THE LIFTS:**

**UPRIDGE QUAD:** Brings you to that ridge up there.
**ABSOLUTE ZERO TRIPLE:** In the PJ Zone, you'll receive a perfect bump.
**MID-DRIFT DOUBLE:** Rip this chair to eliminate your mid-drift.
**Y200 T-BAR:** Pop this between your legs for the ride of your life.

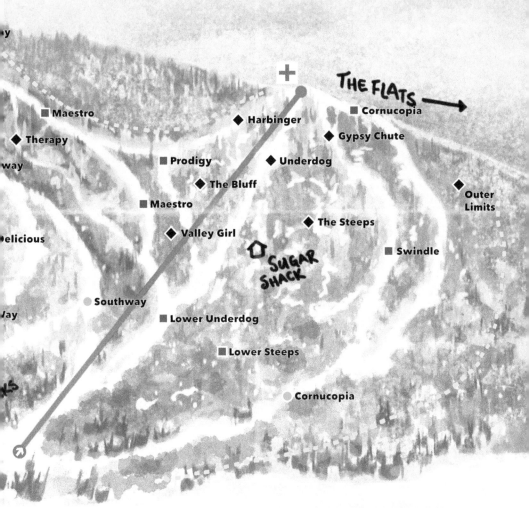

THE FLATS →

Maestro

Therapy

Harbinger

Cornucopia

Gypsy Chute

Prodigy

Underdog

The Bluff

Maestro

Outer Limits

The Steeps

Valley Girl

SUGAR SHACK

Swindle

elicious

Southway

Lower Underdog

Lower Steeps

Cornucopia

DON'T BOTHER

✚ SKI PATROL (802) 326-2113

**WOODS SKIING POLICY:** If you're new, keep to the trails without trees. All woods, whether named or not, are at your own risk. If you injure yourself and require assistance, crawl to a trail, and Ski Patrol will find you during their evening sweep.

TERRAIN PARK

LEARNING ZONE

MOUNTAIN VIEW HOTEL

GENERALLY SLANTED

# Table of Contents

## GENERALLY SLANTED
"Prices as slanted as the foundation"

## MOUNTAIN VIEW HOTEL
"Some rooms overlook the slopes"

## MOUNTAIN VIEW RESTAURANT
"Mediocre dining at resort prices"

## SQUIRREL LODGE
"An old lodge with a classic odor"

## THE BENT POLE
"Perfect place for a beer--for warmth or courage"

## THE SLED STOP
"We don't Stop: open breakfast, lunch, dinner, and late-night!"

## DAFFODIL HARVEST
"Cheap organic produce with a generic taste!"

## THE RED BARN
"An abandoned barn with a dark history. . ."

## ROSEFIELD ELEMENTARY
"Nicknamed the Rez by today's youth."

## CODY'S COUNTRY STORE
"Deli, tools, guns, and light groceries, all a Vermonter needs."

## ENOSBURG
"15 minutes away, closest hardware store.
Oh, and better groceries too."

## SAINT ALBANS
"30 minutes away, home of VerMart and other big box stores.
Plus fancy groceries."

# JOEY ROGERS

GENERATIONAL LEVEL FIRST (ANYONE WHO SAYS LESS IS A LIAR!)

**AGE:** 22, JUST STARTING TO REACH PEAK PERFORMANCE

**FAVORITE SEASON:** ONLY A FLATTY WOULD ASK THAT

**RESPECT LEVEL:** ALMOST-PRO SKIER AND SMALL-TOWN HERO

**WHEN HE SEES A JUMP:** HE HITS IT EVEN IF IT'S THE BIGGEST EVER? MORE AIRTIME FOR FLIPS

# PEGGY MCSTOOTS

GENERATIONAL LEVEL
FOURTH OR SIXTH, HER
GRANDMAS NEVER COULD
AGREE

AGE: OLD ENOUGH TO AVOID
QUESTIONS LIKE THAT
FAVORITE BOOK: SEASONAL
COLORS BY LYDIA MCSTOOTS
OCCUPATION: ROSEFIELD'S
SHERIFF FOR THE PAST FIVE YEARS
WHEN SHE SEES A
PROBLEM: SHE HITS IT HEAD-ON
EVEN IF IT'S BEFORE COFFEE?
NOTHING HAPPENS BEFORE FIRST
COFFEE

# RODNEY
# BURIC II

GENERATIONAL LEVEL: ZERO. RODNEY WOULDN'T TOLERATE GROWING UP RURAL

AGE: YOUNG ENOUGH TO BUILD AN EMPIRE
FAVORITE ENTERTAINMENT: SOUL PESTLE, OBVIOUSLY
THEORY ON THE FINALE: KAPPU DEFEATS LORD KETORU WITH AN EPIC COMPOSITION
HIS GREATEST REGRET: ONLY HAVING ONE RESORT TO HIS PORTFOLIO
WHAT IF HE LOSES HIS BET WITH FATHER? BAH, IMPOSSIBLE!

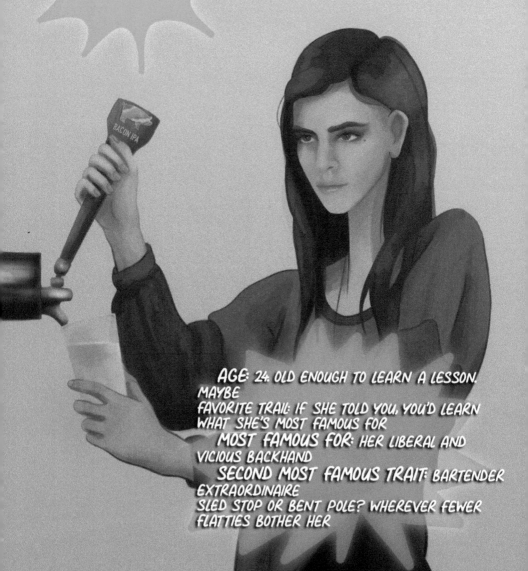

# JANE REACH

**GENERATIONAL LEVEL:** FOURTH AND FINAL, HEADING WEST ONCE SAVED UP

**AGE:** 24. OLD ENOUGH TO LEARN A LESSON. MAYBE

**FAVORITE TRAIL:** IF SHE TOLD YOU, YOU'D LEARN WHAT SHE'S MOST FAMOUS FOR

**MOST FAMOUS FOR:** HER LIBERAL AND VICIOUS BACKHAND

**SECOND MOST FAMOUS TRAIT:** BARTENDER EXTRAORDINAIRE

**SLED STOP OR BENT POLE?** WHEREVER FEWER FLATTIES BOTHER HER

HAPPY SMITH

GENERATIONAL LEVEL:
FIFTH IN A LONG LINE OF SMITH

AGE: 22-YEAR-OLD BACHELOR
FAVORITE DAY OF THE MONTH: GRANDMA DAY
PASS EARNER: RENTAL RAT, TWO DAYS A WEEK
CURRENT HOUSING: A SINGLE ROOM CABIN
DOES HE WANT MORE? HECK NO. THINK OF THE DEER

The first snowstorm hit Rosefield, which meant Joey headed to the mountain. A solid inch greeted him as he stepped out of his house at 9 AM. All he hankered. Joey tried convincing the other Powder Boys into joining him for the hike, but they all responded the same way: not enough snow. Hah! Joey would show them. He whipped together his pack, grabbed his skis, hopped in his truck, and sped east on Route 13.

He slowed to a modest thirty-five mph when he drove through Rosefield. Sheriff Peggy told him he better follow the speed limit in town, or she'd confiscate his skis. He knew her threat was sincere, especially after Joey's minor accident last Christmas morning. Plus, Peggy always ate breakfast at the Sled Stop. She would catch him speeding.

As sure as a January Nor'easter, Peggy strode from her green Jeep to the Sled's front door. Joey stopped to congratulate her. He parked on the street and rolled the passenger window down.

"Hey Peggy, I heard Lyndsay has another baby McStoots on the way."

"Gregory-McStoots," corrected Peggy. She wore her leather jacket, elbows faded from decades of use. Without it, she was a regular Rosefield resident, and unless the fire department caught ablaze again, she wouldn't answer her phone. "Heading up to the mountain for the first snow?"

"I never miss the first snowstorm."

"Only an inch dropped last night."

"That's plenty for an almost-pro like me." Joey laughed. "It just adds to the challenge."

"Be careful. I don't want to drive up there today."

"I'm no flatty!" protested Joey. "I'm familiar with every stream, tree, and boulder on the mountain. No trail could possibly harm me."

"Sorry, guy." Peggy sighed. "Enjoy yourself."

Joey shot her a two-fingered wave, and she returned with the same. He rolled up his window, turned onto Left Mountain Road, and slammed the accelerator. Outside of town, Joey shifted into turbo.

After driving eighty mph and passing three cars, he arrived at the resort in two and a half minutes. He parked at the sign to pay respect to the logo, a rose with its petals shaped like Rosefield Mountain's ridgeline. He raised his arms in an X and shouted, "For snow and for glory!"

Next, he nodded in respect to the distinguished ski tycoon Rodney Buric II. His first act as owner three years ago was installing a second sign with a photo of himself. He might not resemble a skier with his bulbous figure, but he knew everything about the industry. Rodney said so himself. Joey couldn't imagine possessing such tremendous knowledge *and* owning a ski resort at thirty-nine years old. Now that was a man with sharp edges.

With respect paid, Joey straight-lined it to the parking lot. He whipped in so fast, the rear end of his pickup fishtailed out. Nothing announced your arrival like kicking up a dust cloud. He slid his rig into the closest spot to the slope, right next to Timmy Harton's black truck.

"Biscuit my dog. He beat me to it." Joey stomped his boot before shouting up the mountain. "Save some for me!"

Knowing Timmy, he'd scratch off all the best snow—on purpose. A jerk no one liked. He picked fights every weekend at the Sled Stop and cussed out Cody's checkout girls whenever they messed up. Not to mention the incident with his horse a few years back. What drove a man to behave so horribly? Joey shuddered, then shook the memory. He should keep his mind on the snow.

He threw on his bright blue jacket, matching his Scandinavian eyes, with racer white stripes to complement his (sort-of) naturally blonde hair. His snow pants sported a factory smell; Joey always upgraded his gear at the start of a season.

He pressed his hand against the 'POW Life' sticker on his truck bumper and immediately felt energized. He muttered his slogan, his motto, his mantra, "For snow and for glory."

He said goodbye to his unnamed pickup, replacing the Snow Slayer. Joey totaled it last winter. Apparently, the Snow Slayer needed to drop a gear to complete a turn sometimes, especially during ice storms. His new truck had even better handling. It would rip through snowstorms with the same ease as his brand-new Tail skis.

Joey hiked the steps along Squirrel Lodge. Even from outside, he whiffed its signature aroma of sweat, feet, and stale cafeteria food. He breathed in long and slow, letting the familiar scent trigger decades of memories. Ah, what an extraordinary odor.

"I hankered my first whiff, too."

"Jordan." Joey recognized the speaker before he raised his eyes. Only one man possessed a voice that deep. "I meant to call you."

"What for?" He wore his yellow Ski School jacket, a matching helmet, and his eternal frown.

"You know," grunted Joey once he reached the landing. "Just to confirm my position is . . . available."

"If you have a job?" He carried a backpack with strapped-on L3 skis, scraped and chipped from a decade of usage. "After you lost that kid in the Flats last spring?"

"I found him before last chair," protested Joey. "And I *truly* thought he could keep up."

"I'd fire you, but I lack the numbers. Besides, I'd axe Timmy first."

"He's the worst! Remember the horse incident? The broken piece of plywood still haunts my dreams."

"It's the two-by-four for me."

"And now," said Joey, pointing up the hill, "he's scratching off the best snow."

"Timmy's here?" Jordan squeezed his mittens until his knuckles burned. "I missed his arrival while in my office. Which trail did he hike?"

"He's probably heading to the top for the deep stuff." Joey shrugged. "I know that's my destination."

"To Absolute Zero for me, I'd rather avoid a confrontation today." Jordan clenched his jaw until his cheeks bulged. "I'm still angry about last spring."

"What happened?"

"I take great pride in my position as Park & Grill's top culinary judge. My palate is impeccable."

"You've been a fixture of the judging team since the days you taught me to ski."

"Nineteen years," confirmed Jordan. "Timmy spread a rumor I took bribes. I'd never!"

Oh yeppers, Joey remembered the incident. Rodney almost banned Jordan from officiating, but Peter Smith forced a confession out of Timmy before competition day. "Why'd he do that?"

"Because he missed his chance at stardom while I became Rosefield's Director of Ski School."

"Uh-huh." In Rosefield, a Rez established rivalry often endured for life.

"Sorry, guy," said Jordan, tightening his backpack. "I oughta cool off."

"We better hit the snow before it melts," agreed Joey.

Jordan started up Lower Underdog while Joey hiked Greenhouse Way. He cut through Woods Delicious to the headwall on Southway, which he followed to the top.

He required two breaks; only weaklings needed more. During his first stop, he powered down an energy drink produced by his cousin James. Flying Purple flavor, Joey's favorite, featuring a hint of grape combined with cups of sugar and energy compounds. At the Fish Bowl, he powered down an energy bar breakfast, also concocted by his cousin. Cashew Chunk, but James replaced the titular nut with peanuts as they were far cheaper.

Halfway through breakfast, Joey noticed Timmy shredding the next trail over. He waved, but the guy was too busy popping off boulders on his red Astronomics. For a man in his forties, Timmy still skied as though training for the Olympic tryouts. Apparently, he placed five spots shy of the USA slalom team.

Joey would succeed in his place. Maybe next year, he'd solicit some agents or trainers. He had the rest of his twenties.

Timmy never flourished as a pro because he simply lacked style. His purple pants mismatched his bright green jacket, and his goggles clearly came off the clearance rack. He didn't wear a helmet, either. How unsafe.

Joey finished the hike to the top in under two hours. *Boom!*

The sight of the Upridge Bullwheel cresting the top of the mountain always put a smile on his face. Its orange rails encircled the yellow wheel with perfect symmetry. The brown lift shack tilted off the cliff as though ready to ski down the mountain itself. All blessed with two inches of crusty white fluff.

Above towered the Upridge Shelter. As the sixteenth largest mountain in the state, it boasted one of the grandest views in Vermont. A pair of south-facing windows offered a tremendous hundred-eighty degree angle of Mount Mansfield. Breathtaking.

Once he had his fill, he hiked along the ridge to the trail he deemed fit for the first run of the season. He dreamt about it all summer. Usually, he dropped Boulder Chute, the hardest trail on the mountain. However, this summer, a few industrious trailblazers cut the newest hardest trail, Rusch Chute, named after the late ski legend Nick Rusch. Joey might as well send it.

When he arrived at the top, Joey dropped his skis and stepped into his carbon-fiber bindings. He slipped his hands through the straps of his brand-new poles. They enjoyed a couple of massive upgrades from last year's version with auto tightening wrists straps and the deepest racer bend ever crafted.

He put his earbuds in and selected the greatest band south of Montpelier, the Rutland Rotary Boys. A northern rock band with a southern soul, illustrated by their uniform white cowboy hats. The guitarist, Hector Yacoven, strummed chords once considered impossible. The lead singer, Seth Alltheway, possessed a vocal range that hit every octave. When he skied the best, he listened to the best.

He chose 'Small Town Hero," one of his favorite songs:

SMALL
TOWN
HEERO

JONATHAN G. WEEVIL,
HE'S OUR TOWN HERO.

HE CAN SENSE EVIL,
AMID A SLED RETRIEVAL.
MAKE ANY CROP GROW
AND A PLOW DYNAMO.

"BACK OFF!" SHOUTS MR. WEEVIL
AT A TOWN MEETING UPHEAVAL.
"YOU FLATTIES WANT BILLBOARDS?
WE WON'T BOW TO YOUR LORDS!"

THEY RAN, TOO,
FACES ALL BLUE.
THIS HERE'S TRUE,
IF YOU'RE NEW,
DON'T ACT DUE
OR YOU'LL RUE

OUR SMALL-TOWN HERO-O!
JONATHAN G. WEE-EEVIL!
AIN'T NO ZERO-O!

Often Joey felt like Rosefield's small-town hero. He threw the coolest tricks and skied the most challenging terrain. Plus, he taught the Rosfieldian youth how to achieve the same twice a week in Ski School. Was *anyone* more heroic than that?

Embracing the notion, he began his descent. He side slid the top chute to the first turn and swung his skis around with perfect precision. He drifted down into the buttery snow, spraying the white waves against the boulder backdrop. On his second turn, he swooped his skis around the next grouping of pines, greedily scratching off every ounce of cheddar. Turn three, he caught his edge on a rock and launched downhill face first.

He ejected out of both skis and tumbled down the ridge. By jamming his boot heels into the snow, he skillfully dodged pines and maples as he descended. He shielded himself from the boulders with his arms. One snuck through his defenses and smashed up his nose. When he skidded to a halt twenty feet later, both nostrils gushed blood.

The risk every almost-pro skier accepted: when you went big, sometimes you wiped big, too. Whatever. At least his skis skidded to a halt nearby. His poles, well, they sucked anyway, not a deep enough racer bend. And the reason he fell, most likely.

Joey retrieved his tactical folding knife from his bag and cut two strips from his shirt for nose clogging. Then he fetched his skis and slid down an easier trail. The lower grade runs deserved attention, too, and he shouldn't show off every moment. He skied Le Jardinet to Mule Run until the snow thinned to grass.

Instead of taking Whittle Path the rest of the way down, he stomped through the woods off skier's left. Open Glade, where they chopped down ninety-nine percent of the trees for beginners. Disgusting. It could've been a hundred times better, but the flatties ruined everything.

Halfway through, he spotted Timmy's bright green jacket hanging off a branch. Why would he ski a newbie trail? Joey crept closer. A chill wind swept through the trees, raising goosebumps while his knees trembled. Something wasn't right. He *sensed* it. No worries, Rosefield's very own small-town hero Joey Rogers had arrived.

When he located Timmy, however, he was beyond saving. He leaned up against a great white oak with a giant knife stuck in his chest.

"Timmy!" Joey rushed forward, but the guy was a goner. RIP. All those words. Timmy's skin matched the snow. His eyes gazed ahead with an unblinking stillness that weakened Joey's knees. He dropped his skis and crumbled to the ground.

He had never seen a dead person before. For a moment, he considered his mortality. While Joey navigated a fall like a champion, his nose and forehead ached from his encounter with the rock. If he'd connected with one of those trees, he might have broken something permanent.

Ope. An almost-pro couldn't afford to entertain such negativities. Send it big or not at all.

Timmy understood the pressures of being a local ski legend. He couldn't resist the ever-looming urge to pull the next epic trick. He probably attempted to balance his knife while boot shredding on the dusted leaves. Tragically, Timmy biffed the ultimate landing.

Joey wiped some eye wetness and grabbed his second energy drink from his backpack. He ripped off the cap and poured out half. Sure, Timmy would've preferred a Bacon (or some other IPA), but the Bent Pole wasn't open yet for the season. Joey chugged the rest. Then he hiked down to alert security of the tragic accident.

Peggy began her day at the usual 8 AM with a cup of Tootin' from Roaster Dan. She added a healthy pour of Old Gregor's Crude Raw Milk, *less than a week from the teat*. Not her best rhyme, but as Lydia told her, the poem's story outweighed the lyric.

Besides letting Diohgee out, nothing happened before she downed that first cup of coffee. Not even if Bob Hordell rang. Like last Christmas morning, he called eight times because Joey slid off the road and knocked a telephone pole across Main Street. She didn't answer, not once, not until she consumed her first full mug of caffeinated glory.

Peggy reviewed The Facebook for updates on her three daughters and five grandbabies (with a sixth on the way) while she sipped. After Mary Anne graduated from college next year, she'd move back from Burlington and settle down with a nice young man. Then she could pop out a couple of babies of her own. Of course, that was her decision.

After checking in with The Facebook, Peggy read at least one poem from Lydia McStoots' masterful collection, *Seasonal Colors*. Today, she decided on this well-fertilized nugget titled "Pre-Pellet."

The owl glides through the trees,
eyeing the laden forest ground.
The rodent flees
but caught with ease,
and consumed after the prayer sound.

Ah, she loved starting the day with a hunting story. One of Siaytee's favorite poems, too, she purred on Peggy's lap while she read it aloud.

At 9 AM and not a moment sooner, she threw on Robert's ten-year-old leather jacket and exited her house. She strode to her office, a twenty-year-old green Jeep her husband had maintained for her. After he died, she named it after him: Road Runner Robert.

After becoming sheriff five years ago, she installed a couple of modifications in case she needed to arrest somebody. She disabled the inside rear door handles and placed metal fencing between the front and back seats. No arrests yet, but it was better to overpack than return without a new pair of antlers.

She hopped in and turned the key, but the Road Runner just clicked at her. Bad starter. She'd teach it a hard truth. Peggy grabbed the stick she kept in the trunk. Three strikes later, lesson learned; the starter engaged and the engine turned on. She pulled out of her driveway and turned down Left Mountain Road.

While she considered herself officially on duty once she pulled out of her driveway, she still wouldn't answer her phone. It wasn't safe using the ol' cellular while driving. Probably illegal, too, but Peggy didn't need to know those specifics to sheriff Rosefield.

Her first destination was always the same, the Sled Stop. A cafe during the day and an (often raucous) bar at night. She parked next to Frank's black truck out front. After a brief exchange with Joey on his way up to the resort, Peggy entered through the wooden front door.

She claimed her favorite booth, next to the stuffed black bear Uncle James shot thirty years ago. Jane must have noticed her Jeep pull up as a coffee and newspaper awaited. Once settled, Peggy perused the headlines.

"Sheldon Dairy switching to goats next summer." Ope. Another farm planned on ditching their cows, citing the cheaper cost and improved environmental impact. While Peggy enjoyed a goat cheese on occasion, she preferred the cow version.

"Legendary Hornet defense overwhelmed Lake Region in Enosburg's first home game." Go Hornets! The only athletic outfit

Peggy followed, professional or otherwise. The girls' soccer team had several excellent strikers. They might make the playoffs.

"Stoplight to be installed in Jay." Oh no. Peggy panicked until she read it was temporary while they repaired a bridge on Route 242. There were enough of those awful things in northern Vermont already.

What a big news day. *Peggy didn't mind a single potato rind,* as it put off her messages that much longer. Unfortunately, she'd run out of headlines. She set the newspaper aside and picked up her cellular.

Since it was a Monday, she expected a half dozen messages from her fellow Rosefieldians. Maybe a kid drove his four-wheeler over somebody's lawn, or a hunter triggered on their neighbor's property. Maybe some teenager honked and swerved all over the road late Saturday night. Hardly anything more than small-town pettiness, not worth Peggy's energy. Yet she replied to each one, showing the townsfolk their sheriff assisted with their squabbles.

Today, however, Peggy encountered zero messages on her phone. Only spam on her email, too. Not a single issue all weekend? Suspicious. Well, no messages today meant no work for Peggy.

"I haven't seen you this happy since Lindsay's pregnancy announcement," said Jane when she returned for a refill. Her black hair matched her grandmother, the ramen-slinging Nami Reech, who still served her authentic noodles at every farmer's market. "What's up today?"

"Nothing." Peggy pointed at her phone. "Not a single issue for me to deal with."

"Congratulations! It's practically a holiday. Your usual?" Jane pulled a pad and pen from her jeans.

"Actually, in celebration, throw on a side of cheddar."

"Gregory's?"

"Is there any other kind? *A slice of Gregory's cheddar will make your day better.*"

"Hey, that's clever," laughed Jane. "Gregory's coming right up."

While she waited for breakfast, Peggy enjoyed her reprieve. She pondered the car and snowmobile parts adorning the ceiling.

Frank Woodlet shuffled through papers at the bar, occasionally swearing and pounding his fist. He wasn't much of a numbers guy, more of a bourbon guy. How many times had Peggy driven him home after he parked his car in a ditch?

Jane delivered her breakfast, and Peggy's phone remained silent. She picked at her eggs and burnt toast (how she preferred it) and stared out the window.

Full-on stick season. Raked leaves in front of every house, the naked trees readied for winter. John and Wilma's kids, Todd, Amy, and Jordan, set up a cider stand in front of Cody's Country Store. The Viceroy boys occupied the church steps, flicking rocks onto the road. Hopefully, they kept their mischief modest; half of the complaints she received somehow involved either John or Henry Viceroy.

Bear patrolled outside of Slick Mick's for belly rubbings and head scratchings. For a St. Bernard the size of a dirt bike, he was as gentle as a tricycle. He earned quite a few pets from all of Mickey's customers seeking their pre-season tune. Surprisingly, she didn't spot Cody's Tug-Tug, Bear's yellow Labrador best friend. They wandered all around town together, even visiting Peggy halfway up Left Mountain Road.

What a pleasant fall morning. Peggy shouldn't waste it at the Sled Stop. At 11 AM, she settled with Jane and drove down to the Post Office. Postmaster Carol, Peggy's number one informant, enjoyed the best gossip in town.

"Old Gregor lost a cow on Saturday," said Carol. Her freshly curled grey hair matched her work jumpsuit.

"Oh yeah?"

"They spent four hours rounding it up."

"Waste of an afternoon."

"Not for us onlookers." Carol chuckled. "We fetched some ciders and laughed our stomachs red!"

Peggy chuckled herself, then grabbed her mail and returned to the Road Runner.

With no sheriffing duties, she had the whole afternoon for herself. Peggy decided to visit one of her favorite spots, Big Mountain Bridge, just a half-mile west of town.

As she moseyed along Route 13, she passed the recreation center. A sufficient field, with a baseball diamond and backstop in one corner, soccer nets on either side, a pavilion, and a sandy jungle gym. At the center was a bronze statue of Jacques Allen, the Green Mountain Boys hero who died staving off the expansionist New Yorkers. It marked the location of the only northern skirmish to occur during Vermont's Revolution. Considering Jacques's bravery always rose Peggy's cheeks.

A minute later, she arrived at Big Mountain Bridge and parked at the pull-off next to the metal onramp. She hiked down to the massive boulder, which sloped gently into the Mulberry River. From the pinnacle, she observed the water crashing against rocks before the waterfall. At the bottom, the falls carved out a wide bowl, leaving sandy beaches on both sides. Locals coined the spot Jagged Falls, the most popular swimming hole in town. Some of Rosefieldian's most foolish, like the Viceroy boys, would jump from the top of the falls or the surrounding cliffs. Every ten years or so, somebody landed too close to the rocks and broke their neck.

More peaceful here at the bridge, and more fish. One of Peggy's favorite places to drop hook, although she hadn't dug her pole out of the garage in over seven years. Instead, *she lounged on a shaded boulder and let the soft wind hold her*. Not terrible. A peaceful morning often inspired her to write lyrics.

Then her phone rang. She stepped off the boulder before answering. "Yes?"

"Peggy, is that you?" clamored James McJoy, Rosefield Mountain's head of security.

"Yepper."

"Peggy McStoots? Sheriff?"

He'd called her on this phone for years. Who else would possess this number? Peggy sighed again. That helped. One more would put her in the right spot. She filled her lungs with breath, held it for a second, and exhaled through her nostrils. Better. "Yes, Jim. It's Sheriff McStoots."

"Okay. I need you at Squirrel Lodge. There's a humdinger of a situation if you're stackin' what I'm choppin'."

"Calm down and tell me what's happened."

"I ain't heard of anything similar. That's why I hankered your identity. Jeezum Crow, this is one heck of a humdinger."

Peggy waited for him to catch his breath. Jim often grew frantic over an inch or two, but he seemed more distraught than usual. Something serious had occurred.

"Joey burst into my office with his nose busted up. Limping, dried blood, and whatnot. Luckier than a three-year-old hare, I decided to work on scheduling today. I asked Joey what happened to his nose, and he shouted, 'My nose is fine!' It's clearly not, damn near broken if you ask—"

"Is this all because he hurt himself on the mountain? Like he does every other week?" Peggy groaned. "I told him I didn't want to drive up there today."

"Nopers. Well, Joey *did* hurt himself. Those rocks are bullies when you cross them."

"Jim."

"Right, once we concluded his injury assessment, he informed me that he found Timmy. Dead. Up in the woods, that trail with the trees."

"Timmy Harton?"

"Yepper."

"How did he die?"

"I haven't hiked up. Joey said Timmy fell on his own knife while attempting a trick. That doesn't sound like Timmy to me, though."

"I'll be right there, Jim." Peggy hung up before he could say anything else.

She climbed into the Road Runner and drove back to town. What did she know about Timmy Harton anyway? A first-generation Rosefieldian, he was born a couple of years after his parents moved to town. He attended the local elementary and high schools, then he worked for his dad's gravel business until it folded twenty years ago. Afterward, he held various jobs at Rosefield, ultimately ending up as a ski instructor.

He drove a rusty truck with an inspection four years expired, but Peggy never enforced such things. Why put him through the hassle of a ticket? Why not throw a bucket of manure on him, too?

Timmy instigated fights all over town, with Peggy breaking up several incidents over the decades. *If* he was murdered, that wouldn't narrow down the suspect list at all. Without effort, she recalled a half dozen men around town who retained some kind of grievance against Timmy Harton: Jordan Herring, Chef Alex, Mickey, and the Smith Brothers (by family extension, the Roasters, too). Even Postmaster Carol disliked him for only checking his mailbox once every few months. Not to mention the horse incident a few years ago . . .

No sense conjecturing; it was probably an unfortunate occurrence. Murders never happened in Rosefield. Sure, the occasional 'accident' occurred, but not outright *murder.*

Besides, Timmy enjoyed many accident-prone sports. He snowmobiled, four-wheeled, mudded, just about any sport involving a motor. He enjoyed skiing the most, winning various regional competitions, and even trying out for the Olympics. With Timmy's skills, Joey's 'fell on his own knife attempting a trick' theory sounded far-fetched.

Again, no use guessing until Peggy inspected the scene herself. From town, it was an eight-minute drive to the Rosefield parking lot. She arrived by 1 PM and parked next to Timmy's half-black, half-rusted truck. Joey and Jim waited for her next to Joey's new white truck.

Jim told her the same thing he said on the phone, almost verbatim. He actually threw in a few extra 'humdingers.' The whole time, he pulled at his spiral mustache and wiped the sweat from his crimson brow.

After humoring the mountain's head of security, she approached Joey. A trail of frozen blood stretched from his nose to his chin, and he favored his right leg. "What happened to you?"

"When you go big, sometimes you fall big."

About what Peggy imagined. "You discovered Timmy on your way down?"

"Yeah, in Open Glade." He flicked his yellow hair over his shoulder to reveal his brown roots. What a Barbie doll. "I hiked it for the view, no other reason to traverse such an easy trail."

"And he was dead already?"

"Yeah. My bet, he attempted an epic knife trick, and he fell on the blade by accident. He crawled to the closest tree so he could die gazing at the snow-covered branches above." Joey shook his head and wiped a tear. "That's intensity. That's sending it."

Peggy sighed. Speaking to Joey hurt her brain and would reveal nothing useful anyway. She had to hike up and check out the scene herself. Jim insisted on joining her. Thankfully, Joey stayed behind.

"I can't see him again." He shook his head. "Once was enough."

She grabbed a notebook and her phone from the Road Runner before heading up. They climbed the stairs along Squirrel Lodge, which Peggy hadn't ascended in over a dozen years. Even when she skied, she rarely entered the lodge because its odor clung to her clothes for weeks. There was regular sweat, and then there was skier sweat—fermented for decades.

They hiked up Greenhouse Way. Peggy recalled Rosefield Elementary School when the teachers forced all seventy kids to march to the top of the mountain, starting with this trail. They called it an 'outdoor learning experience,' but in truth, the school lacked funds for a real field trip. Peggy enjoyed the hike even less now. She questioned Jim to distract from her searing quads.

"Anyone else on the resort today?"

"I bumped into Mickey before clocking in this morning. He had just finished skiing and rushed to open his shop. He was hurrying down the hill by 8 AM."

"When did Timmy arrive?"

"A half an hour later, I believe. My office window overlooks the parking lot, but I'm not usually gazing out of it."

"Understandable. Notice any other hikers?"

"Joey ripped into the lot at exactly 9:10 AM. I know because his brakes squealed the whole way. That boy's a humdinger." Peggy agreed. "Jordan started hiking around then, too, he had come in earlier to work on scheduling, but the first-snow itch compelled him outside."

"Is Jordan the Ski School Director now?"

"Yepper. He earned his promotion three years ago, shortly after the Burics bought the resort. I reckon he's still skiing, haven't seen him since he set out."

"Sorry, guy." Peggy paused their progression to catch her breath. While she often hiked the stream loop at home, the steep uphill exhausted her. "I need a moment."

"Hey, I'm huffing with you." Jim held his expanded gut. "I've eaten too many of my brother's sandwiches lately. His latest creation involves apples, spinach, cheddar, and bacon, with a maple syrup drizzle, all on top of meatloaf. Delicious! A humdinger for my waistline, though."

"I enjoy Big Top's burgers. When he cooked at the Sled Stop, I ordered one every week. Has he returned from Connecticut for the season?"

"A few weeks back. Big Top's actually out chopping somewhere. He always signs up for fall trail maintenance."

"Anybody else working today?"

"Wilma. Apparently, it's been difficult attracting ski patrollers, so she's brainstorming new pitches. She shared this one with me: 'Ski Patrol at Rosefield, where twelve hundred vertical feels like significantly more.' I told her she can write something better."

"Indeed. Did Wilma hike today?"

"Noper. I'd know. Her office is right next to mine."

"Did you notice anyone else?"

Jim shook his head. "Again, I've only monitored from my office."

"What about Peter Smith?"

"Not today, but he's worked all week, managing the fall reopen routine."

"How about Rodney Buric?"

"On vacation. He flew to the Bahamas to skip the foliage season."

Peggy sighed. "Well, this deer won't strip itself."

They continued their hike and kept their chatter to a minimum so they wouldn't get winded after another two hundred feet. Upon reaching Open Glade, they cut into the woods. A hundred steps later, they encountered his green jacket hanging from a branch and his body a dozen steps further.

'Oh, that's a mess,' said Jim. He wasn't wrong.

Timmy leaned against a great white oak, with his once tan shirt dyed crimson and his tangled red hair unbound by any headgear. Frost spread across his skin and over his eyes, but she could still recognize his pupils beneath. His death stare reminded Peggy of hunting with Pop in her teens and twenties. The bucks gazed upon the forest one final time. Except this was a human being, one she had known since childhood. *Her spine shuddered as her heart fluttered.*

Peggy wiped at misty eyes and stepped closer for inspection. The knife remained lodged in his chest, right by the ol' blood pumper. The oak handle looked like the carver intended a mermaid but ended up with a horrible blocky creature. Identifying the owner should be easy, but Peggy left it alone. She'd upset Commander Strongman and the Staties if she disturbed the crime scene. Instead, she retrieved her cellular and captured the entire area.

As she snapped, she recalled the other fatality she had investigated since becoming sheriff. Another of the Harton clan, was their family cursed? Four years ago, John Harton (Timmy's cousin) suffered a heart attack while chucking logs into his woodchipper. He collapsed mid-throw, launching himself forward. His arm landed inside the feeder, a chicken feather from the grinding blade and getting chipped himself. What was with these Harton fellas dying in such gruesome fashion?

She should stay focused on Timmy and *this* scene. She surveyed the surrounding area. The green jacket he wore every winter hung on a tree branch twenty feet away. His bright red skis and matching poles leaned against the neighboring birch. All of which appeared intentionally placed, like he stopped for a break. How did the knife end up so deeply sunk into his chest?

Despite Joey's evaluation, Timmy's death wasn't accidental. Only one possibility remained. Murder.

She rested on a cut log and sighed, noting the recent trail maintenance. Had one of her fellow Rosefieldians killed Timmy? A strong possibility. In a small town, the largest cocks often battled for dominance of the den. And Timmy maintained a lot of enemies. If a local murdered him, then this case could cause even more personal loss. Her heart wrenched in preparation.

"Jim?"

He stared at Timmy, muttering, "Humdinger, humdinger, humdinger." Over and over, always in sets of three.

"Jim!"

"Oh . . ." He shook his head, breaking his stare. "Uh, yes, what do you hanker, Peggy?"

"Call the Staties. And—" Peggy stopped when she noticed cloth in Timmy's right hand, a torn piece of a yellow flannel. He wasn't wearing any flannel. Maybe he ripped it off his attacker. Who wore yellow flannel in town? Not a popular color . . .

"Call Rodney Buric," continued Peggy. "If you can't reach him, then Peter Smith. They should prepare for a long winter."

# A Marketing Strategy

When he received the call from his GM, Peter Smith, Rodney Buric II was vacationing on a Bahamas beach. He always spent October someplace tropical, too many colors in Vermont.

"Sir?"

"Yes, Peter?"

"An incident occurred at the mountain."

Of course it occurred at the mountain. Why else would Peter disrupt his vacation? Rodney held his tongue because Peter was his longest-lasting General Manager. The first four had been complete failures.

Rodney turned off *Soul Pestle* and swung his feet off the lavender plush sofa. He strode to the sliding glass door. He might as well suffer some sunlight while dealing with Peter.

"Tell me."

"A local skier named Timmy Harton was discovered dead a few hours ago on Open Glade."

"Is that some kind of trail?"

"Yes," said Peter. "A few hundred feet up from Squirrel Lodge."

Did Rodney detect a tone? How was he supposed to memorize every trail on the mountain? Rodney didn't have time for skiing. Unlike Peter,

41

who enjoyed mingling with the tourists in those lift lines. He consorted with the lowest employees, too, changing sheets like a housekeeper and doing trail maintenance. Wasted effort. As Father said, 'Great leaders rule from above."

Rodney shook off his annoyance. If he let Peter tell him what happened, he'd sooner return to *Soul Pestle*. "This Timmy, uh, Harta-whatever, who is he? Some loser who broke his neck?"

'A local, I've known him most of my life. Can't say we got along, especially after a snowmobile incident with my brother." Rodney could've done without the life story. "Excellent skier, he once tried out for the Olympics. They found him with a knife in his chest."

Rodney coughed. "What did you say?"

'A few locals found him with a knife in his chest. A large hunting knife meant for butchering game in the wild. Sheriff McStoots was among them, and she suspects murder."

When the 'M' word struck Rodney's ears, he suffered a severe muscle spasm, and the remote popped out of his hand. "I'll catch the next flight."

'Sir, you don't have to cut your vacation—"

"It's finished, Peter. The Bahamas just became a wasteland of disappointment. When I return tomorrow, I expect a full report with an action plan prepared." Rodney paused, and Peter possessed the smarts to keep quiet. "And don't say 'murder.' In fact, ban the word, a demerit for any employee who utters it. Understand?"

"Yes, sir. See you tomorrow."

It actually required two travel days. The negligent fools who managed airlines had yet to establish a first-class direct flight to Burlington. No matter, with the extra travel time, Rodney considered what Peter told him.

Simply devastating. An icon of the mountain perished on the slopes, right before the winter season. How would this affect ticket sales?

His layover in Miami was adequate. A decent hotel for an airport, with an above-average restaurant. Although, Big Top cooked a better steak. While attractive, the waitresses often lingered. Francis, his favorite waiter at the resort, never idled by the table and only ever appeared after a snap of the fingers.

Rodney possessed a couple of quality employees. Maybe he should tell them sometime. Bah! Enhancing a worker's ego corrupted them faster than offering them a union. Another lesson Father taught him.

For his evening entertainment, Rodney completed season two of *Soul Pestle*. Rogue tea composer Kappu defeated Lord Ketoru's top enforcer in a battle of herbal concoctions. With a mix of red willow and night perennial, a combination no one had ever considered, Kappu encapsulated himself in blue flames. After a decisive uppercut, he vanquished his enemy. With the enforcers destroyed, Kappu could now focus on taking down Lord Ketoru . . . in season three.

Of course, Rodney knew what would happen. This was his fourth rewatch, after all. However, he noticed new details every time, like how Kappu muttered "steep" over his fallen foe. Typically, he said that when delivering a powerful attack, but Kappu used it after the battle. Why did he mourn the enforcer? Was this a clue to the revelations coming in the series finale? Rodney would find out in March.

The next morning, he awaited his flight in the 'executive lounge,' a dull room with a tarmac view. Like he'd want to stare at planes when he'd soon be stuck in one. They should install a few palm trees and a water garden. His resort apartment offered more impressive views and larger TVs.

*Steep, steep, pestle! Steep, steep, pestle!* Rodney retrieved his phone and glanced at the screen. UNKNOWN CALLER. He should probably ignore the obvious telemarketer. On the other hand, yelling at someone might improve his mood.

"I don't want whatever you're selling, giving, or scamming! Get a real job instead of pestering people with nonsense!"

"I have a job, Rodney."

He almost dropped his phone. "F-Father? I-I didn't recognize your number."

"As I intended." His voice matched the bitterness of burnt toast. "An adept businessman imposes unease on his opponents."

"Opponent?"

"Even as my son, our wager makes us enemies."

"Oh. That."

"Did you forget, Rodney? This upcoming season marks the fourth since I bought Rosefield Mountain. For three years, you've operated the resort. Have you managed a profit?"

"We enjoyed a few successes. Last season, we recorded the fewest injuries in the history of Rosefield. And they've figured out the issue with the hot tubs."

"Hot tubs? Injuries?" Father laughed. "How about the profits?"

Rodney gulped. "Well, I don't carry the numbers with me every—"

"I requested them from accounting. To summarize, they're abysmal."

"I still have one more season."

"To undo three years of losses? *And* profit this season as well?" Father flavored his chuckle with the bitterness of liver. "Not to mention the murder."

"You know about that?"

"I knew before the town constable."

"Peggy?" How was that possible? According to Peter, she discovered the body.

Father often exaggerated. Like how he claimed ownership over twenty business entities when really it was eighteen. Or when he insisted Mother disappeared because of Rodney. He probably exaggerated the seriousness of their wager, too. "About the stakes of our bet . . ."

"Rodney, my son. If Rosefield isn't profitable by Closing Day, I *will* take everything from you, including your pathetic resort."

"Of course I remember. I'm not worried because of my tremendous plan," lied Rodney. "Actually, I set it in motion years ago, and in the next few months, I'll earn every dollar I need to win our wager. Then I *will* own Rosefield outright." None of this was true. Rodney would figure something out, just like Kappu during a climactic battle.

"Hm. I enjoyed that vigor. Maintain it through the season, and maybe you'll win." Father clicked his tongue. "I suppose I win either way. You earn enough; my son is less of a loser. You don't, then my original plan will come to fruition."

'Original plan?' Father often dramatized situations. "I'll prove myself, Father. After all, you taught me everything about managing a business."

"I attempted." Father laughed with the bitterness of gasoline. "Goodbye, Rodney. Try not to watch too many cartoons."

'Cartoons? I don't—"

*Click.*

Rodney lowered his phone, red in the face. Anime wasn't the same thing as cartoons! he wanted to scream. With mature plots and complex characters, *Soul Pestle* rivaled any live-action drama. Take Kappu's backstory: his mother died while birthing him, and his father was slain by Lord Ketoru during the Freepolk Rebellion. The orphaned Kappu was then enslaved by the Kuki Tea Company, where they forced him to compose for the very man who killed his father. Primetime television had nothing on that.

Still, few people understood the depth of anime, Father very much included. So Rodney kept his passion to himself. Many people hid their hobbies.

What Rodney really needed to think about was earning enough to win the wager with Father. He stared at the planes. Despite their bland appearance, the repetition both calmed his mind and bolstered his thinking.

The dead skier complicated the scenario. The local constable already called it a murder. Soon the newspapers would spread her nonsense across the state. No one wanted to vacation where a murderer still lurked. If Timmy's death remained an 'accident,' everything would be fine. Accidents happened, no big deal. He probably fell on his knife after skiing the closed trails. Hence why they were closed. Rodney had attempted to abolish all hiking on-premises because unfortunate things like knife impalement occurred. And because hikers didn't buy lift tickets.

If Rodney considered the situation anymore, he'd develop a migraine. He ordered a scotch and swallowed a sleeping pill. The perfect combination to forget both his problems and the impending flight. Worked, too. The only thing Rodney recalled from the trip was the size of the stewardess's breasts.

His limousine awaited him at the Burlington airport. Peter provided a glass of scotch set in the beverage holder of his leather seat. What a talented little General Manager, always paying attention to the details. Not really 'little,' though, Peter held a farmer's build, his shoulders straining the fibers of his black leather jacket.

Bah! For such a tough guy, he begged a lot. A year ago, during Peter's performance review, Rodney played an innocent joke on him—inspired by a similar prank Kappu pulled on his assistant Baggu.

"You're fired!" shouted Rodney the moment Peter entered his office. His face fell to the floor, and his body followed. How hilarious. Peter cried, too! He begged for his job like his *wife* depended on it. Oops, how insensitive, considering she died a few years prior.

Between recalling his prank and drinking his scotch, Rodney felt better. He held out the empty glass, and Peter refilled it. "Tell me about this Timmy situation."

"First, sir, let me say your employees worked a hundred and ten percent across the mountain to ensure we open in mid-December. They are tremendously motivated since the accident."

"As for Timmy?"

"The press wasn't great. Nearly every publication uses the 'm' word.

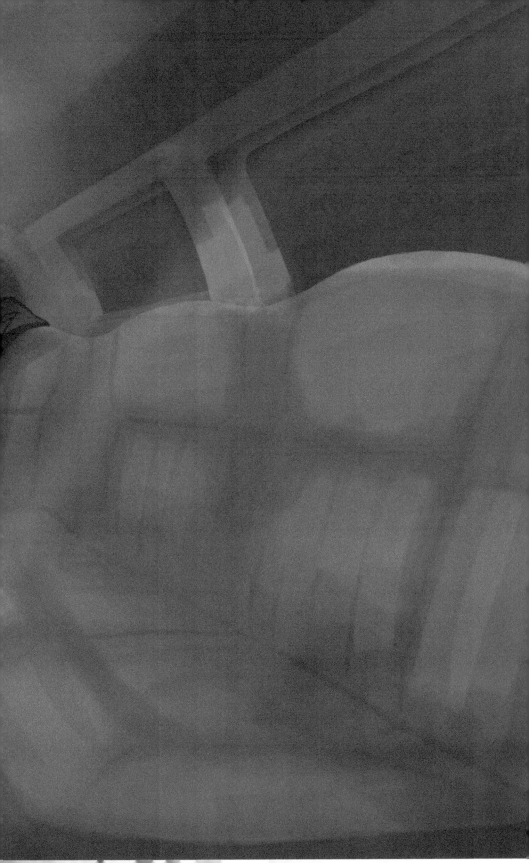

The Rosefield Town Letter, the St. Albans Times, and the Burlington Free Press. I've lobbied for them to call it an accident—which it most certainly was—with little success."

Rodney spit. Right onto the floor. The cleaners would scrub it out during its weekly servicing. "What of the investigation?"

"The Staties searched the entire area but discovered little. No signs of a struggle, so they're considering suicide."

"What about the constable? McStoots?"

"She believes Timmy was . . . 'm'd. That's all she's saying."

"Now, the serious business." Rodney set down his scotch. "How are pass sales? Bookings?"

Sweat dripped down Peter's brow, and his mustache lacked its usual sharpness. A GM of a prestigious resort should shave frequently. "It's a little early to tell, but not much."

"Not much of what?" Rodney didn't pay this fool for riddles.

"Of anything. Sales, bookings, the phones are quieter than a hunter's stand."

Rodney coughed on his scotch. He needed this season to be their best, by multiple degrees. Otherwise, he would lose everything—even his limo.

"However, I have a plan," continued Peter.

Rodney almost interrupted to fire Peter, for real this time. While terminating employees always elevated Rodney's mood, he listened to Peter's final speech.

"A couple of years ago, Jordan mentioned a—"

"Is that the maintenance guy?"

"Jordan Herring, your Ski School Director."

"You sure he's not in maintenance? He's not the quiet one I like?"

"Are you thinking of Larry?"

"Bah!" Peter's story dragged. Maybe he should just fire him already.

"So Jordan mentioned a resort in the Rockies, where a skier died suspiciously. The employees and managers anticipated losing business, but the opposite occurred. They more than doubled their ticket sales from the previous year, fully booked hotels all season."

"You're fi—" Rodney caught himself. What did he say about doubling ticket sales? "You think we can capitalize on this?"

"I've already drawn up a marketing plan, along with employee policies, to create a spooky ambiance for our guests. We'll corner the market for a haunted ski resort. Maybe—pardon the word, sir—we rebrand to: 'Murder Mountain.'"

The idea had merit, like something Rodney would have concocted if he tried. Desensitized by sports, movies, and even animes, people might *want* to visit a mountain featuring a ghastly murder.

Rodney decided to keep Peter Smith around a little longer. He recognized some of himself in the GM, seamlessly turning this terrible situation into a gold pot. Similar to how Rodney transformed Rosefield Mountain from a forgotten hill into an esteemed resort.

One significant difference, though: no one fooled Rodney. Which reminded him of another time he'd tricked Peter—essentially Rodney's Baggu.

Peter arrived for his initial job interview, and after a brief discussion, Rodney hired him. Negotiating salary remained. Rodney tricked all of his GMs into accepting a lower amount by offering a six-figure bonus should the mountain attain massive profits. He chose a virtually unachievable total, but they all took the salary cut in hopes of a big payday. Peter Smith included. What an idiot.

Though not on par with Rodney's intellect, Peter excelled at reading a situation, and in this case, he understood the importance of silence. All the way to Rosefield, he didn't produce a single noise, granting Rodney the necessary quiet for intense contemplation . . . about all the money he'd earn with this 'Murder Mountain' idea! His bank account would swell until he needed landscape mode to behold the full figure. He'd win the bet, and Father would finally accept his worth.

When they drove through the tiny speck known as Rosefield, they passed Constable Peggy McStoots, the so-called 'sheriff.' Who voted her in? Maybe the townsfolk, but no one asked Rodney, the largest local business owner. She looked like an overripe plum in her ugly brown jacket. She didn't even wear a uniform. How unprofessional.

She fueled her Jeep at Cody's Country Store, a dump Rodney never entered himself. If he required something, he sent an employee to pick it up.

They turned left onto the mountain 'road,' so covered in cracks and bumps it barely qualified. Rodney paid significant taxes to upkeep this highway. How was he supposed to sip his scotch while jostling around—

A massive creature dashed by his window! Rodney dropped his glass in surprise, splattering scotch across his ruined leather shoes. "What was that? Were we attacked by a moose!?"

"A town dog, sir," said Peter. "Bear lives on Main Street with his owner—"

"Shoot it. Wild animals will scare away my customers. Order the constable to track down and kill the beast."

"Of course, sir."

They ascended the final few miles and turned into the resort, right past the Rosefield Mountain sign. He remembered the first time he regarded it four years ago. "Look at this gold pot," he muttered to himself. "A rundown resort needing a cash infusion, and then *endless* profits." Sure, Father originally picked the mountain, but Rodney agreed to manage the operation.

His driver parked at the hotel side entrance. A corridor once leading to the cafeteria, Rodney blocked off the whole section for his private access. Plus, this forced lodgers to trudge outdoors for the cheap cafeteria grub, so they chose the more convenient (and expensive) Mountain View restaurant.

A private elevator ushered him to his modest condo. He'd combined three of the five penthouse suites into one living space: an office-suite, a home-suite, and a lounge-suite. While he admitted three kitchens felt unnecessary, the extra bathrooms required less traversing so he could return to work faster, and the spare bedrooms meant fewer steps to the nearest nap.

After fixing himself a scotch, he relaxed on the ten-person leather sofa at the center of his lounge-suite. He stared out the wall-spanning windows overlooking the chair lifts and ski trails. Except for the sunset, the view was perfect.

"Murder Mountain," he said to himself. He chuckled and sipped. "Murder Mountain." The more he said it, the more he appreciated it. What a great idea. Who conceived it back in the limo? Peter and himself had brainstormed together, but who said the words "Murder Mountain"? Or was it the maintenance guy's idea? His uncertainty grew with each sip of scotch.

Could this be Rodney's Soul Pestle? In the first episode, during Kappu's attempted escape from his enslavement, Lord Ketoru's enforcers surrounded him. Then the Soul Pestle appeared, and together they composed the mythical Air Light Brew. With a "Steep, Steep, Pestle!" Kappu flew to safety. Maybe, with the ideal composition, Murder Mountain would deliver Rodney from Father's grasp.

When he finished the scotch, he decided his rebrand began tomorrow. First thing in the morning, he'd call the busty girl in marketing. What was her name? They'd meet at Mountain View for breakfast and discuss his grand ideas. He'd even pay for the meal.

When Jane saw the Rosefield Mountain Resort sign, she almost drove home. A crappy sheet of plastic covered the usual logo with a cartoon of a grim reaper on skis and the words, 'Murder Mountain.' What moron would name a ski resort that? Rodney Buric, of course, and she stared right at his round face and clueless eyes. They should've covered his sign instead.

She knew to expect something, of course. Around town, people gossiped about two things: the murder and the resort's new name. Every local newspaper covered the story, too. For the first time in Rosefield's history, they filled headlines all the way to St. Albans. For reasons Jane couldn't fathom, the papers applauded the rebrand decision.

One headline read: 'Rosefield Mountain? She's dead! Murder Mountain's slicing up her slopes!' Another wrote: 'A villainous rebrand? Only if originality is considered evil." A third penned: "To honor the dead, Murder Mountain rises from the powder." What complete nonsense.

After she parked her Subaru outside Generally Slanted, she spotted the other differences. They changed the general store's slogan from 'Slanting Prices' to 'Slaying Prices,' and an additional banner read 'Will she fall today?' They tagged an '-ish' to all the 'Ski Safe' signs along the Squirrel Lodge stairs. How did Ski Patrol okay that? They replaced the hotel's logo of a rose on a pillow with a skeleton hanging in a closet. They even superimposed grim reapers and bloody daggers into the background of the Opening Day banner in the cafeteria.

Who would bring a family to this ghoulish resort? How would she earn tips with the custies scared away? While fewer flatties meant more snow for Jane, it wasn't worth the humiliation.

They changed the name of her bar. The mountain might own it, but Jane *owned* the Bent Pole. Every winter, she called (and took) the shots. She secured the best shifts, too, as the longest-lasting bartender at a contemptuous three years.

They didn't bother producing a new sign for the bar. They just slapped up a piece of construction paper with a handwritten 'Knife' covering 'Pole.' Bent Knife? What did that mean?

Jane would not tolerate this rebrand. She'd return her mountain to its original name, even if she had to incinerate the entire resort and rebuild it from scratch. She started by ripping down the 'Knife' sign and tossing it into the trash.

She began her opening ritual. She wiped down most of the stools (built from old skis) and half of the bar. She restocked the refrigerators with beer and dollied the kegs up from the loading dock. All the while, she hummed along to the Rutland Rotary Boys. Not her favorite southern Vermont band, but a custy left one of their CDs, and the twenty-year-old stereo's antenna broke off last season. The best song was "My BRT":

RIDING (RIDING)
RIDING (RIDING)
RIDING MY BIG RED TRACTOR.

GOTTA SIXER IN MY LAP,
ON THE WAY TO SET A TRAP,
I'M COLLECTING ALL THE SAP,
FROM ALL MY DRIVEN TAP.

AIN'T GONNA MAKE A-NAP A FACTOR,
WHILE I'M RIDING MY BIG RED TRACTOR.

RIDING (RIDING)
RIDING (RIDING)
RIDING MY BIG RED TRACTOR.

MY NEIGHBORS SAY 'GOLLY GEE,'
WHEN I'M RIDING MY BRT.
DON'T ASK ME FOR A FEE;
I'LL TILL YOUR FIELD FOR FREE.

AIN'T NOTHIN' BOTHERS ME ON PASTURE,
WHILE I'M RIDING MY BIG RED TRACTOR.

BIG

RED

TRACTOR

When the CD finished, Jane set down her rag. Good enough, cleaner than most things in Squirrel Lodge. She jogged to the cafeteria for her traditional Opening Day snack. While she avoided eating the overly greasy and questionably sourced food they served, their corn dogs tasted too darn good. In fact, she ordered two.

She brought them to the Bent Pole to enjoy. Their crispy breading still glistened from the fryolator and provided a satisfying *crunch* with every bite. She scarfed down the first corn dog in under a minute, with the second already in hand. So focused on her Opening Day treat, she didn't notice Helmet Joe stroll up to the bar until he slid onto a stool.

'Heya, Jane!' They called him Helmet Joe because he perpetually wore a bright green helmet, even in the lodge, even after the lifts stopped spinning. 'You hear about Timmy?'

'Hard not to. It's the only thing anyone talks about.' She poured him a Bacon, an IPA from Pig's Foot Brewery and Swinery. 'That or this stupid rebranding idea.'

'What do you think happened?'

'He died from a knife in his chest.' Jane shrugged. 'Everyone has a theory, of course. Rosefield is full of detectives.'

'Was he wearing his trusty helmet?'

'Not sure I've ever seen Timmy wear a helmet.'

'Well then, that's what killed him. You should always wear your trusty helmet.'

Jane rolled her eyes. 'Hanker another?'

'And a whiskey chaser. I oughta loosen up before returning to the slopes.'

She obliged, and soon Helmet Joe stomped out of the Bent Pole— *not* the 'Bent Knife.' What a stupid name. Jane would sooner relinquish her four-wheeler than call her home 'Murder Mountain.' She fisted the bar, rattling stacks of pint glasses.

No reason for excitement. Jane would fix this. She plotted while munching on her second corn dog and plotted.

PJ stopped in around noon, wearing the same red liftie jacket he received six years ago on his first day of bumping chairs.

"Just on lunch, I figured I'd say hi."

"How was your summer?" asked Jane.

"Relaxing. I studied anatomy to improve my bumping abilities. I missed my lift, though." PJ only ever spoke about one thing, the Absolute Zero Triple for which he bumped. "Oh! She's looking pretty. They serviced her thoroughly this summer; you should listen to her spin."

"Not too screechy?" Jane laughed. "Sometimes that lift makes my ears wanna fall off my head."

"She sounds thirty years younger." He chuckled. "They probably burnt out several sanders removing her rust."

"What's your opinion on Timmy's killing?"

"It doesn't make any darned sense." PJ shook his head. *Hiking?* Wait for the lifts, bud! It's all about the chair ride; bring a pocket burger and appreciate the views. Once at the top, race down as fast as possible for the next ride."

"We'll never agree, bud." Jane shook her head. "The chair is a necessary evil. It's all about snowboarding."

"One day, you'll understand the truth." PJ coughed. "Did you, uh, attend the funeral?"

"I hardly knew him," said Jane. "And . . ."

". . . He was a jerk. Whenever he skied the Zero, he purposely waited too far forward, forcing me to hold the chair longer."

"You should've released it, let the chair snap right into his legs."

"Against the bump code. Karma repaid him, anyway. Did the Sled Stop even throw a Parting Party for him?"

"Yepper." Jane chuckled. "About a dozen people attended. Neither his uncle or cousin showed. The Farney brothers came for the free pour."

"A shame." PJ hopped off the stool. "Well, I shall return to the PJ

Zone. If I stay away too long, my inept coworkers will tarnish my chair's reputation."

"Thanks for stopping in. Bump 'em good!"

"Bump out!"

Around 2 PM, the self-labeled 'Powder Crew' arrived. They each ordered a Bacon and proclaimed their theories on Timmy's death.

"Simple, he went too big." 'Sendy' Joey wore his shiny blue ski jacket, and his hair appeared freshly bleached. "He attempted a crazy new trick, balancing a knife while ski-boot ripping. Case closed."

"On a trail with a dusting of snow on it?" Even though he discovered the body, Joey formulated the *worst* idea of how it happened.

"That's Grade-A manure, three seasons cured," said Happy, wearing the proper Rosefield snowboarding uniform, Carpartt jacket over a red flannel, Kinkys gloves, and camo ski pants. "I reckon when he moved out of town for those few years, he messed with a flatty and returned home to hide. Except, the easiest place to catch prey is in their den."

"A revenge murder?" said Jane.

"You hit that deer head-on, bud," said Happy. "He stole something valuable, drugs or money."

"Or he stole someone's girl," said Tall Brad. "It's a problem well-endowed fellas struggle with. I'd know." He removed his helmet to reveal sprayed hair and gag-worthy cologne. "My reckoning? He brought a lady friend with him. He became a little too handsy, and she stabbed him. Where's the girl? Far away, Maine or even Canada."

"You're all wrong," said Handy Jesse. He could fix anything, but you had to listen to his conspiracies the whole time. "It goes to the top. Not just the supervisors, their managers, or the folks above them. This plot involves Mr. Buric himself."

"Rodney Buric?" scoffed Happy. "He's a sun-ripened turd, but he ain't no murderer."

"He hired someone. But it wasn't his idea; this travels further up the chain. A state senator ordered the hit. Why?" Jesse turned towards the cafeteria. "You hear those crowds? I can't remember a busier Opening Day."

"They killed Timmy to sell more lift tickets?" questioned Jane.

"Who knows why?" Jesse shrugged. "Big oil, most likely."

Jane knew better than to ask any more follow-up questions. "How's the skiing, boys?"

"Perfect for bombing cliffs, hitting jumps, slicing glades, and ripping trails," said Joey.

"I've carved better rows of corn, but the groomers try their best," said Happy Smith.

"I'd enjoy seeing more snow bunnies," said Tall Brad.

"Ruined by the secret snowmaker agenda," said Handy Jesse.

They finished their Bacons and geared up. The Powder Crew skied bell-to-bell on Opening Day. As they pushed through the double doors to outside, they passed Charlie Smith. He paused for a moment to speak with his son, Happy, before approaching the bar and ordering a Lard.

"We only have Bacon. We'll receive our Lard keg next week."

"I only enjoy their stout," grunted Charlie, removing his helmet and jacket. His curly brown hair matched his son's, but he was taller with broader shoulders. Strong like his brother Peter, Jane heard plenty of stories from their rougher days. They engaged in monthly fights at the Sled Stop. Not anymore, not since Charlie settled down with his family and Peter started full-time management at the resort.

"How about a scotch?"

"You know me better than your snowboard."

"You only ever order the same thing." She poured a double and slid it to him. "No rocks."

"Ice ruins the scotch."

"I haven't seen you in a few months. Out-of-town work?"

"I got a big job in Albany, finished a few weeks ago." Charlie smirked. "Paid big, too."

"What type of work?"

'Oh, I won't discuss it. My employer paid big for a reason . . ." Charlie chuckled menacingly while stroking his fully maintained beard. 'I'm joking. Construction stuff, I managed a crew. They wanted my sizable brains."

'You sure they weren't after your brother?"

'Peter? He can't even handle his own bills." Charlie motioned Jane closer. 'I wasn't home a week, and he came asking for cash. I handed it over, of course. I always support my family."

That didn't sound like Peter. Maybe she'd ask him about it later when he showed up with the rest of the Rosefield employees at 5 PM. Charlie stayed for another drink, but the après ski crowd arrived, so Jane had little time to chat.

Plenty of other familiar faces stopped by. Roaster Dan with his wife Molly and their toddlers Little Dan and Sugarsnap, all wearing their skiing uniform of red flannel and hunter orange hats. They told Jane about their new coffee brew and its slogan: The Brown Bomber, *'if you gotta poop, this is your scoop.'*

Boston Tony showed up with a beard full of snow, a smile even whiter, and red hair to crown it all. He talked and talked. Jane pretended to listen, but she didn't understand his language. 'I banged a uey, my cah rippen about like a hahd ass, then *boom*! I'd gone too fah. What a pissa, shoulda popped by the Dunkie. What am I, new to the Hub?" Fortunately, with so many custies, he couldn't trap her into a conversation.

Annie and George stopped in for a while. Montrealers, but Jane never held that against them. They were friendly, gracious when she messed up their order, and most important, good tippers. Jane also appreciated their sense of fashion, wearing colorful scarves and sleek jackets. Plus, they were some of the few people on the mountain who showered once a day.

Plenty of unfamiliar faces stopped in as well. Flatties upon flatties, which should've added dimension, but . . . nopers. Had the rebrand brought them to Rosefield? Jane asked one couple with an overwhelmingly flat appearance.

"Why are you here?" she questioned after delivering them two pints of Bacon.

"We ordered a—" started the male.

"A drink I don't know how to make." Jane tapped her fingers on the bar. "Answer the question."

"Uh," stammered the female, "w-we wanted . . ."

". . . A vacation with more excitement," finished the male. "Honey, she's part of the 'Murder Mountain' act, play along."

"Oh. I *was* scared for a moment, how thrilling!"

Jane stomped away before she slapped a flatty. She questioned several others, whose responses only increased her frustration.

"My hubby and I skied a Magic Mountain, a Presidential Mountain, Buttermilk, Powder and Bald Mountains. Never a Murder Mountain!" Flat.

"I'm a murder mystery writer, here for research." Flatter.

"We're spiritualist skiers. We carve with the dead." Flattest.

Jane felt her backhand tighten up. Could she keep herself contained? She almost flew over the bar at a custy wearing his jeans tucked into ski boots, a helmet-mounted MyView, and a twenty-year-old pad of wickets. But when he dropped a twenty-dollar tip, Jane forgave all those offenses. Actually, despite their vertical challenges, most of the flatties tipped well. Maybe she should share this chair.

At 5 PM, the sea of custies filtered out, as a tide of employees replaced them. Ever since Rosefield's first year of operation, all resort workers received a free beer on Opening Day. Cheap ass Rodney ordered it to stop, but every year Jane kept pouring out freebies. Employees from every department showed up for the party: Ski School, Ski Patrol, Housekeeping, Security, Slanted Staff, Snowmaking, Groomers, and most of the Administration, including GM Peter Smith.

When he stepped up to deliver his speech, Jane considered what

Charlie said earlier. From the stories and what she observed herself, the opposite was more likely true. Charlie instigated trouble, and Peter protected his little brother from the reprisals. Besides, as GM of the resort, he earned a sizable paycheck. He even took in their mother Margaret to spare her the old folks' home.

Peter knife tapped a mug until the crowd quieted. "I hanker your ears for a moment. First, let's recognize our tragic loss. Timmy Harton lived here his whole life, a true Rosefieldian. Cheers to Timmy!" The crowd roared loud enough to put a lion's pride to shame. "Another cheer for our best Opening Day in Rosefield history!" This roar made the last one sound tame.

"Now, it might appear like we are attempting to profit off of Timmy's ill-fortune. However, I prefer to think of it as his memory guiding us into a more successful future." Peter nodded. "It's what he would have hankered."

"Kick it back, friends!" shouted the Food and Beverage Manager, Jeremy McJoy. They called him Big Top because he wielded a wrestler's shoulders but a desk jockey's legs. "Cheers to Murder Mountain!" The crowd cheered and drank.

Jane noticed a few folks who kept quiet. She wasn't the only employee who disapproved of the rebrand.

"It's reckless and a humdinger. The murderer still runs free!" said James McJoy, Rosefield's Head of Security.

"We can barely save people from themselves," said Head of Ski Patrol Wilma Johansson. "Now we have to save them from each other? What a disaster!"

"They intend to rename my lift?" said PJ. "A celebrated name for fifty years, the Absolute Zero! That's its identity, its soul."

However, it appeared most employees embraced the rebrand.

"Rosefield Mountain is boring. Murder Mountain is exciting." Ski School Manager Jordan Herring didn't care for elaboration. "I'll . . . miss Timmy."

'It's fun redecorating the store. I love new themes!" said Yelsa Hodinker, Manager of Generally Slanted. She dressed in costume, replacing her usual bright colors with an all-black dress and matching accessories. The only exception was the rainbow-colored scrunchie she wore every day since she moved to town ten years ago.

'I enjoy seeing a full parking lot for a change," said Maintenance Larry, who resembled a smart guy. He raised a valid point. Despite Jane's earlier reservations, she never earned more on an Opening Day, raking in over four hundred in tips alone.

At 9 PM, she shut down the Bent Pole, and folks filed out. Since she didn't work tomorrow, she neglected to clean as she closed. The next shift could handle wiping a few things down and restocking the refrigerators. Besides, during her brief stint in housekeeping, she learned two important things. First, others would complete her work if she simply didn't do it herself. If Jane failed to scrub the toilet, someone would. Even if it was the custy when they checked in.

Second, she learned how to use a hair barrette to prop open a hotel door without the custy noticing. She used this trick to great profit until enough flatties complained about their missing belongings and upper management fired Jane. Only to be rehired at the Bent Pole a year later.

Pretty much the standard job rotation at Rosefield Mountain Resort.

After locking the last door, she started towards the Squirrel Lodge exit but stopped when she heard voices echoing from the cafeteria. Always interested in a little eavesdropping, Jane crept down the hall until it turned. Any further, and they'd notice her.

'Somebody suspects us, I sense it," said Yelsa. Jane recognized the squeaks. "What will we do?"

"Quiet," returned a voice too quiet to identify. 'Do you want every squirrel in the lodge to hear us?"

'I don't care. We can't keep this a secret. Not forever."

'It's not forever. We keep to your plan. At the end of the season, when we've saved enough, we skedaddle." The man coughed, and Jane instantly recognized him. Only Roger Elwood phlegmed at the beginning of their cough. Gross! He spewed loogies worse than a llama. He launched spittle Jane's direction several hours ago. If it weren't for all the other resort employees, she'd have smacked him from across the bar.

"They won't know the truth until we're far away," continued Roger. As head cashier of Generally Slanted, he worked directly under Yelsa. In more ways than one if the rumors proved accurate. "Your plan is perfect."

"You're right. We'll keep it together for a few more months, and then no more snow." Yelsa giggled, which sounded like a cornered chipmunk. "Where will we travel?"

"Someplace warm. Just us, a beach and a whole case of fruity beers."

"How about North Carolina?"

'I love BBQ. Now let's leave before anyone sees us."

Yelsa's giggles receded until they disappeared entirely.

Were they involved with Timmy's murder? Jane would figure it out, just like she'd put an end to this 'Murder Mountain' nonsense. Rosefield was *her* town, and she'd protect it. No matter the scheme or who deserved Jane's famous backhand.

Peggy completed Cody's in under twenty minutes, a new record. The Country Store was the central hub for Rosefield; she couldn't buy a cup of coffee without bumping into eight people who warranted a 'howdy doody.'

Today she grabbed a coffee and donut. She hankered something quick with the long day ahead of her. First, she had to stop in for a chat with Rufus, Timmy's roommate. Then she drove to St. Albans, as the Staties were finally sharing their autopsy. Weeks later was better than not at all, Peggy supposed. Instead of simply sending her an email with the report, Commander Strongman insisted she retrieved them herself.

She shouldn't complain about the Staties keeping to their side of the county; after the murder, they parked one of their troopers by Cody's every night. As Rosefield's sheriff, Peggy patrolled her town. She grew so tired of their presence she almost called Commander Strongman, but they stopped on their own a week ago. So lovely when issues resolved themselves.

As usual, Tug-Tug waited by the Road Runner for his ear scratch. Peggy obliged and snuck him a bite of donut before climbing into her

Jeep. She didn't fire up the engine immediately, as it wasn't safe operating a vehicle while eating. Especially a strawberry-filled donut, those were *explosive*. Instead, she perused a Lydia McStoots classic titled "The Pond":

Flatwater in peace,
Do we dare jump in?
To ripple and crease,
the beauty ceased
by bodies foreign
by even us geese.

It felt like a pond kind of day. Peggy finished the donut and poem simultaneously and turned on the Road Runner.

As she moseyed down Main Street, she noticed Yelsa's two daughters, Harvesta and Karma, in front of the Daffodil Harvest. They both wore floral dresses with matching bows in their yellow hair. They operated the organic grocer during the winter while their mother managed Generally Slanted. What responsible children. Peggy couldn't compel her daughters to stack a pile of wood, never mind handle a business.

Maybe because Yelsa raised them as a single mom. They needed to help out their whole lives.

Banker Henry spoke with the girls, wearing his usual bowler hat and grey pea coat. Was he dropping off a foreclosure notice? He enjoyed delivering those himself. She hated when local businesses went under, especially one bringing healthy food to Rosefield at such affordable prices. Over the last few months, their prices dropped close to Cody's General Store. Yelsa must have found a new supplier . . . or they were selling off their inventory before a foreclosure. No, Peggy overreacted; based on Harvesta and Karma's broad smiles, Banker Henry just paid them a compliment. Nothing to worry about.

Instead, she should worry about the murder investigation. She better solve it by summer, especially with her grandson due in early June. Once Robert (they named him after Grandpa!) was born, she wouldn't have time to sheriff, not while assisting Lyndsay with the baby. *Peggy sighed so deep and hard, she drove right over Sammy's yard.* No, she'd solve it before her favorite green months, even if it meant working six days a week.

Peggy pulled into Timmy's old driveway and parked next to Rufus's rust-covered car. She had questions for the roommate, along with an update on his hunting knife. She paused before exiting Road Runner, hankering a few more moments to consider the case.

Investigating his rivalries around town revealed nothing. Timmy simply maintained too many. Between skiing, sledding, four-wheeling, side-by-siding, and Sled Stopping, he pissed a lot of his fellow Rosefieldians off. At the infamous Red Barn Incident, he got into two fights on the same night. One with Charlie Smith, which naturally drew in his brother Peter, and another with Bill Viceroy of all folks. In both instances, they beat up Timmy harder than whipping cream.

After the Red Barn Incident, Timmy fled town to regather his pride. He stayed away for five years, and when Peggy asked around town, she only learned he traveled "out west somewhere." The Staties used their databases and out-of-state connections to track down his whereabouts. Peggy awaited their findings.

When Timmy moved back, he returned to the late-night fight scene at the Sled Stop. With his cousin John, they instigated fights with anyone who glanced at them. This behavior lasted a year until John suffered his fatal heart attack. Afterward, Timmy kept to himself, with the noted exception of the awful horse incident. As sheriff, Peggy reviewed the scene. She'd never forget the pile of milk crates.

After folks in Rosefield heard what happened to the poor horse, Timmy lost his remaining friends. Probably why so few people showed up to his Parting Party. His landlord hated him enough to kick him out. He beseeched his family for shelter, but they denied him. So then he moved in with Rufus.

Few Hartons remained in Rosefield. Timmy's mother and father retired south, and his sister soon followed. His uncle Rogen lived on Gregory Road by the plow turn around. Twenty years ago, he built his cabin on the mountainside, and he rarely left. In fact, Peggy hadn't seen him in a couple of years. Rogen's daughter Amy married a St. Albans farmer, and she refused to speak with Timmy since he released a pig at her reception.

Investigating his family and past hadn't helped, but neither did the evidence at the crime scene. First, the ripped piece of yellow flannel seemed promising, except everyone in town wore flannel. Yellow was unpopular, though. No one had donned the color since the murder.

The knife appeared a promising lead with its unique 'mermaid' handle, but Timmy simply borrowed it from his roommate, Rufus Redwood. The day after the murder, Peggy sorted it out. At least she attempted to. Rufus smoked more weed than an entire Rutland Rotary Boys concert. Better than the alternative: when he stopped smoking, he acted crazier than a squirrel who lost his acorns.

Peggy sighed, hopped out of the Road Runner, and sauntered up to the two-bedroom cottage with green siding and brown trim. She appreciated the color combination, very tree-ish, but preferred the brown siding and mauve trim at home. After knocking three times, she let herself in. Like most Rosefieldians, Rufus never locked his door.

He lay on his couch a few feet away, clothed in a Carpartt jacket and overalls. Closed eyes as drool dribbled down his chin. His face resembled snow. Was he breathing? Uh oh. She rushed over. "Rufus!" Had the murderer struck again?

His leg kicked, his hand fluttered. He grumbled, and his eyelids popped open. "Jeezum crow . . ."

Yepper, totally fine.

"What an amazing dream," continued Rufus. "I flew over the tundra, but I swam, too . . . my muscles wearied, so I hitched a ride on a seal to Europe . . . but the seal informed me of a Nazi submarine . . . I boarded and—"

"Good morning Rufus, I stopped by to . . ." She trailed off because Rufus continued rattling on about his dream.

"—all of a sudden, I'm standing . . . naked. In front of Bob Dylan!" He shook his head and closed his eyes. "Now I just wanna watch what happens next . . ."

"Hold on, you'll find out later. I have a couple of questions for you." When his eyes remained shut, she reached down and shook him by the shoulders. In the process, she regrettably caught a whiff of him. Sweat, piss, and mold, all wrapped in manure. She held her breath and shook him until his eyes opened.

"Hey . . . Is that you, Bob?"

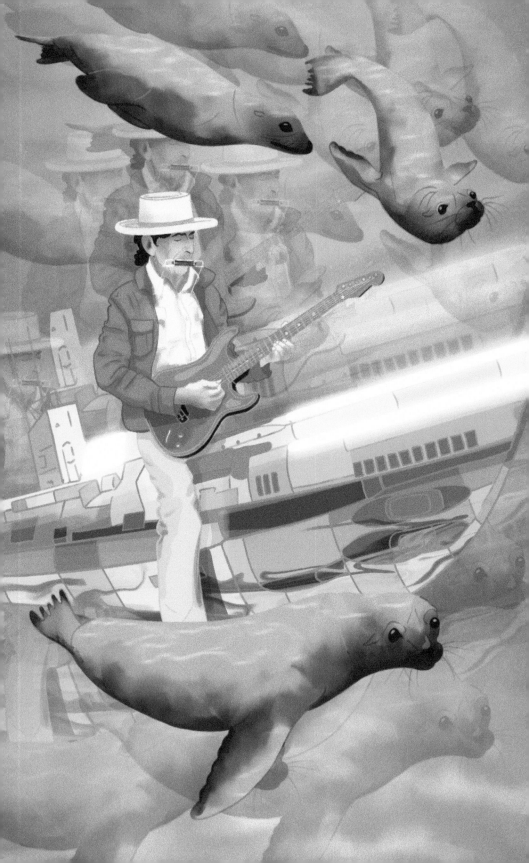

"It's Peggy. Sheriff McStoots. Come on, sit up." Once she oriented Rufus into a semi-vertical position, she sat down on the coffee table because she refused to touch that couch. She repositioned two pipes, a bong, and a tray full of roaches to create space. "First, the Staties intend on keeping your knife a while longer. Sorry, guy."

"What?" He popped up with wide eyes. "That's my favorite hunting knife!"

Peggy sighed. The idea of Rufus with a rifle put an acorn-sized knot in her stomach. While he *had* served in the army, he smoked substantially less weed back then. "They will keep it until we catch the murderer. The trial too, you know, for evidence."

"Come on, Peggy . . . I love my knife. I carved it myself."

She knew about his mermaid knife from her last visit. He carved the handle in Iraq when an explosion trapped his team in a basement. Three days transpired before his unit discovered them, but their batteries only lasted the first night. Two whole days they lived in complete darkness, so Rufus carved a mermaid to keep sane. At least he attempted to; the outcome resembled a female troll.

"It's a murder weapon, after all," said Peggy. "The Staties gotta follow their procedures. They'll return it by next hunting season."

Rufus grunted, then slid down the couch. "Well, I guess I'll return to Bob Dylan, he carried something in his—"

"Ope, not yet. I have more questions." Peggy waited until Rufus reopened his eyes. It required two shakes and a pinch on his ear.

"Ouch! Okay, what's your question?"

"Timmy borrowed the knife, correct?"

"Yeah, yeah, he borrows them a lot. Sometimes he grabs two or three. I can't figure out why he hankers so many . . ."

The way he spoke about Timmy in the present tense put a second acorn-sized knot in Peggy's stomach. "The morning he died, did you personally hand him the knife?"

Rufus frowned and stared at Peggy like she was a cow wearing a tutu.

"That happened months ago, almost a year now, man . . . How am I supposed to remember so far back?"

'It's been a month. C'mon, Rufus, what happened the morning of Timmy's murder?"

He gazed at her, blank-faced, but his ears twitched in what Peggy assumed was his version of fierce thinking. After a full minute, he finally produced something. 'I do, I remember. I lay here . . . but not really."

Peggy blinked.

'I chilled on the couch all day, but I wasn't *really* here." He gestured towards all the paraphernalia on the coffee table.

She sighed. Why had she bothered stopping by? 'Do you remember anything about the knife?"

'Nah, that knife?" Rufus reached over to the coffee table and picked up a large glass bong. 'I never gave it to him. Actually, I don't think . . ." He trailed off as he grabbed a lighter.

"Now hold onto that cow a second longer," said Peggy, snatching the lighter from his hand. The immense sadness in his eyes rivaled a puppy on ball choppin' day. 'What were you about to say? I'll return it when you tell me."

"Okay, okay. Deal." His face contorted into a deep frown as he recalled once more. After another minute, he relaxed and said, 'Yeah, I hadn't seen the knife in days. I hankered on cutting some tubing, but I couldn't find it. I needed to use a different knife. What a pain!"

"Timmy borrowed it?"

"Timmy says no, but who knows?" Once more, Rufus referred to Timmy in the present tense. 'Who knows why the wind blows? Or why have my poops turned red?"

'Eating too many beets?"

'Is that why?" Rufus frowned. 'Even pickled?"

'Surer than a five-legged goat."

'Ohh man, I love those pickled beets."

'Back to the knife, who else might've taken it?"

Rufus shrugged. "How can I keep track of who comes and goes?"

What she should've expected from Rufus. A wasted effort, but at least it delayed the drive to St. Albans. She handed Rufus his lighter. He immediately ignited his bong and inhaled a backhoe-sized hit.

"Well, I'll let you return to Bob Dylan and those Nazis." She opened the front door, but before she stepped out, Rufus finally said something useful.

"You know, somebody else stopped by . . ." he slurred, drifting into his couch. "This guy wearing yellow. A weird yellow, though . . . with black lines."

"Yellow with black lines . . . Do you mean yellow flannel?" Like the piece of fabric in Timmy's hand?

"Bumblebees." Rufus giggled, now thoroughly horizontal.

"Oh no, don't make me fetch the cattle prod." Too late, his eyes closed, and no matter how hard she shook or pinched, he wasn't reviving anytime soon. *Equal to blowing a tire en route to the qualifier.* Well, she'd try again when she returned from St. Albans.

She drove the twenty minutes, encountering two (two!) stoplights. At least the Statie barracks resided on the northeast side of town; she hated city traffic. She parked on the curb and strode into the brick entryway.

"Constable Peggy!" Cassie lounged with her legs crossed on the reception counter. "Welcome to our humble barracks."

"Nice to see you." Peggy smiled. "With that attitude, they won't promote you out of rookie."

Cassie shrugged, then pointed. "He's waiting for you."

Peggy followed the hallway beyond the counter until she reached the end. She opened the left door and entered Commander Strongman's office.

"Hi, Bob." She could barely spot him behind his shiny oak desk covered in framed achievement awards. Peggy sat in the opposing over-cushioned chair.

"Hi, Peggy." He removed his wide-framed glasses and cleaned them with his green Statie uniform.

"Your troopers are finally using my proper title."

"Who, Cassie?" Bob laughed. "She's a rule follower. I don't care if the folks in Rosefield want to call you 'sheriff.'"

"I never asked for the title, but they've used it since the day I started."

"I've always liked 'Sheriff McStoots.' Although, 'Sheriff Strongman' is a little . . . stronger."

Peggy sighed. She dated Bob when they attended Enosburg high school together, a mistake she still regretted. Forty years, a marriage, and three daughters later, Bob thought some chemistry remained between them. "About the autopsy report . . ."

"I have it." He tapped a folder on his desk. "How about I tell you what's inside?"

Peggy considered grabbing the folder and stomping out, but she risked offending him. Then Bob might order his troopers to resume their Rosefield patrol. "What did you find?"

"Timmy died within moments of the knife severing his aorta."

"A knife to the ol' blood bumper." As Peggy diagnosed a month ago.

"No signs of struggle. Whoever stabbed Timmy caught him by surprise. *If* somebody murdered him." He sniffed. "My detective nose points to a suicide."

Bob's 'detective nose' was about as valid as his actual one. "Timmy didn't struggle at all?"

'No bruises, scrapes, nothing under his fingernails." Bob stuck his hands out, then thrust them towards his chest. 'Suicide. Bag it, tag it, and call the game warden."

'What about the piece of flannel?" Peggy debated telling Bob what Rufus described earlier, but then she'd have to reveal her source. Bob would laugh her out of the barracks. 'If he killed himself, how did it end up in his hand?"

'Maybe it was his lucky fabric." He flipped open the folder and searched through the pages. 'Like you, my forensics guy's convinced someone murdered Timmy. He's excited about a hair he identified on the flannel. Nonhuman. *Canis lupus familiaris*."

'Black or chocolate?"

'Yellow. Did Timmy own a Labrador?"

'Noper. Tell your forensics guy to contain his excitement, as it's most likely Tug-Tug's. Everyone who visits Cody's General Store rubs his belly on their way in, even jerks like Timmy. Did he discover anything on the knife?"

'No other DNA discovered besides Timmy's."

'Anything else?"

'Nothing of note." Bob shut the folder and slid it across his desk. 'There's your copy."

'Thank you." Peggy stood up.

'I don't know if you've heard," said Bob, hopping to his feet. 'A new Italian/seafood restaurant opened in St. Albans. I reckoned you might wanna taste. My treat, of course."

'Sorry, guy." She had prepared a lie for this eventuality. 'I promised to watch Lyndsay's kids so she could rest for a night."

'You can be a little late." He trotted around his desk and grabbed her shoulder. 'Remember the nights we shared in high school? Cruising dirt roads in my green van with the white racer stripes and vinyl interior. I still maintain it, you know."

"No," said Peggy, recalling the van—mostly its stench. Wet dog mixed with body odor and a pinch of urine, not too dissimilar to how Bob smelled. "A grandmother's duty never ends. Maybe next time." She turned and stepped to the door.

"I almost forgot, we heard from our out-of-state connections about Timmy's missing years." Peggy stopped. "He ski-bummed up and down the Rockies, working at most of the major resorts."

"Which leaves a lot of holes in his timeline." She sighed. "Do you have a list of all the resorts?"

"I do." Bob smirked. "Plus how long he worked at each. I'll email it to you."

"Thanks. Goodnight." She stomped back down the hallway. Cassie snoozed, so Peggy didn't bother her with a farewell. She hopped into the Road Runner and drove home, encountering two (two!) stoplights.

Upon returning to town, she stopped to question Rufus. He remained incapacitated. She attempted the next day, and the one after, and on the third day, she finally caught him in a conscious state . . . but with no recollection of anyone wearing a yellow flannel. She questioned him for a full hour but received nothing except several more acorns in her gut.

Not a complete loss, in that one moment of clarity, Rufus said 'someone else' wearing a yellow flannel stole the knife. If true, the murderer planned the crime in advance. This wasn't an accident, nor a random fight escalating into a lethal encounter, further confirmed by the lack of bruises or scrapes.

Someone wanted Timmy dead for a reason. They must possess a compelling motive, too, to drive a knife through his heart. He garnered a lot of enemies around town. Did someone hate him enough to kill him?

The ripped yellow flannel made no sense. How did Timmy tear off a piece of his attacker's shirt when there wasn't a struggle? No matter how it ended up in his hand, tracking its owner could provide an important clue. If she scanned old pictures on The Facebook, she'd discover something.

Peggy sighed. She might have to call in reinforcements. Recalling Yelsa's daughters inspired Peggy to employ her own. While Lyndsay and Georgia were busy with the grandbabies, Mary Anne had only her college courses to worry about. However, should Peggy involve her daughter in an active murder investigation? Would it violate some kind of law enforcement ethics?

She'd consider it. Meanwhile, Peggy scoured The Facebook on her own. She could figure out the search bar. Whatever was required to finish this investigation by little Robert's due date.

They called it a murder, and Helmet Joe agreed. Now when they said a helmet wouldn't have stopped the knife, that was a whole other thing.

As a very athletic young man, Timmy did the flippies and the spinnies, the grabbies and the railsies. He skied the upper glades. And the glades above the upper glades. Plus the glades beyond there. He spread the butter and skipped the rope. He skied backward, sideways, and probably upside down, too.

Now, the helmet blocked ice chunks, hardpack, trees, and branches—all from bashing in a skier's brain. Wielded properly, the helmet was every bit as powerful as Captain America's shield.

So, when they said Timmy would've died whether or not he wore a helmet, Joe took exception. Someone as athletic as Timmy, with enough helmet training, could've easily blocked the knife.

Was he murdered? Yes. Would he still be alive if he wore a helmet? Almost certainly. Lesson over.

Happy loved Grandma Day. On the last Saturday of every month, he'd truck over to Uncle Pete's farm for a visit.

She needed the company since she fell off the sled and cracked her knee. She cruised around the house with her four-wheelin' walker but rarely ventured to town with all the hassle. At least Uncle Pete's wide house contained plenty of moseying hallways.

A dozen horses greeted him at the bottom of the driveway, stocky from a long summer graze. Uncle Pete raised them tough. They never wore blankets because they grew thick coats, not even on a toe-freezer of a night. Not on a lip-shriveler, either. A couple of years ago, on an eyelid-sealer, Uncle Pete dressed them all in wool blankets. *Neigh!* They shook them off within twenty minutes.

Happy spotted his favorite, a bronze mustang mare with a white star on her forehead, white socks, and a white tail. All of that blended in with the snow, so she appeared like a fluffy pillow floating about the field. Happy waved to Bess, and she neighed back. He wished he could ride her today, but he already committed to a sunset skin with the Powder Crew.

He passed by the hundred-year-old moo-moo barn. The sagging roof threatened to cave in during the next blizzard, and the wallboards slanted so severely, Happy cricked his neck looking at them. Uncle Pete kept mostly dairy moo-moos, plus a few oinkers and a clucker coop on the far side.

He puttered up the quarter-mile driveway and parked in front of the massive horse barn, shinier than last week. Every summer, he repainted the outside and scrubbed the interior until the lumber appeared fresh off the mill. Uncle Pete insisted his herd sleep in pristine stalls, as Laura had maintained.

"Happy!" Uncle Pete stepped out of the barn dressed in his riding attire: jeans, a black leather jacket, a brown cowboy hat, and pointed leather boots. More John Wayne than the legend himself.

'Uncle Pete!" After a handshake, Happy noticed Banker Henry step out of the barn and strut to his Prius.

'Good day to you." Henry tipped his bowler hat before squeezing into the driver's seat. 'And no more delinquency!" He shut the door and sped down the driveway.

'What's that all about?" asked Happy.

'Oh, your father . . ." Uncle Pete shook his head.

'Ope. Is he behind on the mortgage again?"

'Don't tell your mom, I don't hanker Charlie living on my couch. Again."

'Not a peep. I'll be quieter than a mouse in the cat jaw. I'm actually here for Grandma Day."

'Already? The mountain's so busy, the month's over before I flip the calendar page."

'I meant to tell you, nice job on the new name, bud. All the Powder Boys agree. 'Slaying those drifts!' That's Joey's new motto."

'I'll tell Mr. Buric you approve."

'We know it was your idea," said Happy. 'Rodney Buric couldn't figure where to put the udder on a cow."

'Or where to put the cheese on a poutine."

'Or the gas on a bonfire."

'Or the maple on the snow."

'That's two foods," observed Happy. 'You must be hungry."

'Hungrier than a pig at chow time. I store jerky in the barn so Mom won't eat it." A sparkle emerged in Uncle Pete's eyes. 'Also, I need to clean out Dancer's old stall because a new horse is arriving."

'Biscuit my dog!" Happy whistled. 'What breed?"

Uncle Pete giggled like a schoolgirl receiving her first rifle. 'A Percheron!"

'No! You said 'Never again.'"

'I had made that declaration." Uncle Pete removed his hat and placed it over his chest. 'Percheron was Laura's favorite breed. After she passed,

I couldn't bear owning another . . . until I gazed upon Laura."

"Same name!?"

"Yes. *Laura*." He sang the name with a heartbreaking melody. "I had to buy her, no matter the cost."

"It's destiny. Reminds me of when I first beheld my sled and learned its name was 'Harry.' If the name fits . . ." Happy whistled. "I look forward to meeting her."

Uncle Pete nodded, but his eyes remained downcast, and he wiped a tear. Laura was beautiful and kind, and their horses were her final manifestation. He'd do anything for them.

A few months ago, the Viceroy boys reckoned they might joyride one. Nopers, bud. They hadn't even mounted the horse before Uncle Pete confronted them with his favorite shotgun and a line straight out of an old western. "You gonna step off the stirrup, or will this gun do it for ya?" The Viceroy boys scampered off with their pants a little browner for the experience.

"Sorry, guy," said Uncle Pete. "I miss her."

"Ain't nothing for you to apologize about." Happy wrapped an arm around his uncle's shoulder.

"Get off," laughed Uncle Pete. "Go on, say hi to your grandmother. I have stalls to muck out."

"Yeppers, bud."

Happy entered the front door and called, "Grandma!"

"Happy?" Her voice echoed down the hallway with the gentleness of a baby's fart. She wore her favorite yellow dress and a matching hat over her grey curls. "Is it already Saturday?"

"Grandma Day!" He hurried down the hall and delivered a bear-sized (but hen-strength) hug. "Best day of the month, better than Cody's Pie Day."

"Oh, Cody's pies . . ." She rubbed her belly and smiled. Then she pointed out the bay window to the grazing horses. "Did your uncle tell you he's buying a new horse?"

'Laura the Percheron! I love her already."

"Me too. I usually tell Peter that he oughta reduce his herd, just for the financials. Once I heard her story . . ." Grandma dropped jaw. "Welcome to the farm!"

"He's had a difficult few years."

"Your father's instigations don't help. Did Peter share his latest tomfoolery?"

"Yeah. I saw Banker Henry on my way in."

"I thought I beat enough sense into Charlie, but I too often listened to your Grandpa's soft heart." Grandma smirked. "At least he supported Peter through his loss. No matter how much my sons fight, they're the closest of brothers. Whichever fool tries to hurt one of them will gain the other as a lifelong enemy."

"Foolishness that deep only exists in the flatlands."

"Thankfully." Grandma glanced out the window again. "Will you ride Bess today?"

"Actually, I'm meeting the boys at five for a night hike."

"You'll snowboard in the dark?"

"Our headlamps shine brighter than Mo-Vegas."

"Just be careful, especially with this murderer in town."

"The murderer isn't from Rosefield. My guess is a southerner, from Rutland or even Bennington."

"Don't count out Burlington," chuckled Grandma. "Plenty of flatties attend the university."

"A few Rosefieldians do, too."

"Ah, yes. Your beloved Mary Anne attends UVM."

"She's not my 'beloved,'" grumbled Happy.

"You've crushed on her since kindergarten. Maybe you should adjust your sights. I heard the Sled Stop hired a new waitress."

"I'm waiting for the right doe."

"Sorry, guy. A grandma must tease her grandson." She laughed and slapped knee. "Let's move to the kitchen for coffee and dominoes."

"Yeppers." She brewed the best coffee, from beans roasted by Happy's cousin Dan, plus her own secret ingredient. Today they drank the Deuces blend, a French Vanilla that Grandma favored, but Happy preferred Cardiac's bold taste. Heck, he couldn't conduct his morning 'unload' without guzzling a cup of Roaster Dan's first.

Once the coffee finished brewing, they moved to Grandpa's oak dining table he chainsaw-carved thirty years ago as a wedding anniversary present.

"Before we play," said Grandma, once comfortable. "I hanker a favor."

"Anything." Happy laughed. "Ope. Not *anything*. Remember when you dared me to shoot a rifle from horseback like the cowboys? I almost broke my neck!"

"*Whatever doesn't break you will make you.*" One of Grandma's favorite sayings and a mantra she drilled into her two boys. The primary reason Uncle Pete and Happy's dad grew into two of the toughest guys in Rosefield.

Grandma grabbed an envelope from her purse and slid it across Grandpa's table. "I need you to deliver this to Peggy."

"Sure." Happy scratched his head. "Uh, which Peggy?"

"Sheriff McStoots, your 'beloved' Mary Anne's mother."

"Hah." Happy flipped the letter over and felt the seal. She licked the glue, but he could probably steam it open. "What's it about?"

"I'll only tell you if you swear to bring it right to Peggy. No peeking."

He nodded vigorously. "I swear on the soul of my favorite shotgun."

Grandma raised an eyebrow.

"Okay, okay." He contemplated his sweet baby Remi. "I swear on the soul of my favorite hunting rifle."

She raised her other eyebrow. "And?"

This required the ultimate deal. Happy would stay strong. His curiosity wouldn't overpower his love for Remi. "If I peek, she's yours."

"All right then." She gazed out the window. "You know Diane

Robbitet? She manages Cody's deli."

"Yepper, she prepares the best sandwich in town, large enough to dislocate your jaw."

"Well, Diane and I partnered for team cribbage, and she learned this from her cousin Florence. You might know him from the Sled. He lives in Stowe."

"Unrung bells."

"Doesn't matter. Florence told Diane about a new version of cribbage, brand new rules." She giggled and squirmed in her seat. "Two cribs. Two!"

"Why don't you tell Peggy when she's at cribbage night?"

"She hasn't attended since the murder investigation began. She's determined to identify the killer by summer. No distractions. A shame, Peggy's my favorite partner when we play team cribbage."

"You could call her."

"I hate these new phones, worse than computers. Too many buttons and pictures. Besides, I want Peggy to witness the official rules, printed out." Grandma giggled and shook her arms in a happy dance. The last time Happy saw her this excited was when Uncle Pete bought her a new four-wheeler. "She's gonna jump right out of her truck!"

"Why don't you deliver it yourself, then?"

"Because I'm old. I only leave this house to kick your ass on the way out. Or the occasional cribbage night. Just complete the task and no more questions, or I receive your rifle."

Happy bit his lip and nodded. Grandma always cut a shrewd but fair deal. "Okay." He put the envelope in a pocket. "With that deer tied to the grill, shall we proceed to what's important?" He reached over to the sill and grabbed the cloth bag.

"If I remember, I won the last two weeks in a row."

"Your dementia just turned on." Happy spread the dominoes across the table. "You haven't won since they invented electricity."

"You insult *my* memory? When you've clearly forgotten how well I

crack a belt?"

They laughed and slapped knee. They chitchatted through three games, addressing every essential topic: snow accumulation, the upcoming sledding season, the Powder Crew's exploits, and gossip from cribbage night.

Grandma won every match, and she bragged about it all the way out of the farmhouse. "Come back after you watch one of them YouTube things," she called from the porch. "It's spelled D-O-M-I-N-O-E-S."

"Love you, Grandma." He pulled out of the driveway with his head hung.

He never stood a chance, no way he could focus on dominoes with that letter in his pocket. What did it really contain? Grandma could out-lie a lawyer, but Happy knew her since he popped out of his Mama. The letter didn't involve Deli Diane, her cousin, *or* cribbage. She needed to send Peggy a message, but why not deliver it herself? It required all of his willpower not to open the letter on the drive home. Whenever he felt his fingers scrape at the seal, he considered his dear Remi. He couldn't abandon her after all their hunts together.

He hiked with the Powder Crew, and he forgot all about the letter. Nothing like a twelve hundred foot vertical up and down to work the worms out of the hay. Well, at least until he returned home and noticed it on his dining table, once more calling to his natural curiosity. No, he'd remain steadfast, for Remi's sake. He'd bring it to Peggy in the morning on his way to work.

He brought it to his car, at least, but he forgot to stop as he drove up Left Mountain Road. No problem, he'd drop the letter off after his rental shop shift. Except that didn't happen, either. He had a month before the next Grandma Day. He'd decide by then what was more important, his favorite hunting rifle or discovering his grandmother's secret.

An epic New Year's Eve party raged at the Sled Stop tonight, and Joey prepared all week. While driving to St. Albans proved difficult with one arm, he ventured for the legendary VerMart Everything Store. What happened to his other arm? Wrapped up in a cast after snapping (like a bitch) when he skied into a tree. The *humerus* bone they called it . . . hah! Nothing funny about it.

He'd power through this injury like a chest-high snowdrift. Joey had broken many bones over his storied career: cracked both hips and nearly a dozen ribs, hairline fractured a shin or two, hyperextended his right knee, chipped seven teeth, and popped his left shoulder out more times than he remembered. Oh, and memory loss due to the eleven or so concussions. He recovered from all those. This new injury was no different.

While a broken arm might prevent him from ripping runs for a couple of weeks (doctors said a few months, but they didn't know Joey like Joey knew Joey), he still partied in pro form. Which brought him to St. Albans, home of the historic VerMart Everything Store. It began as a humble country store carrying groceries and general goods but expanded over the century. Twelve additions later, the rambling structure spanned an entire block, rivaling the department stores down the road.

First, he hit the beer section, then the snack zone, before finally firing over to the best part of VerMart, Party Central. Two full rows of Glow Stix, sparklers, poppers, funny glasses, face paint, body paint, soul paint, Buddha statues, beer helmets, shotgun pokers, enough glitter to blanket Town Hall, and LEDs with more spectrums than a TV. After three hours of deciding, he realized none of it sufficed. What would Jonathan G. Weevil do? Something so explosive no one would ever forget this New Year's Eve! In the end, he bought a case of beer and a bag of chips.

He drove to Richford next, where his cousin James manufactured amateur fireworks in his garage. The same place he concocted his energy supplements.

"I need you to construct the Big One!" Joey exclaimed as he burst through the front door.

"Affirmative, bud," said James. "It'll take me six days, and I'll require a small fortune for parts."

It cost Joey all of his three-figure savings, but for the Big One? Worth all of it and more. He picked it up the morning of New Year's Eve. James secured it in a paper bag with a staple.

"Thanks, bud."

"Yeppers, bud."

When New Year's Eve finally arrived, Joey reminded himself right at the beginning to pace. If he intended to endure until midnight, he couldn't drink every shot handed to him at the first pre-party. Except Handy Jesse provided jello shots with his homemade moonshine! Distilled in the basement from corn and barley. Of course, Joey tried one. A second came naturally when the crowd gathered for cheers. The third because they tasted delicious.

Frederico hosted the second pre-party, and he prepared every drinking game imaginable—possibly more dangerous than jello shots. He filled a table with cards, quarters, and beer mines. In the living room were both beer pong *and* flip cup. He arranged stump, trick-shot darts, and paddle pong in the basement, plus drinking cornhole in the garage. Joey limited himself to only two hours at Frederico's because one stop remained before the Sled.

He smelled Rufus's house from the other side of town. The eruption of smoke when Joey opened the front door almost knocked him over. He walked into a haze of cantaloupe, purple, and g13 by the smell of it. Bowls, bongs, and rigs of every shape and size lined the coffee and dining table, the kitchen counter, and the floor. It felt weird being in Timmy's old house, so Joey departed after twenty minutes. Besides, if he inhaled too much, he'd never survive until midnight.

From there, he sauntered to the Sled Stop, stopping at his truck briefly to grab the Big One (which he kept concealed in its brown paper bag) and a beer. As he staggered down Main Street, he contemplated Timmy Harton's demise. Every Rosefieldian harbored ideas of what happened to him, but Joey harbored better ideas.

Timmy left town for five years and returned with enhanced skiing skills, so he traveled someplace snowy. What about Japan? Timmy heard about their legendary mountains where snow stacked higher than houses, and he desired it for himself. He bought a one-way ticket.

Except, only those mastered in the ancient Japanese arts could wield the mighty parabolics. After several years of intense samurai training, he attained enlightenment and gained access to their mountains. He fell in love. Bikinied women lounged about every lodge, and endless snow dumped throughout the year. Paradise.

Timmy biffed it, however, when he committed an unforgivable offense. He slighted someone important or skied with impure form. Whatever his transgression, they banished him.

The pain of his failure consumed him over the years until he couldn't bear it. So this fall, Timmy hiked up for one last run. At the bottom, he committed *seppuku* on himself. It also explained why he hung up his green jacket beforehand, no reason to waste functional snow gear by drenching it in blood.

Maybe he should have Peggy's job. While 'Sheriff Joey' sounded very official and heroic, it was more responsibility than he hankered. For instance, could he enjoy himself on New Year's Eve, or would he have to patrol the streets? Joey should stick to the two things he performed best, skiing and partying.

Frank and Mary thoroughly decorated the Sled Stop, as they did every holiday season. Christmas lights hung across the bedroom balconies and around all the windows, a wreath covered in red bows hung on the front door. They mounted the old New Year's flag, the same one from forty years ago when they bought the building. A little tattered around the edges, but the colors appeared freshly dyed.

Marvin checked IDs and collected money out front. While expected, Joey never paid cover charges on principle. Besides, when he won the next big air competition, he'd give the Sled a shoutout. Should more than cover him.

He snuck around and climbed the fire escape. A locked door confronted him at the top, so he drew his health insurance card and targeted the space between the door and the frame. He missed, way too high. He tried again, this time too low. Finally, on his third drive, he lined his credit card up at the correct angle. He pushed it through the lock until the door popped open. He should slow down on the drinking if he required three attempts to bypass a simple door lock. He slipped his social security card into his wallet and charged down the stairs.

Joey bumped into a Powder Crew brother the moment he entered the bar. "Mr. Happy Smith, happy New Year!"

"Happy New Year! I just ordered a shot, bud, you hankerin'?" Happy threw up a mogul.

"Does a Powder Hound huck a cliff?" Joey popped two fingers over his friend's fist.

"Yeppers, and he'll straight-line a chute, too. Pour another, Jane!"

Of course, Jane worked the bar. The busiest party of the year demanded their best and prettiest bartender. She served the whiskey shots in moments, along with a freshly poured pair of Bacons.

"Happy New Year!" they cheered and slammed those shots.

"All right, I'm gonna mingle," said Joey.

"Brad's on the dance floor, already chatting up Rosefield's finest bunnies."

Joey spotted his friend, looming a full foot over the rest of the crowd. He wore a tight-fitting Carpartt vest, a pink lei, and his hair slicked. Tall Brad had accumulated quite the nest: party twins Dixie and Trixie from Bakersfield, the waitress from the Enosburg barbecue spot, and the French girl Danielle—one of the best telemark skiers to drop knee. Joey should step in, say what's up, and mention his ski skills, but he told Jesse he'd buy him a shot. "What about Handy?"

"He just arrived, out on the deck."

"Three more, Jane!" One for Happy to repay him, one for Jesse in return for those jello shots earlier, and one for himself. Pacing was for Jerries anyway.

"Coming right up." Jane trounced those blue square girls. She was a triple black diamond, with eyes prettier than a blizzard rolling in. Her black hair brushed her shoulders in a gentle outward wave like the perfect jump ramp. She was tough, too. Whenever a brawl broke out at the Sled Stop, she'd break it up, often landing a couple of her famous backhands in the process.

Only one flaw, she snowboarded.

Jane returned with the shots in moments. Joey handed one whiskey to Happy and escorted the other two onto the porch.

Jesse and Crazy Bob hollered their conspiracies over each other. What morons, Joey couldn't wait for their dropped jaws when he delivered the *seppuku* twist.

". . . which led to Westminster, and then the American Revolution!" shouted Jesse. He wore his usual brown pullover and red fedora.

"Jacques Allen?" Bob laughed. He flicked his red overalls against his camo dress shirt. "A *Quebecois* infiltrator, Ethan Allen recognized the traitor in his cousin. That's why he ordered Jacques to defend his post alone."

"Traitor? The French and Indian War ended a decade prior. Quebec was our ally at this point. No, the *hero* Jacques Allen defended this region from loyalist New Yorkers, killing three and causing the rest to flee!"

"As written by the Green Mountain Boys, who didn't want their reputation tarnished."

"Jeezum crow, fellas," broke in Joey while handing Jesse a shot. "It's New Year's, not July 4th."

"What's in the bag?" asked Jesse.

"First bud, cheers." They drained their shots, and then Joey opened the bag. "Some party favors."

"Ohhh, that ain't *just* party favors . . ."

"It's the Big One. For years Cousin James dreamt of building this rocket, and I handed him the cash to achieve it."

"I don't know, Joey." Here came Jesse's objections. "He also mentioned a 50% failure rate."

"It's New Year's. We gotta send it harder than a two-foot dump. Step in and step off, right? Why spin when you can flip? Grab some ski, make it official." Joey slammed the rest of his Bacon. "I'm gonna fetch another, and then I'll tell you how Timmy died."

He marched two steps towards the door, but a cloud of smoke blocked his path, followed by Rufus. How had he arrived so fast? He was just at his house with a bunch of people. Joey didn't notice before, but Rufus looked pale and smelled like fermented lemons.

"Hey man, you know how Timmy died?"

"Oh, prepare your mind for some melting. First, I require a Bacon, but when I—"

"Have mine." Rufus handed him a full pint glass.

"Okay." Joey shrugged. His knowledge came with a price, and he accepted Rufus's offering. He drank a quarter of the pint before starting. "It began in Japan. Remember when he left Rosefield for a while? That's where he went. He learned under a guru or whatever, who taught him a samurai code . . ." He delved into the whole thing, right to the tragic ending.

"Wow," said Rufus. He put out his joint. It smelled lawny, like actual grass. Maybe he discovered the ultimate strain. "Right on."

"Well, I'm gonna—"

"Hey man, Timmy's old skis . . . who gets those?"

"A superb question." Joey scratched his head. Timmy owned some fine alpine. "Did he leave a will?"

"Noper. Makes you hanker one, right?" Rufus coughed as he relit his joint, which once again smelled like a fresh-cut yard. Not the usual smell for high-quality weed, but Rufus knew his ganja better than anyone. "But about those skis. I've tried them all just to see. I'll, uh, take them if that eases things."

"They're in your possession," reasoned Joey.

"It's what he'd choose. I'll actually use them. His family members? They'll probably stick his skis in their basement until they rust out."

"His uncle won't use them, not unless he leaves his cabin on Deep Gregory. And Amy hasn't skied since she moved to St. Albans. Perhaps Timmy fathered a Japanese love-child, but they wouldn't want an exile's skis." Joey finished the half-pint and handed the empty glass to Rufus. "Now I hanker another."

Rufus continued about a plan, but Joey was already moguls beyond him. He charged inside, straight-lining to the bar with a hockey stop finish. "One Bacon!"

Seconds later, Jane refilled his pint, served with a wink. What he'd sacrifice for just one run with her . . . from top to bottom . . . into every chute—Ope. So busy fantasizing, Joey wobbled like a newbie. Pace, pace, pace, he chanted to himself while sipping on his beer. He should find Tall Brad and those ladies, tell them all about Japan.

Joey weaved his way to the dance floor, sliding between folks like slalom gates on his way to a first-place finish. When he arrived at the packed dance floor, he strutted through the crowd like a champion.

'Brad!" he shouted while busting out his best series of dance moves, a shifty to the left, another to the right, with an eagle finale. All in perfect sync to *Highway to Hell*.

Tall Brad accepted the challenge, popping an ollie three-sixty into a flawless nose mute. *Boom!* Joey conceded, he lacked the dance skills to keep up with Brad. 'Happy New Year!" They clinked their Bacons together and drank down half a pint.

'You seeing these bunnies?" shouted Brad over the music.

'Doin' the boys proud!"

'I have hare to spare if you wanna join!"

Danielle's sway caused her blonde hair to brush against her rounded skier's rump. Dixie and Trixie danced close to each other, wearing tight white dresses and their hair in identical strawberry bobs. All very sexy, but Joey couldn't risk Jane seeing him with the French girl or the Bakersfield twins.

"There's something long-term! I'm hitting the pool table."

They cheered once more, then Joey one-eightied off the dance floor. No sidetracking, not even by the waitress from the BBQ place. Midnight approached, and the Big One required preparation. Since he passed by the bar, he might as well order another shot.

As he pushed through the thickening crowd, he brushed Yelsa Hodinker wearing a slinky red dress. For a mother of two grown daughters, she wielded curves matching a world championship slalom. Others wagged their jaws, too, including that creepster Roger.

So distracted, Joey stumbled right into Jordan Herring. 'Sorry, guy!"

'I'm not a guy. I'm your boss." He wore his black and white Park & Grill Head Judge outfit, with the matching poofy hat. 'I heard about the kid on Rusch Chute."

'Oh . . . that."

"His parents requested your termination."

"Well, that's off-trail," protested Joey. "He claimed to be the best skier since Nick Rusch himself. I figured what better place to test his claim?"

"He's nine."

"The same age I learned the importance of proving my boasts. Besides, all of the greatest skiers sport facial scarring. It's a mark of commitment."

"If only I had the numbers to fire you," groaned Jordan before stomping away. He just couldn't handle Joey's truth bombs, not yet. One day they'd explode his mind in the ultimate revelation.

Joey advanced to the bar. He raised his hand, and Jane brought him a shot. He should tell her his theory on Timmy's murder; she'd appreciate it due to her Japanese heritage. Jane must have learned about *seppuku* and the mountains packed with powder and samurais from her traditional grandmother. Her mind would explode!

Afterward, he'd invite her to his place. He owned vodka, some flavor of juice, a frozen pizza, and a full-sized floor mattress—the perfect way to cap off the night. He'd ask her . . . after a confidence shot. Down the hatch and courage instantly spread from his gut, but not quite enough. He'd wait until after he launched the Big One. As the hero of Rosefield, Jane couldn't resist his offer.

Big Top interrupted his fantasy with a rough hand on the shoulder. "Joey!"

Joey turned and raised his glass. *Clink!* "Happy New Year!" they exclaimed in unison. Despite his tiny legs, he skied with some serious skill.

"I haven't seen you since last season," said Joey. "How was your summer?"

"Pocketed deep money from my rafting gig down in Connecticut, my usual offseason drift. I love floating down a quiet river with my fishing pole, a case of beer, and a bucket of bait." He whistled. "Like peering down unscratched corduroy."

As Joey stared at Big Top, he realized something differed from last season. Nothing in the face, the same orange beard sprawled across his cheeks, joining his burgeoning ear hairs. His broken nose remained crooked.

"When the river froze," continued Big Top, "I returned to Rosefield for trail maintenance. I chopped a couple of nice lines in the Steeps and Open Glade. Plus, in Outer Limits, I cut a line so deep, I bet Ski Patrol has to rescue a dozen custies from the Flats this season. Wilma will be furious!"

His flannel jacket! For years Big Top wore the same yellow flannel jacket. Wait. There was something significant about a yellow flannel.

"I rarely ski the trees myself. I'm a speed hound these days, top to bottom and back on the lift. It's how I cook at the restaurant, slinging out burgers as fast as I can toast the buns." Big Top laughed. "Especially this winter, we've filled every table, every night, for *two* weeks. We've already served more plates than all of last season."

Like a dozen water shots at once, Joey sobered up. Timmy held a yellow flannel in his death grip! Big Top said he cut trees in Open Glade this fall. What if he witnessed Timmy's death?

"It's just the time of year. When spring comes, I'll dip into the glades for some shade." Big Top glanced at his watch. "The countdown will start soon. I'm gonna head over to the stage."

"Yeah, man." Joey stared at Big Top as he lumbered away. A whole new feature just dropped on the Timmy mystery. Was he involved? Or even the killer? But why? Joey stared through the crowd at Big Top, dancing with Dixie, Trixie, and the rest, adjusting his *seppuku* theory with this new information.

When midnight arrived, everyone shouted the countdown except for Joey. He even forgot about the Big One. For the next two hours, he barely acknowledged anyone. No way Big Top killed Timmy, no way! But maybe . . .

So lost in thought, Joey didn't notice when John Viceroy and Thomas the Train began fighting. When Jane backhanded Thomas off John, Joey barely raised his eyes. He considered his theory and how Big Top was involved. Did he work for the Japanese?

His New Year's spirit only returned at the first after-party at Mechanic Joe's house. Probably because Big Top wasn't there, but the multiple kegs of Pork Chop certainly helped. Joey preferred Bacon, but as a stronger IPA, he re-drunk faster.

At the second after-party, he recovered completely, downing shots and chugging beers. He'd remember what he learned and improve his theories. He'd crack the case.

At the third after-party, he fell asleep on Crazy Bob's couch an hour before sunrise.

After days of reflection, Joey ranked this New Year's Eve as seventh on his all-time greatest list. If he'd lit the Big One, it would've ranked way higher.

Joey would wait until the *perfect* moment. How about when he announced to everyone in town who killed Timmy and why? First, he needed to prove Big Top was a Japanese assassin.

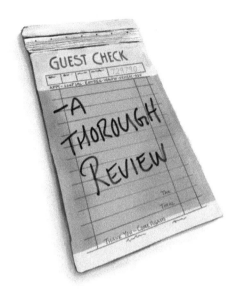

The Crimson Sentry guarded the second key. Clad in full armor and armed with a sword wider than a tree trunk, he was also one of the greatest tea composers in the entire nation. This would be Kappu's most formidable adversary yet.

"You've come for your final steep?" growled the Crimson Sentry.

"I've sapped every henchman so far." Kappu drew the Soul Pestle. Its neon glow brightened with every episode. "Your flavor will soon join the rest."

"Lord Ketoru has ruled over this island for the past three centuries. He won't be defeated by a squirt like you."

"Every fifty years, his enforcers and sentries are defeated, and he is challenged." Kappu dropped several pinches of meadow root and a dollop of horsespruce into his enhanced mortar. "I'll ensure he never taints another ounce of this nation again!"

"You'll dry out like the rest!" The Crimson Sentry lunged forward, swinging his sword around as though it was as light as a sapling. The earth yielded to the blade in an explosion of soil and roots, a dozen feet deep and wide obliterated in a moment.

Except Kappu had dodged already, managing to sprinkle a few drops of buttersap onto his composition simultaneously. A single strike from the Soul Pestle and the ingredients combined. Alamant vines burst from the mortar, twisting upwards in a weave so fine it formed an edge sharp enough to cut through steel.

Kappu raised his weapon and charged. He parried the Crimson Sentry's second attack with enough force to shatter his sword! With his opponent disarmed, Kappu readied for the final steep.

Except the Crimson Sentry produced a backup blade, precomposed with enhanced piercing. He flicked it directly at Kappu's heart. He couldn't defend in time, was this it?

"Dropping in!" In a flurry of steps, Baggu extended his eternal shield and blocked the dagger. Of course, the writers had to give the lowly assistant *something* to do.

The point-of-view panned back to Kappu, the star. He thrust, piercing the Crimson Sentry's armor in the weak spot above the hip.

Within moments, Kappu drained every ounce of composition from his enemy, and he glowed as neon as the Soul Pestle.

He then performed his post-battle ritual. Kappu held his mother's purple pendant to his heart and meditated. He saw flashes of her dancing in a field of rosegrass, her silver hair whipping with the wind, and her song swirled like a tornado. Then his mother disappeared, like a memory that lost its validation.

Kappu pocketed the purple pendant. Then he retrieved the second key and continued on his path towards the showdown with Lord Ketoru.

In a couple of months, they released the series finale. Surely, Kappu would triumph, but what then? Would he absolve the Kuki Tea Company and return the land rights to the commoners? Bah! So they could squander their wealth?

No, Rodney had the perfect prediction: Kappu would assume Lord Ketoru's position as owner and operator of the Kuki Tea Company. Sure, he'd institute some anti-monopoly rules or whatever the peasants wanted, but Kappu was too smart to let the foolish masses operate on their own.

Similarly, the Rosefield Mountain managers required constant supervision. Today, Rodney had an afternoon packed with meetings. Each of his department heads needed their monthly review.

He glanced at his phone. When was the first meeting scheduled? Ten minutes ago. He might as well mosey down to Mountain View.

He considered changing the restaurant's name to fit the rest of the mountain's murder theme. Murder View, perhaps? Or Mountain Homicide, Death Food, Is There Arsenic?, Die-In or Takeout, etc. All excellent options, but he decided on keeping Mountain View's name. As the fanciest restaurant in town, it should retain a respectable title.

Apparently, Rodney's sensibilities held merit. Tourists filled every table. They smelled like sweet, sweet money. Rodney disliked their noise, however, so he usually dined in his living-suite.

When he arrived, he climbed to the best table on top of the old stage. Who liked live music anyway? Once he settled, he signaled Francis to commence with the meetings. The Mountain View Head Waiter hurried out of the restaurant, and Jordan Herring strode in shortly after.

He wore his yellow Ski School jacket and carried his helmet like he just stepped off the slopes. Which meant he smelled. Jordan should shower before meeting with his boss. He enjoyed a full thirty-minute lunch break.

"Thank you for coming," said Rodney.

"Can't refuse a meeting with the boss." When Jordan sat, his rotted onion stench overwhelmed Rodney.

"No, you can't. Order whatever you desire." Rodney snapped his finger, and his favorite server materialized.

"May I take your order?" said Francis. A sharply folded bowtie filled out his wrinkle-free black and white uniform.

"Whatever?" Jordan laughed with an obnoxious drawl. "I'll have the smothered steak. Extra mushrooms."

A superb choice. In fact, the smothered steak was Rodney's favorite dinner. But for lunch, what was Jordan trying to prove? He might've earned himself a demerit.

"Excellent choice," said Francis and disappeared. What perfect service.

"I've decided to meet with all the managers about this murder thing," began Rodney. "First the good news, profits are up! Way up. Murder Mountain, my idea, recorded more profits this holiday week than ever before. Weeks later, we're still on track for our most profitable year ever. Keep it up."

"I support the Burics in every capacity." Odd, he used the plural for Buric. Did he have a lisp? Another demerit.

"I must ask, where were you when Timmy was murdered?"

"Well, I, uh . . ." Jordan coughed. Sweat formed upon his brow. How disgusting. "I hiked around the—"

"It doesn't matter. It's a required question." Peter thought it would increase morale if Rodney pretended to care. What a *Baggu* idea. "Lastly, how can I assist your department?"

Jordan's eyes lit up. "We need fencing for the bunny slope. Plus, the Park & Grill judging uniforms have faded over decades—"

"Another required question. Here's your food." Francis arrived in perfect timing, as always. "Pay the bartender on your way out."

"Pay?"

"Of course." Rodney waved him away. "Send in Yelsa. She should be waiting outside."

Jordan departed, taking his stank with him. Rodney snapped his fingers twice, and Francis appeared with an air freshener.

While he waited, Rodney considered Kappu. How did he remain patient when interacting with Baggu and the other commoners? That was probably a greater struggle than any of his battles with Lord Ketoru's enforcers.

Yelsa promptly filled Jordan's chair. She wore a purple dress and tied her hair in an elaborate bun secured with a rainbow-colored scrunchie. Considering her alternative attitude, Rodney had once thought about asking her if she liked anime but decided it was too risky.

"Mr. Buric," she squeaked.

"Thank you for coming." He snapped his fingers, and Francis appeared. "Order whatever you desire."

'I ate lunch already." Yelsa fidgeted with her dress cuff and avoided his eyes. Rodney often instilled anxiety into his employees when he met with them personally. A sure sign of respect. 'Is this meeting about the Staties? They patrol Generally Slanted sometimes. Do you know what they're searching for?"

"Their presence is annoying," agreed Rodney. 'No one buys booze with cops around."

'Are they looking into financials? Checking books? I heard the SEC often pokes around budgets and money allocations. What about the Staties? I only ask because Generally Slanted's numbers might appear a little strange to someone who doesn't know how to read—"

"You won't order anything?" What kind of person didn't order *something* when seated at a restaurant? Of course, Francis waited with the patience of a statue.

'Well . . ." She studied the menu for so long Rodney considered a quick nap. Meanwhile, poor Francis waited for her, unable to check on his other tables. How insensitive. 'I'll order a cup of soup," she finally squeaked.

She chose the cheapest thing on the menu. Had Jordan said something to her? Yet another demerit, Rodney might have to fire his head of Ski School.

'I've decided to meet with all the managers about this whole murder-thing," began Rodney. 'First, the good news. Skyrocketing profits! Higher than ever, my Murder Mountain rebranding idea continues to draw the crowds. Keep it up."

'Fantastic! Generally Slanted's sales are *shockingly* strong, as well." She giggled ever so squeakily. 'Halloween's my favorite holiday. I love the spookiness."

'Uh-huh, high sales." Rodney flashed her a thumbs up. Like the Kuki workers from *Soul Pestle*, Rosefield's employees appreciated physical affirmation of their success. 'You're doing great."

'Although, I miss the old name occasionally. 'Rosefield Mountain

Resort' has a little ring to it, and—"

"Great, Yelsa." He cut her off because, if allowed, Yelsa would tell him everything from her favorite yoga position to the type of tea she drank on her hiking trip in India. Besides, why change Murder Mountain when they earned a pile of cash daily? That was the stupidest idea since carpooling.

Bah, these interviews soured his mood. "I gotta ask, where were you when Timmy was murdered?"

"Hm, I, uh . . ." Odd. Usually, she chatted endlessly but shut up for this simple question. "Such a long time ago, and so much has happened. I might've conducted inventory at Generally Slanted. Or maybe . . ."

"Interesting." Rodney didn't care as long as she kept producing profits. "Lastly, how may I assist your department?"

"Since you mention it, Roger Elwood really stepped up. I know your NOPE—No Overtime Permitted Ever—policy, but Roger has clocked out and kept working on over a dozen occasions." Yelsa tugged at her rainbow-colored scrunchie. "Could we repay him with an end-of-season bonus?"

"Bonus?" Rodney almost spat his drink at her. "You're joking, right? I assume you haven't heard of my BOOT policy?"

Yelsa shook her head, and he enjoyed watching her eyes tremble.

"Bonus Offer Obligates Termination. In simple English, if you ask for a bonus, you suffer the BOOT!" Rodney let Yelsa squirm in her chair for a full minute before giving her the good news. "Since it's your first offense, I won't fire you today."

"Well, I heard about a deal with your GMs. If resort profits reach a certain amount, they earn . . . additional wages."

He grunted. How had she heard about that? If Yelsa knew, *all* the other department managers knew, too. If he didn't break this idea now, they'd all come begging.

"We will reinvest all profits back into the mountain," lied Rodney. "Even if we do extraordinarily well, we require infrastructure repairs, plus new hotels to build. The hot tubs need an upgrade, as they're barely warmer than my bath. Et cetera. Perfect timing, Francis."

The top server handed Yelsa the soup in a to-go cup and disappeared. Who wanted a lingering waiter? Again, perfection, Francis was the only competent employee Rodney possessed. "Pay the bartender for your . . . meal. And send Jeremy in when you see him."

She protested, so he coughed and waved her away. Yelsa slumped off, defeated. And Peter thought Rodney might improve his employee management skills. Bah! What a *Baggu* suggestion.

Soon after, Jeremy McJoy entered the restaurant and sat opposite Rodney. He resembled a toy top, hence his nickname Big Top. He wore a red slicker. Odd, didn't he usually wear a flannel jacket? Something more lumberjack to compliment his thick red beard and tangled hair. How unprofessional. Murder Mountain needed to tighten up its dress code. "Thank you for coming."

"My office is in Mountain View kitchen, not far at all. Although, I rarely have time for paperwork this season. When a customer yearns for a meal, they receive one no matter what, even if I cook it myself."

"I appreciate what you do. The steaks taste incredible lately. I enjoy the gravy's beer-ish flavor. What have you changed?"

"To allow Head Chef Rob creative control, he writes the menu. I'll ask him and let you know." Big Top clapped twice. "F & B! We're the backbone of the mountain, as I tell my team. Cook delicious food and serve strong beverages."

"Not too strong," Rodney pointed out.

"Yepper. Strong as in strongly watered beverages. Two inches of foam on a beer and two seconds of water in a cocktail. Two & Two Rule we call it. Two & Two!"

Always shouting his slogans, Big Top was the loudest person Rodney ever met. "Perfect. Order anything you desire." He snapped his fingers, and Francis arrived.

"I'll chomp on a burger. Tell Rob it's for me."

Francis nodded, and he left without an unnecessary word or gesture. Why couldn't Rodney own a mountain full of Francises? "I've decided to meet with all the managers about this whole murder-thing. Good news first, our profits soar higher than ever. Apparently, people love Murder Mountain. My idea."

"Busy, as I mentioned, but we handle it." Big Top beat his chest. "At F & B, we thrive with adversity because we studied at the hard-knock university."

"I'm supposed to ask, where were you when Timmy was killed?"

"On the mountain cutting trails. I spent all day in Outer Limits chop, chop, chopping."

"I don't care," yawned Rodney. These meetings exhausted him. How many more were scheduled? Too many. He'd cancel the rest and take a nap. "How may I assist your department?"

"No hankerin' here. F & B is self-sustaining, self-regulating, and self-pollinating."

"Right," yawned Rodney.

"I gotta say one thing. Folks love Murder Mountain. It's new and steamy, hotter than the fryolator at full blast. More customers than ever before, too. Rosefield will run out of cows with all the burger orders. It's just . . ." Big Top tugged at his oversized beard. "We kind of miss the old name. It's not flashy or dangerous, but it was the name for sixty years. There's history."

"Are you insane?" Rodney almost threw his drink at him. "Did you not hear when I mentioned the profits? Rosefield Mountain never earned any money. We'll milk this murder thing until the teat falls off. Imagine how massive we'll become! New hotels and hundreds of condos! We'll build a waterpark so enormous, Jay Peak's will resemble a lap pool. We'll construct a village so grandiose, Stowe will resemble a truck stop. We'll become ski industry kings!"

"I'm tasting what you're toasting. We love the money." Big Top shrugged. "Just felt I oughta tell you what folks are grillin'."

"Enough of that nonsense." He snapped some furious fingers, and Francis materialized. Rodney waved Big Top away as he couldn't even speak.

Too much talk of 'Rosefield Mountain,' maybe he should ban the phrase. Or better yet, with his riches, he could bribe the select board into renaming the town 'Murder.'

Even Kappu couldn't tolerate this amount of idiocy. Rodney canceled the rest of the meetings, instructing Francis to inform those who waited out in the hall. He tossed a dollar on the table and slipped out the back door to avoid exposing himself to tourists and their foreign germs. Same reason he blocked off one elevator for his private use, no sense in enduring unnecessary risks.

When he entered his suites, he regarded his office for a moment. The red phone on his desk remained quiet for over a month. None of his employees ever called Rodney on that phone, not even Peter Smith. Only Rodney Buric Sr. used the number.

Certainly, Father heard of Rodney's success with the rebranding. On track to cover all the losses from the previous years, he would win their bet and secure his position as the resort's sole owner. Yet, each day Father didn't call, Rodney felt more unease. Had he missed something important?

Bah. Father simply recognized Rodney's impeccable management skills. Finally.

He spent the rest of the day reclined in his lounge-suite by the wall-spanning window overlooking the packed ski lifts. He imagined each customer as dollar bill signs as they passed through the gate scanner. *Cha-ching, cha-ching.* It helped him calm down. As Father repeated, money was most important. Always.

Francis knew who killed Timmy: the biggest psychopath of them all, Rodney 'the modern Jesus' Buric. Of course, he didn't carry out the deed himself, as he was conveniently in the Bahamas. But he hired someone.

Rodney 'king above all' Buric's father was even worse. Francis had the displeasure of serving him once. Rodney Buric Sr. complained about his steak for several minutes but still devoured the whole thing. He called Rosefield a 'decades-old haven of liars and whores', whatever that meant. Hypocritically, he told the waitresses they should exercise more and wear shorter skirts. And like Jr., Buric Sr. never tipped more than a couple of bucks.

Also, whenever Rodney 'lord and savior' Buric dined in the restaurant, Francis waited nearby for him to snap his fingers. Which meant Francis made no tips at all because he couldn't serve any other tables. Rodney also required the stupid bowtie, so anytime Francis heard Rodney 'God among mortals' Buric was dining, he would dash out to the staff locker room and tie it on.

Francis secured his revenge with a little special sauce in the steak gravy. It produced the 'beer-ish' taste Rodney 'eats dishwater' Buric found so appealing.

117

THE PLAID

Peggy couldn't figure out the search bar. Bowhunter fair, she could run searches, but she didn't find anyone wearing a yellow flannel jacket. Except, someone around town favored the style, and the answer existed within The Facebook. Peggy needed assistance. So after her first cup of Tootin', she called her youngest daughter Mary Anne.

"Good morning, Mom," she answered with a familiar sigh.

"Hey, sweetie." Peggy paused. *She should just whack her with the big smacker.* "Can you come home and help me with my computer? It's important. You don't have classes on Sunday, anyway."

"I have friends."

"Are they boys? As you've heard, Lyndsay's baking her fourth—"

"Mom! No." Mary Anne sighed. "I could do laundry."

"Perfect. See you soon."

"Fine. Give me a couple of hours."

While she waited, Peggy hiked the mile-long trail through her backwoods with Diohgee. She paused by the bend in the river where the water cascaded down truck-sized boulders. The blue jays sang their eloquent tunes *from their perches in the birches*. One chipmunk hopped between branches, his cheeks puffed up with an extensive collection of nuts.

118

Peggy conducted some of her best thinking here. Today, she considered the yellow flannel and how it seemed too perfect. Somehow Timmy ripped off a piece of the murderer's jacket and yet didn't struggle once during the encounter? As her only lead, however, she would follow this evidence wherever it pointed.

When Peggy returned home, she cleaned the kitchen, tidied up the living room, dusted several fixtures, and restocked the woodpile. She set up her laptop on the table next to the cast iron stove, the warmest spot during winter.

"Mom, you know how to use Facebook!" shouted Mary Anne, after letting herself in. "You like all my posts."

"Not *all* of your posts," Peggy protested before hugging her youngest. "Not the ones involving that nudist group."

"A couple of my friends lived there. They usually farmed with their clothes on. It was all very spiritual."

Peggy chuckled. "Right. *Spiritual.*"

"Hey, I've heard about your wild years. What happened at the Park & Grill of '93?"

"As I've told you before, folks exaggerated the details over the decades. Did you also hear Ben and Jerry showed up with an ice cream cow? Or that Jacques Allen rose from the dead to reenact his heroic deeds?" Peggy sighed. "May we start on the computer?"

"You chop 'em, I'll stack 'em."

They settled by the stove and logged into The Facebook.

"And don't say, 'The Facebook,' Mom. It's just 'Facebook.'"

Had Mary Anne read her mind? No, she was just smart, always reading, staying late at school to earn all those A's. Since she moved to Burlington, she spent all of her free time on homework and never visited her mother anymore. Ah, the cluckings of a hen who lost her chicks. Peggy should embrace her new role as Rosefield's sheriff.

"What are we searching for?" When irritated, Mary Anne raised her right eyebrow like her grandmother, Helen. They resembled each other, too, from the light brown hair to the meadow-green eyes.

"Somebody wearing a yellow flannel jacket."

"That's it? No other teats to work?"

"They might be a local or resort employee."

Mary Anne squinted and smirked simultaneously, like her great aunt Lydia McStoots, scrunched freckles included. "This is about Timmy's murder, right?"

"I can't tell you about my investigation when you're not an officer yourself."

"What if you deputize me?"

"Even if I can, I won't." Peggy sighed. "Yes, it's about Timmy's murder. Now, will you help me?"

"All right. We'll start with last year's Closing Day photos; every local skier shows up." Mary Anne laughed, high-pitched and sing-songy, like her godmother Josephine. "Thirty-three unread messages? Do you ever check them? What if someone sent you something important?"

"I dislike the messenger. It puts these confusing bubbles on my screen."

"Bob Hordell sent you a message."

"He emails the important things."

"Yeppers, it's a Christmas card with a cute reindeer." Mary Anne giggled. "Bob is a troll, right? With his tiny wisp of hair and permanent scowl . . . Couldn't he find a better profile pic?"

"He's always wearing a polo turtleneck, too. Even for the Fourth of July Parade."

"Here's one from Dana Shoeman," continued Mary Anne. "Is she still the principal at the Rez?"

"She'll never retire." Peggy liked Dana. She principaled all three of her daughters at Rosefield Elementary School. "What did she write?"

"Something about some punks ripping donuts on the soccer field."

"Oh yeah, those Viceroy boys about a month ago caused substantial damage. I interrogated them already. I can't prove it, but based on how

their cowered responses, they're guilty." Peggy laughed. "Eyes wider than a chicken when it's staring at the chopping block."

"John's the worst. He once lit a firecracker taped onto a cow's tail. Another time he slingshotted moose turds into Mrs. Henderson's classroom." Mary Anne clicked her tongue. "Henry isn't as bad. He looked out for Harvesta, Karma, and me in high school. And they didn't pick their parents."

"The whole family is more rotten than last year's apples." Mary Anne carried a soft spot for Henry because they attended elementary school together, but his apple fell from the same Viceroy tree as the rest.

"Oh, you received a message from Joey Rogers." She chuckled. "That idiot fell off his four-wheeler one too many times as a kid."

"Headfirst onto gravel," agreed Peggy.

"He's a few flags shy of a slalom," continued Mary Anne.

"A couple of pallets short of a bonfire," concluded Peggy.

"Huh." Mary Anne frowned, like her cousin and best friend, Jackie McStoots. "Aren't you searching for a yellow flannel?"

"A jacket, yeah."

"Joey's message might involve your case."

"What are you saying?"

"According to him, his legendary ski skills somehow led to an epic breakthrough in Timmy's murder case. He remembers who the yellow flannel belongs to. Big Top." Mary Anne frowned once more. "He writes about how Big Top doesn't wear it anymore, then continues on about cliffs and rails for two whole sentences."

"It's not easy translating idiot," commented Peggy. "Now that Joey mentions it, Big Top's the one I've been trying to recall. He's worn a yellow flannel for the past several winters, but not this season."

"That's certainly suspicious." Mary Anne sighed. "This comes from Joey, though."

"I'm not exactly teeming with leads." Peggy shut the lid on her computer and prepared herself for a high noon confrontation in the

Mountain View kitchen. "Well, I'm gonna breath deep and holler at Big Top."

"No way he murdered Timmy." Mary Anne shook her head, her brown bangs bobbing about. That look was uniquely hers. "I worked for him, remember? When I served at the Mountain View Restaurant. A little racy, but Big Top never behaved inappropriately. He fought against Rodney when he ordered us to wear short skirts and Hooters shirts."

"No other leads and I'm not spending quality summer hours on this investigation. Especially with baby Robert on the way." Peggy strode over to the entryway and whipped on her old leather coat in one smooth motion.

"I'll come, too." Mary Anne whipped on her coat in one smooth motion, like how . . . Well, Momma should take *some* credit.

"*Oh no, little doe,*" said Peggy. "I can't bring you to a potential murder interrogation."

"What?" Mary Anne stomped her boot. "You wouldn't have this lead without me."

She continued to plead, but Peggy remained steadfast. "I'll tell you how it goes," she promised and departed for the mountain. Well, the Road Runner couldn't figure out how to start, so Peggy delivered a quick lesson with her stick. Three strikes later, the starter turned over the engine without issue—what an excellent student.

As she drove up to the mountain, she thought about Big Top. She agreed with her daughter that didn't seem like a killer. Peggy met him over twenty years ago, and while excitable, she never witnessed Big Top trade punches with anyone. Besides, what was his motive?

A Statie pulled out of Rosefield Resort as Peggy turned in. She waved, and the trooper returned with the appropriate two-finger greeting before speeding down Left Mountain Road. She noticed an increase in their presence lately, but they only appeared interested in the resort. Did they suspect the murderer was an employee? Like Big Top?

Peggy sighed when she saw the packed parking lot. There were more cars than a Rutland Rotary Boys concert, and they filled a stadium. She couldn't understand why. She never enjoyed their music, a little too pop-country.

She drove past the lot, around the backside of Generally Slanted, and parked by the Mountain View loading dock. Peggy hesitated in her driver's seat. *Best to prepare for moose, even if you only hunted goose.* She popped open her glove box and snatched the cuffs.

She marched into the hotel, past the front desk, through the Mountain View kitchen, and into Big Top's office. "I have questions." She slammed the door on six jaw-jangling cooks.

"Hello, Sheriff McStoots." Big Top resembled a red-haired bulldog and barked even louder. "No reason to turn the grill to the max. Why are you cooking so hot?"

His plastic desk and two chairs filled the tiny office. Peggy settled on the green chair before commencing her interrogation. "Where were you when Timmy was murdered?"

"On the mountain, I was clearing trees in Outer Limits."

"By yourself?"

"I always cut trails alone. I enjoy the solitude. It's just me, my chainsaw, and a pile of trees." Big Top coughed and leaned forward. "The Staties already grilled my one side. Why are you searing the other?"

"What happened to your old jacket? The one you used to wear every day."

"I miss my jacket. It fit better than anything else." Big Top's frown was visible through his massive red beard. He held up his arms and the sleeves hung to his belly. "Every other jacket squeezes too tightly on my shoulders or hangs too loose on my arms."

"Will you remind me of its color?"

"A plain yellow jacket."

"Flannel?"

"Yes, exactly. Standard yellow."

'Were you wearing it the day of Timmy's murder?"

'No, because it disappeared a week earlier. After a long day of cutting trails, I dropped it on that hook." Big Top pointed to an empty red hook above Peggy's head. 'Due to the rain, I wore my slicker home instead. When I returned in the morning, my jacket had disappeared. I can't understand why anyone would steal it. Not many folks possess these shoulders."

Stolen? Convenient, like his alibi. Still, she knew Big Top for over twenty years, and even on the rowdiest nights at the Sled, he never popped jaw. 'Who can vouch for your story?"

'Anyone I've shared a kitchen with has heard me complain about it, ask any of my chefs. Since I've simmered for a minute, I called Head Chef Rob the very next day to ask him if he'd noticed my jacket. He's out there right now. Question him yourself." He fisted his desk. 'Come on Peggy, what's got you baking?"

She sighed. 'When we inspected Timmy's body, he clutched a ripped piece of yellow flannel. It matches your jacket."

'I didn't kill Timmy!" Big Top pulled on his beard so hard he nearly ripped out a handful. 'I barely knew the guy."

'Rufus, Timmy's roommate, said he witnessed someone wearing yellow flannel steal the murder weapon from his house." While Rufus hadn't confirmed this, Peggy believed it. 'That wasn't you?"

'Noper. Rufus's brain is crispier than a fresh chicken tender. I once hired him to flip burgers in the cafeteria. I fired him after one week. He couldn't operate the toaster!"

*His brain's burnt worse than a Nordic hearse,*" agreed Peggy.

'More baked than a twice-baked potato." Big Top stroked his beard. 'Even if Rufus witnessed what he did, maybe the killer wore my flannel when they snatched his knife."

'Sorry, guy." Peggy sighed and pushed herself to her feet. 'I didn't mean to cause a fuss."

'I wish I could've been your man." Big Top rose and reached out a hand. "If you ever hanker a perfectly cooked burger, however, I'll be your chef."

"If you remember anything else, call me," said Peggy as they shook. "In particular, anything about the flannel."

"Yepper. I miss it. I haven't found anything that fits since. Might never again."

Peggy left the resort with no new information and no direction for her investigation. *Wasn't that like cooking with cast iron, but its grease coating was soaped on.* A horrible rhyme that reflected her mood. She returned to no suspects halfway through winter. Spring arrived next month, and then little baby Robert soon after. She *needed* this investigation finished.

When she pulled into her driveway, Mary Anne's truck was gone. If she was so interested, why hadn't she waited until Peggy returned? She probably forgot about the whole case; children have the shortest attention spans. No matter, now Peggy could ponder without distraction.

What if Timmy was involved in a drug deal? Maybe one of his shady business partners wanted him silenced. While Peggy hadn't heard of Timmy dealing drugs, it wouldn't surprise her. If his murder involved criminal activity, she knew who to talk to. Bill Viceroy.

The idea lined her stomach with extra-pointy acorns. She preferred to avoid the entire Viceroy family like a burdock bush, especially the parents. While the boys caused significant mischief around town, they respected her title as sheriff and generally feared the law.

Bill and Judy Viceroy, however, followed their own rules, disregarding what governments passed down. They bought a thousand-acre lot, the largest in Rosefield, to erect their gothic estate.

Peggy shuddered when she remembered her only visit to their mansion. After that horror, she vowed never to return. Hopefully, she wouldn't have to. She retrieved her phone and called Bill Viceroy.

# The Red Barn

He held the beauty of his life tight to his chest, right next to his heart. She glistened after a full-bodied bath, with curves both petite and rounded. Her solid butt called for a nuzzle against Happy's shoulder. Remi was his first bolt action rifle, and as they said, 'Once you went bolt, you cranked for life.' A Remington Model Seven with a Leupold VX3 scope, she fired .308 caliber and weighed less than eight pounds altogether.

Happy and Remi dropped five deer, a moose, and two bears—by far the most kills in his arsenal. He brought her everywhere with him, safely tucked beneath his seat just in case. Nearly every day, he held Remi in his arms, if only to feel her grip and peer through her scope. Sometimes he aimed at a spot on the wall and pretended to fire. *Pow!* It could've been an eight-pointer.

He packaged her in the original carrying case along with two boxes of ammo. After a final kiss on the muzzle, Happy shut the lid and secured the lock. He slid Remi underneath his bed, where she'd remain until the next Grandma Day.

Then Happy ripped open Grandma's letter to Peggy. Two notes slid out onto his kitchen counter. She addressed the first to him:

Happy,
Your favorite rifle is
mine! You can deliver it
after your mourning
period. It's a few months
until hunting season
anyway. Now bring the
other note to Peggy.
(You'll never figure out
its meaning, so don't
bother.)
Grandma

He set the note down, cheeks already wet. How? Classic Grandma trickery, she knew Happy couldn't stop himself from peeking . . .

Once his fingers stopped shaking, he read the second note:

Peggy,
Remember the Red Barn
Incident? Check the
rafters; who lost their
head? And against who?
Check under the gold
cushions, which became?
Put it all together.
Margaret Smith

Happy didn't comprehend a single sentence. He read it over and over, upside down and backward, but still nothing. Grandma never worried about him reading the letter at all because she knew he wouldn't understand it, anyway. She just hankered Remi! Sneaky Grandma.

The next day he drove around searching for red barns, but it turned out half the barns in Rosefield were red. Besides, farmers scorned trespassers, usually greeting them with a shotgun in hand. Two days after opening Grandma's letter, he decided he might as well deliver the note.

He drove up Left Mountain Road to Peggy's house, a large wood cabin built for a family of five. Now she lived alone, probably feeling like the last moo-moo in a butcher barn.

'McStoots' Autoservice' still hung on the separate two-bay garage where her husband had operated his mechanic shop. Robert could fix any engine, no matter how rusted, and he charged way less than Mechanic Joe. When he succumbed to lung cancer six years ago, everyone in town attended his funeral, and the proceeding Parting Party at the Sled Stop was the largest Happy ever witnessed.

When he knocked on the red front door, he hoped to find Peggy. He'd hand over the cursed letter which cost him his dear Remi, return home, and fill a creek with his tears. When Mary Anne swung open the door, all his thoughts about Remi evaporated faster than that same creek in July.

She wore jeans and a t-shirt as usual. When the other girls wore summer dresses, she sported cutoffs and a t-shirt with a funny image.

'Happy! Why are you here?'

'I-I was looking for Peggy.'

'She just left after *I* discovered an important clue for *her*. Where's the gratitude?' Today, Mary Anne wore a shirt featuring a Great Dane wearing a Santa Claus hat. Her light brown hair (golden in the right light) dressed her fair shoulders, not scrawny like the flatties. She stepped back for Happy to enter and shut the door behind him.

129

'Uh, my grandma asked me to deliver this note to Peggy. Is she home?"

"What does the note say?"

'She wrote it in code. I can't figure it out." Happy handed it to her. 'Hi, Diohgee!" He only met Peggy's yellow lab once before, but he never forgot a puppy's name.

'I understand a little bit." Mary Anne laughed, a sound more beautiful than a sled finally catching after twenty pulls. 'You don't remember the Red Barn Incident? We were six or seven. A bunch of folks threw a party in Farmer Rick's brand-new red barn."

'Biscuit my dog, I remember. A year before Rick's house burned down, right?"

'Yeppers." She whistled with the elegance of a blue jay on a snowy porch. 'What a fire."

"The whole town came out for it."

'It happened on a beautiful summer day. Might as well watch a house fire."

'My folks brought the grill and hot dogs," laughed Happy. 'Okay, I remember the barn, but what happened at the Red Barn Incident?"

'I don't know. The adults kicked the kids out before any real action. I heard a bunch of fights broke out, and two guys ended up missing."

'Missing? You mean, never found again?"

Mary Anne shrugged. 'I tried to unearth what happened—I can't resist a mystery—but nobody will discuss it. It's like the whole town represses the event as an unfavorable memory."

'I remember a sweltering summer, reaching a hundred once or twice."

'Folks joked about the end of days," agreed Mary Anne.

'My dad fought with someone that night," said Happy, recalling the shiner his dad wore for the second half of the summer. 'Actually, I think it was with Timmy."

'You mean the murdered Timmy Harton?" Mary Anne slapped

knee.

"Yeppers. Their feud started over a decade ago. They'd fight, and Uncle Pete broke them up. I know of at least four or five incidents."

"Huh," said Mary Anne. "What if Charlie . . ."

"My dad's not a murderer!" Happy's turn to slap knee. "He has a temper, but he punches for the head, not the gut."

"Yepper." Mary Anne sighed. "After helping my mom with the murder case, I feel suspicious of everyone."

"Does she have any suspects?"

"Yeah," scoffed Mary Anne. "A suspect I discovered for her!"

"Who?"

"That's 'official sheriff business.'"

Happy almost objected but stopped when he noticed her devilish half-smile. Ope, nothing good followed that.

"Let's roll."

"Roll?" Happy blinked. "Where to?"

"To Farmer Rick's barn, of course."

Not too grim, Happy prepared for something more reckless or dangerous than visiting an abandoned barn. When they found nothing, he'd follow Grandma's orders and deliver the letter to Peggy. Besides, after she tricked him out of his Remi, he didn't owe her a match, never mind the birch bark.

"Wait, I thought it burned down."

"Farmer Rick's house, not his barn." Mary Anne leaned forward, her lips inches from his ear. She smelled like the snow-covered evergreens on a mountain summit, and Happy's knees buckled. "I heard not a single plank singed. Spooky, right?"

Happy grabbed the counter to keep upright. Now that Mary Anne mentioned it, a lot of townsfolk considered Farmer Rick's haunted. Some Rosefieldians (like Handy Jesse) refused to drive on Deep Gregory because they feared passing by the property. Happy never believed in such things, but . . . what if it *was* haunted? "Maybe we shouldn't."

Too late. Mary Anne accompanied her mischievous half-smile with an eye twinkle that convinced him every time. Like when she persuaded Happy to jump from the highest spot at Jagged Hole, he missed the rock wall by a chicken feather! Or when she coerced him into sticking the chewing gum in Mrs. Henderson's hat before English class. Their poor teacher had to shave her head, and Principle Shoeman suspended Happy for two days.

Had he learned his lesson? Nopers. "Fire up the truck."

Mary Anne drove her V8 because who knew *what* they might encounter up there. Two extra cylinders might save the day. Plus, her heated seats felt like a warm bath for his bum.

After a mile on South Road, they turned onto Gregory. The old dirt road wound through Gregory Notch and all the way to Enosburg—but only in the summer, as they didn't plow it.

They passed Gregory Farm, where hundreds of moo-moos grazed one of their massive pastures, and fifty or more bah-bahs browsed another. A giant mural of Swiss cheese decorated the cheesemaking barn, which Happy considered strange because they specialized in cheddars. Their moo-moo barn sprawled across the hilltop, and the two-hundred-year-old mansion loomed above it all. The Gregorys built the original farm, and they still operated it ten generations later. Now that was true Rosefieldian lineage.

A few hundred feet further, they reached the plow turn around, just past Rogen Harton's driveway. Happy last encountered the old man at his son's Parting Party several years ago. He lived off-grid in his cabin a mile deep, and by the pristine powder on his driveway, he hadn't descended since the beginning of winter. Rogen didn't even come down for his nephew Timmy's funeral.

They parked and slapped on some shoes. Of course, Mary Anne stored several sets in her truck. Who didn't? They hiked up what folks called Deep Gregory Road. With the sun shining and no wind, it felt like spring. Happy shed his jacket, and Mary Anne unzipped her blue puffy.

132

"Farmer Rick used to plow this road," said Mary Anne. "I wish he still did."

Happy actually enjoyed the trek. Since Mary Anne moved to Burlington three years ago, they'd only hung out a few times.

After a mile, they reached Farmer Rick's old driveway, marked by a red mailbox that hadn't tilted a degree in all these years. Its paint remained untarnished as well, and its wood post resembled fresh lumber.

A sudden gust of wind whipped through the trees, and the mailbox door opened with a *clunk*. Happy yelped and retreated a step but his snowshoes tangled together. He crashed into the snow.

"You okay?" laughed Mary Anne.

What a scaredy-cow. "The mailbox door . . ."

"That *was* spooky." She stepped over to Happy and hoisted him up. "It popped open at the scariest possible moment. Creepy."

After Happy brushed the snow off, they tromped up the driveway. White birches arched overhead, creating a tunnel of darkness. Several fallen maples impeded their progress, especially with the shoes on. Was this nature's attempt at barring folks from the evil beyond?

"I heard Farmer Rick lost his acorns after the Red Barn Incident," said Mary Anne. "Crazier than a squirrel who lost his nuts."

"Did he grow a bushy tail, too?"

"His snout elongated, and his eyes bulged." Mary Anne stopped and pointed up the driveway. "There it is!"

A large red barn dominated the hill despite acres of cleared land. Only a few weak-limbed trees sprouted in the past decade, as though the soil couldn't support growth. Yet another sign evil lingered here?

The carcass of the old house remained, charred up worse than a forgotten pig roast. Two opposing outer walls still stood, arched and jagged like a set of picked-through ribs. The stone foundation was thoroughly blackened.

On the other side of the clearing, the red barn emanated with the brightness of a recent paint job, and not a single window was cracked. A burnt section of the sidewall represented the only blemish.

"Didn't you say none of the barn boards burned?"

Mary Anne shrugged. "I guess it isn't haunted then. Let's go."

As she led them through the clearing, an icy wind howled and cut through their clothes. A cloud eclipsed the sun, and the darkness thickened with each step. When they reached the wide barn door, Happy couldn't distinguish the tree line. He fought against a full-body shiver.

Upon arriving at the half-buried barn door, they set to shoveling it out. Of course, they shoed with collapsible snow shovels. Who didn't? Once they cleared enough to fit within the doorframe, they pushed it open to an empty barn.

"I don't see any cushions, bud," said Mary Anne, turning on her headlamp.

"Ain't much of anything, bud." A couple of long troughs, a few buckets, and a frozen hay bale remained. "Someone already harvested this road moose."

"Soup was cooked, eaten, and composted," agreed Mary Anne. "I'll check the rafters at least."

"You sure?" At eight-feet high, she required a boost. "The beam's slippery with dust, and I've already spotted a dozen spider webs. I bet a whole bunch more live up there."

"The letter said to check the rafters, so that's what we'll do."

He kneeled, and she stepped up. He lifted, and she grabbed the beam, a cloud of dust bursting out.

"You all right?"

"Okay," she coughed, pulling herself up. "I don't see anything. Some bird nests, I think."

"What kind of bird?"

"I dunno, it's a pile of sticks. It's too dark to—"

Suddenly the whole building shook as howling winds assaulted the outer walls. Icy breaths erupted through open windows.

"You okay?" shouted Happy.

"Fine. I almost lost my balance, but I'm secure now. Where'd that wind come from? It's been calm all day."

"The weather's declined since we arrived—"

Curdled screeches interrupted him, blaring throughout the barn. His ears throbbed, but he resisted the urge to cover them in case Mary Anne required assistance.

The shadows erupted in a feathered frenzy as two owls ripped and screamed at each other. The fighting birds bolted from the other side of the barn and flew right at Mary Anne. She blocked, but they crashed into her outstretched arms. She tumbled! She grabbed the beam with one arm, which slowed her fall enough for Happy to step under her.

*Boom.* She collided with him.

*Boom!* They both smashed into the ground in a dusty haze.

Hurt worse than when Bess launched him from his saddle into a rocky stream. Hurt worse than the tree he rammed in Outer Limits three seasons ago. But unlike those instances, this was totally worth the pain and shortness of breath.

"What happened?" grunted Mary Anne.

"Those owls lost their eggs and started fighting."

"Why?"

"I dunno. Where did that crazy gust come from?" While they recovered from the fall, the wind once more calmed. The owls had vanished, along with their awful *hoots*. "And where did it go?"

Neither had any ideas, except one. "Let's get out of here," they said in unison.

They rose to their feet and brushed off the dust. Happy led them towards the barn door but stopped when he heard voices outside.

"You son of a bitch!"

"You're dead! You hear me?"

Two voices raged just outside, both masculine and belligerent, like certain folks at the Sled when they drank too much whiskey. Timmy Harton came to mind.

*Oh shit,* mouthed Mary Anne.

*Who are they?* returned Happy.

She shrugged.

"You've screwed up now!" raged the first voice.

"No one's getting out alive," returned the second. "Not after what you did to my daughter!"

*Daughter?* mouthed Happy.

*Are they shouting at us?*

Happy shrugged and shook his head. He pointed to the other end of the barn and mouthed, *Run.*

They dashed to the back door and stopped to listen. No voices, so they swung open the latch, but *woosh.* An avalanche of snow burst through and knocked them over. They fell onto their butts, and the snow kept dumping.

Happy wiped furiously at the powder covering his face. Was Mary Anne okay? He spotted her, struggling just as hard against the flow.

Fortunately, the snow stopped, but they remained buried to their chins. No problem, even without shovels, they dug themselves out faster than a tractor-mounted snowblower; they spent a hundred recesses at the Rez building snow structures with just their mitts. Once free, they crawled up the snowbank and out the opening at the top of the doorframe.

The sun beat down without a single cloud in the sky. The stormy weather had disappeared as quickly as it arrived. Not that Happy complained. He preferred bluebird to the gloom, especially while on this freaky property.

He shouldn't consider the weather, not with those thugs on the other side of the barn. Happy trudged through the snow, waist-deep without snowshoes, until he reached the side. He peered around.

Nobody there. He looked to Mary Anne at the other corner. She shook her head.

Happy hadn't heard their shouts in a while. Maybe they entered the barn. He backtracked to the door and peeked inside. Nobody there, either.

"Where did they go?"

"This place is creeping me out." Mary Anne trembled.

"We should leave, around the outside." Happy never wanted to step foot in the barn again. He'd rather post-hole through feet of snow.

"Yepper."

As they progressed, he once more noticed the scorched siding in the shape of a triangle, a point at the top and then widening as it dropped beneath the snow. For a fire to spread like that . . . It reminded Happy of his childhood burning pallets with kerosene. Had someone attempted a fire? Had the barn refused to burn? He shivered at the notion.

Happy should've saved that shiver for when they reached the other side—and discovered unblemished snow, not a *single* footprint besides their own. He shook so hard, he would've fallen over if not for his half-buried legs.

"No one was here?" Mary Anne exclaimed. "That's impossible. We definitely heard those voices."

Happy agreed, but he'd rather discuss it once off this property. "Let's get back to the truck."

One of them needed to fetch their shoes from inside the barn, however, and Mary Anne's half-smile and eye twinkle already persuaded Happy to volunteer. He gulped once, twice, hocked a loogie, and spit it out. With the speed of a raccoon in a floodlight, Happy hopped down, tossed all four shoes up, and climbed out.

After fastening them to their feet, they hiked down to her truck in complete silence. Only once in the embrace of those heated seats did they speak, and no louder than a whisper.

"Never again," stated Mary Anne. She put her truck in gear and drove down Gregory Road.

"Something evil happened. Remember Jeremy Yackers?"

"Was he the one they arrested for farming wolves?"

"Caught rabbits and turkeys to feed to those beasts."

"I heard even worse," said Mary Anne while turning onto South Road. "A few of his neighbors lost their pets."

"Yepper. Something similar to Jeremy Yackers happened in that barn." Happy shook his head. "Maybe Farmer Rick's house burned down because of what happened."

"We should speak with Farmer Rick."

Happy glared at her. He hankered nothing more of this mystery. He just wanted to hand the note over to Peggy and not miss any more sheep counting.

Mary Anne laughed and elbowed him in the shoulder. "I'm messing with you. That was enough heartburn for me." Then she whispered, "At least for today." Happy chose not to hear.

Without warning, she slammed the breaks. Happy almost popped through the windshield like a hedgehog out of his hole. His own fault; he should've known to wear his seat belt with Mary Anne at the wheel. She ripped a hard right, and if he hadn't grabbed the 'Oh Shit' bar, he would've flown right into the driver's seat. She coasted down the short access road and skidded to a stop at Abscond Pond.

"W-what's happening? Why are we here?"

"On such a nice day, we oughta grill by the water."

"I can't eat after what we just experienced." Except, as soon as he said the words, his stomach rumbled with the opposite answer. "I might down a dog or two."

"It's important to appreciate these spring-like winter days." While her near-instant recovery concerned him, Mary Anne presented a valid point.

"This is the nicest afternoon since November," agreed Happy.

"What better way to spend it?" She hopped out of the truck and grabbed the grill while Happy carried the cooler. Of course, she stored dogs and buns in her pickup. Who didn't?

They stayed until dark, joking, laughing, and listening to the ice crack. They watched for wildlife. Abscond Pond was notorious for its wild moose sightings, but they had no luck. They saw a family of deer, though, investigating the saplings at the water's edge for some tasty twigs.

Neither mentioned the Red Barn nor what happened. Maybe if he never brought it up, Mary Anne would forget. Not likely. When she sank her teeth into a good mystery, she chewed it thoroughly—even with ghosts involved.

Another day, another crowd at the Bent Pole. Jane loved the cash. She already earned double what she had the previous year. She *hustled* for it, though, with few opportunities to chat up locals. This proved problematic for her investigation into Yelsa and Roger; her primary method of gathering information was talking to locals while serving them drinks.

She still caught snippets throughout the season. Roger Elwood himself delivered a juicy bit when he came in for a drink around Christmas. "Today, we achieved our most profitable day at Generally Slanted. The register line reached all the way outside! People waited in the cold for our products."

"Wow." Everywhere on the mountain was packed, especially the slopes. Barely any snow remained for Jane. Her hatred for 'Murder Mountain' deepened with any mention of its success. "Bacon?"

"Actually, I'll have a Pork Chop to celebrate this historic day." The clown grin stuck unpleasantly to Roger's face. Why so happy? He wouldn't earn any extra money from it. Unless, of course, he knew something Jane didn't.

"What's up with you and Yelsa?" No time for pleasantries when the bar might fill up at any moment. "You hang out more than banging

141

rabbits."

"Nothing, nothing at all." He phlegmed and then coughed, spraying his bacteria-filled spittle across the bar. Jane resisted smacking Roger for his poor hygiene. "She's a good boss."

"I don't care if you're tossing the pork roll to your boss."

"It's against company policy!" He fisted the counter, which shook significantly. Despite his feeble personality, he was physically quite strong. "Mr. Buric disapproves of managers dating their employees. And I love my job. No one wrangles a register better than me."

"So there is something between you two."

"I never said that."

His eyes revealed the truth. Jane let him drink in peace afterward, even buying him a Pork Chop to elevate his mopey face.

Her investigation was nowhere near complete. Even if they fooled around in the hay, that didn't explain the conversation she overheard on Opening Day. They were up to something worse than a sly pokey-poke.

A few weeks later, Montgomery Joe delivered another critical detail. He strode into the Bent Pole with icicles in his beard and a face red from laughter.

"Ripping those deep turns, Joe? Lap it up now. The flatties will ski it off by tomorrow."

"I've never waited in a line before today, not at Rosefield."

Montgomery Joe removed his ski jacket to reveal his grey sweater, and as usual, it reeked of body odor and weed. "Still, some of the best skiing of the year, thanks to this two-day blizzard."

"I had yesterday off." Jane laughed. "I'm not even sad about working today. I rode from first chair to last, and my legs are stiffer than an 80s snowboard."

"I'll be stiffer than brand-new ski boots tomorrow." He removed his helmet, letting his wavy brown hair fall to his shoulders. Attractive, but he possessed one of the most annoying personality traits: never-ending hometown pride.

"The cliffs in The Foot?" he continued. "Insane! Twelve-foot drop into a cloud, softer than your bed at home. Boulder? Steepest chute this side of Jay Peak, and I barely turned. Therapy? I'll say so! I slayed it all. Reminds me of home, skiing the epic Jay range."

Oh no, if she allowed him to continue, he'd tell her about every landmark, restaurant, trail, or covered bridge in Montgomery and Jay. "I have beers to pour."

"Oh Jane, I heard an excellent piece of gossip. You'll hanker this."

She teetered between ignoring him and engaging. She risked being sucked into ten minutes of useless Montgomery trivia, but what if he learned something relevant? She rolled the pinecones. "Whaddya hear?"

"Earlier, I hopped on the chair with Jake Lobster from Maine. With the nose."

"Nice guy, tough nose," agreed Jane. "I've only seen him a couple of times this season."

"He talked about that, too. He said it's the tourists, Rosefield's too crowded."

"I sympathize," sighed Jane. "Schools of flatties clogging up trails like trout stuck in a dam. I can't avoid trawling a few as I rip by."

"Sometimes, I'll pop out of the trees and flatties loiter on my landing. Where am I supposed to touch down? I'm not about to hurt myself for a southerner."

'Or one of those northerners, either. Let them eat the ski, not me."

"The west is just as bad," said Joe. 'Weird accents."

'I like the east," pointed out Jane. 'Nice folks in that direction."

'Nice folk," confirmed Joe. 'Anyway, Jake told me something else, too, from when he shared a chair with Annie and George a few days ago."

'From Montreal?"

'Yepper. They heard this interesting tidbit from Mickey on the chair several days prior."

"The good ol' chair network."

'Better than the local newspaper," agreed Joe. 'Mickey spotted Yelsa on the resort the day Timmy died."

Jane almost dropped the mug she was filling. 'Generally Slanted's Yelsa?"

'Yepper. Apparently, her little fetcher-pheasant Roger was with her." Montgomery Joe chuckled. 'Right behind her, if you're stackin' what I'm choppin'."

'Oh, she's definitely receiving those off-trail face shots. Do they think they're fooling anyone?"

Montgomery Joe shrugged.

"Those two are up to something," considered Jane. 'But a connection to Timmy's murder? Unlikely."

'Nothing makes sense in Rosefield anymore. The mountain changing its name, murderers running free, flatties around every corner . . . I'm not sure *what's* possible of who, never mind *who's* possible of what. In the Jay area, this would never happen. They'd never change the name of Jay Peak." He laughed and slapped knee. "They'd sooner remove one of their famous covered bridges. Hah!"

He kept on about his beloved hometown. Though Jane wouldn't tell Joe, she actually liked Montgomery. In high school, she hung out most weekends over there, mostly because of the guy she dated. And sure, Jay Peak was a superior ski resort, but Jane didn't want to hear it while stuck at the Bent Pole. However, he brought her valuable information, so she pretended to listen.

While Montgomery Joe blathered on about swimming holes, mountain bike trails, and free concerts, Jane applied this new clue to her case. Maybe they killed him because he discovered their secret. Except, what *was* their secret? Jane overheard them talking about warm beaches, fruity beers, and traveling far from Rosefield. Were they attempting to flee from the murder investigation? Why wait until the end of the season? Too many questions and few answers, she'd keep her ears alert and the customers intoxicated.

She caught another clue a few weeks later when Peter Smith visited the Bent Pole a little before closing. He shook his head, causing the dark rings beneath his eyes to jiggle, and his mustache lacked its usual crispness. Had he gained a little weight?

'Looks like your day slipped on some ice." She slid him a Pinot Grigio in a Mason jar with three ice cubes. 'What's bruisin'?"

'I'm surrounded by morons, that's what."

'Do these morons have names?"

'My brother, for one."

'Charlie?" While the Smith brothers sometimes feuded, they usually resolved it with their fists and moved on. 'What did he do?"

'It began when I lent him money last fall to repay Banker Henry."

"*You* lent money to *him*? Charlie told me the opposite."

"I'm not surprised. He told everyone a story about this lucrative contract in Albany." Peter laughed. "You know where he really went?"

"Phish tour? Montreal?" Jane snapped her fingers. "Skiing in Argentina?"

"Close. A hunting and fishing tour across Alaska. Charlie spent so much money on rentals and guides, Banker Henry almost foreclosed on him."

This made more sense than Charlie's story. Peter protected his younger brother, not the other way around. "What did you do?"

"He's family. I paid off Banker Henry, and I even glanced at Charlie's trophy pictures." Peter chuckled. "I enjoyed my revenge. In exchange, I made him sign up as a judge for the Park & Grill cook-off."

"Why?"

"Because I'm a judge, and I might as well force him to suffer as well."

"How were you stuck with that 'honor'?"

"Old man Johnny retired, said he couldn't shoulder the pressure anymore. And then Mickey quit because of Jordan Herring."

"That stacks." Jane laughed. "Jordan's obsession rivals PJ and his Absolute Zero chair."

"Apparently, he's a real bully when assigning scores. After Mickey wrote a six for the Lobsters, Jordan intercepted his scorecard and turned it into an eight." Peter sipped his wine. "With two positions open and no volunteers, it fell on me to fill them. At least Charlie will endure it with me."

"A just punishment."

"He's not even the worst moron in my life."

"Who earned that title?"

"Who else? Rodney Buric." He spat the boss's name. "He's riding this whole place off a cliff without stopping to check the landing."

"I figured the mountain was earning tons with all the flatties. I've never been busier."

"The money's great, but the murder investigation . . . The Staties suspect the killer is an employee."

"Like Big Top?" Jane tended bar three days ago when Sheriff McStoots stormed Mountain View kitchen and nearly left with his head. "No way he's the murderer."

"Of course not, but the Staties have a lens on him and some others." Peter chuckled. "They might be watching the two of us right now."

"Watch away." Jane laughed. "All they'll discover from me is undeclared tips."

"I want them to conduct their investigation. Let the Staties catch their guy and leave by last chair. Not Rodney. He's jamming up their investigation by blocking them from the resort. He's convinced it'll create a 'bad image.' Like that hadn't happened when he changed the name to 'Murder Mountain.'"

"I miss the old name. Rosefield Mountain. Simple and plain, no reason for greater aspirations." She clicked her tongue. "And what an idiot to tangle with the Staties. It's like he's skiing a black diamond on his first day."

"Yepper," chuckled Peter. "Somebody quick, grab a camera!"

"I wager Rodney assumes his bindings broke because the heels are up."

"He probably wears his goggles an inch from his helmet."

"I bet he sets his DIN on his computer monitor."

"Speaking of his computer, he writes his password right next to the keyboard." Peter laughed. "Owner of a resort and his maids can access all of his documents."

Jane blinked. If she knew that while working in housekeeping, she would've made better use of her barrette trick. What secrets might she uncover? Maybe some blackmail to use against Rodney and force him to restore Rosefield Mountain's name.

"Rodney's too addicted to the profits. He'll never change Murder Mountain." Peter set down his wine and fidgeted with his stallion key chain. It belonged to his wife, and he fiddled with it whenever he possessed a juicy bit of town gossip. 'Especially this year . . .'

'What does that mean?'

'I shouldn't.' He finished his wine and slammed the jar down, the bar groaning in response.

'Now, Peter, no mentioning syrup without passing me a sample. What's up with Rodney?' Jane leaned over the bar and hushed her voice. 'I'll reveal my stash if you share yours.'

He stroked his mustache. 'What's your information?'

'I'm close to uncovering something huge.' Jane smirked. 'I'll tell you what I've learned.'

'All right, a secret for a secret. We tell no one, right?'

Jane refilled his Mason jar and slid it back to him. 'On me.'

'Okay. I'll drop first.' Peter leaned forward. 'If Rodney doesn't earn enough for the mountain to become profitable, his father will cut him off. And after years of losses, he has to recoup a tram-load, or he'll forfeit everything.'

'What'll happen to the resort?'

'His father will manage it himself, I suppose. Meanwhile, Rodney will be penniless, which makes me wonder . . .'

'Don't stop right before the headwall.' Jane poured them both a whiskey. 'Send it, bud.'

'Right when Rodney needed a tremendous year, he got one. What if he's connected to Timmy's murder?'

'Rodney couldn't kill anyone.' Jane lifted her shot glass to Peter's, then down the chute.

'Noper, but he might *hire* someone. Rodney's stupid enough to hire an employee, too, like Big Top.'

'Or Roger Elwood.' When he raised a brow, Jane smirked. 'My turn.'

'I thought you'd never drop in.'

'Roger and Yelsa were on the mountain the day of the murder. No one knows why, either." Jane considered telling him what she overheard on Opening Day, but she wasn't ready to share her whole investigation.

"Huh." Peter finished his Pinot Grigio and slammed the Mason jar, once again shaking the whole bar. "That explains a lot. They've been nesting chipmunks all season, and I'm not talking about their affair. Do they think they're fooling anyone?"

"Everyone knows!" she blurted out. In Jane's excitement, she overpoured a custy's drink. Lucky winner. "Why bother hiding it? Does Rodney care?"

"Why indeed?" Peter laughed, his cheeks redder and broader than when he arrived. Another fulfilled customer. "Thanks for the ski report."

"Only a fool rides without one." Jane nodded. "And I'll keep my ears un-muffed."

"Let me know if you discover anything, and I'll return the favor." Before Peter moseyed out of the Bent Pole, he dropped a generous tip, which Jane pocketed without counting. Hopefully, no Staties spotted that.

Was Rodney involved in Timmy's murder? Jane decided she couldn't conduct her investigation from the Bent Pole anymore. She needed to *Put on her after-work boots, for them second shift scoots.* Or whatever the lyrics were to that new Rutland Rotary Boys song.

After her bartender shifts, Jane staked out Generally Slanted. She even sacrificed her non-work days. She sat in the corner of the cafeteria, overlooking the general store's loading dock and back entrance.

She brought her laptop and told folks her internet was erratic at home, which was a common occurrence, so no one suspected a thing. Plus, she could write an email to every resort employee, townie, and passholder, requesting their signature on a petition to restore Rosefield Mountain's name.

Jane hated 'Murder Mountain,' and most folks in town hated it, too. If everyone signed, Rodney Buric would acknowledge it . . . at least she hoped so. If not, Jane would happily get fired (for the third time) after slapping sense into that round idiot. Her knuckles itched for some action; she hadn't extended her backhand since New Year's Eve.

Yelsa and Roger might require that beating first, though, once she uncovered their scheme. She noticed nothing unusual for the first few weeks, except they always closed up Generally Slanted together. At first, she assumed they simply packed late-night salami. But then they grew sloppy.

Roger usually backed his truck into the loading bay and out of Jane's view. On the first night of spring, a maintenance van blocked the entrance, so instead, he parked outside. They carried boxes of vegetables from the store and dropped them in his truck. Once they finished loading, they locked up and drove away. Where were they bringing all that produce?

The following three days, Jane watched from her Subaru, parked in front of Mountain View. From there, she observed the entire loading bay. She recorded them carrying out dozens of food boxes, even packaged goods and deli meats. They robbed Generally Slanted by the pickup-load!

Should she inform Peggy or the Staties? Except, they'd receive all the credit for the bust. Besides, they might interfere with her investigation before Jane uncovered the connection to Timmy's murder, and hopefully Rodney Buric too. She should at least discover where they brought the food.

On a dark night, she followed them into town. She kept her distance, but it hardly mattered. Only Left Mountain Road descended Rosefield Mountain, so everyone ended up with someone on their tailgate. They turned right onto Main Street and then left into Daffodil Harvest. Of course, Jane knocked herself one for not realizing that on her own. She parked in the same spot by Slick Mick's she used on busy Sled Stop nights, so they wouldn't suspect a thing.

Jane recorded every moment of Yelsa and Roger unloading the stolen goods. Their scheme appeared simple. They robbed Generally Slanted and sold it here, with a serious 'organic' markup. Which explained Daffodil Harvest's recent success but didn't connect them to Timmy's murder. And then, right after they locked the store, the case blew open wider than Tuckerman Ravine.

A black BMW pulled up and parked right next to Roger's truck. Who stepped out? Rodney friggin' Buric! Was he part of their scheme, too? Except, why steal from his own resort?

What if Rodney had discovered their scheme? In exchange for his silence, he required they murder Timmy Harton. An exceedingly long turkey stretch, Jane admitted. She'd continue to investigate. For the sake of Rosefield, Jane would uncover the truth; if she eliminated Rodney Buric, 'Murder Mountain' would soon follow.

The nightmares returned, so he smoked, and they disappeared. Where was he again? Oh yeah, the couch. He should hit the mountain and play with the skis he inherited from Timmy. He ripped the bong for motivation. Ah . . . The new stuff tasted more bitter than the medical, but it was hard to earn money from the couch, so he bought what he could afford.

Suddenly, snow surrounded him on all sides, a blizzard. Somebody loomed a few feet away, but who? The storm raged too thick . . . long red hair with a green jacket. "Timmy?"

Black holes for eyes, sewn-up lips, and blood gushed from his chest. Timmy raised a withered hand towards Rufus. "Why? We'll never hike again."

Before he responded, a ninja star flew past his nose. Rufus spun and found a blood ninja equipped with a pair of katanas.

The ninja charged, blades swinging. Rufus calmly grabbed his mermaid knife, dodged with a side roll, and struck. The knife sank into the blood ninja's soft chest, killing him instantly. Except his face changed into Timmy's.

"Why?" he repeated. "We'll never hike again."

The nightmare ended when he woke up. He should smoke, then he'd head up to the mountain with his new skis. Except he remembered his mermaid knife, still locked up with the Staties. They better keep it safe, or else!

Oh, he forgot to chief the bong, the best cure for rage. *Puff puff.*

CHÂTEAU VICEROY.

The Viceroys lived off Low Street, which ran parallel to Main Street by about a hen's throw. Their driveway climbed the steep hillside that formed the southern barrier of town. After a thick patch of woods, she drove through a mangled metal gate.

John and Henry lived in the apartment above the garage right at the beginning of the property. Usually, Peggy stopped there. She would've preferred giving those boys another tongue lashing, but she needed to speak with their father, Bill Viceroy. Which meant ascending the rest of the driveway to the ghoulish mansion he shared with his equally unsettling wife, Judy.

Peggy visited them only once, ten years ago, and still had the occasional nightmare. It wasn't too late to turn back. No, she should hit this deer head-on. Summer approached, and she hankered progress on the case.

She waved to the Viceroy boys clearing the snow off their truck (didn't they live in a garage?), and they flicked her off in return. What a pair of wolf pups. Peggy sighed and drove past.

She rolled through another broken metal fence, with barbs on each side resembling pointed teeth about to devour her Jeep. *Best not wither to that shiver.* She drove up the rest of the winding driveway.

The spidery mansion loomed on the hilltop. Two round windows gazed down from the third floor, watching over the entire Rosefield valley. The porch beneath curved upwards in a hungry grin. Eight stone columns held up the broad second floor. Plywood painted black covered every first-floor window, presumably to prevent any light from entering.

Peggy drove past the second garage, which held a dozen broken elf statues on its roof. She parked next to the crooked front porch. As she stepped out of the Road Runner, she shivered. A dark cloud covered the sun, and a burst of wind howled.

She had chosen this particular time to visit Bill Viceroy because of the clear forecast. When she departed the Sled five minutes ago, the noon sun thawed an inch-per-hour. Did they cast some kind of weather-blocking spell over their property?

She climbed the soft wooden steps, each sagging more than the previous. As Peggy planted one foot on the porch, a sharp *creak* cracked through the suddenly frigid air. *A shocking sound to get her all wound.* Ah, a quick rhyme always calmed her nerves. When the next step creaked even louder, enough to wake the rooster himself, she didn't flinch.

Peggy rapped the black knocker on the arching wooden door. It opened immediately with no one on the other side. "Hello?" she called in, but only her chilled echoes replied. "Anyone home? It's Peggy, Sheriff McStoots. Bill? Judy?"

Nobody responded.

She should turn around. Peggy hadn't visited Carol at the post office in several days. Who knew what gossip she learned? Also, Old Gregor messaged earlier about a fallen tree that originated on his neighbor's property. Typically, Peggy wouldn't interfere with feuding neighbors because it was never about the tree. Old Gregor would complain about Frederico's late-night parties, and Frederico would pretend he didn't speak English. With nothing resolved, Peggy would learn new ways to sigh. However, *that* might be better than setting foot into the Viceroy mansion.

She recalled a Lydia McStoots poem titled 'Satisfied Chip' that consistently inspired courage:

If it's rain on your sunny day,
or the battery gone dead.
Maybe your money's withdrawn,
now how to buy bread?
Reckon a meadow, of love birds,
your hardship rebut.
Soon you'll be happier than a chipmunk,
cheek full of nut.

Better. Peggy stepped inside with renewed confidence and shut the door behind her. Where might Bill—

"Greetings!"

Peggy jumped higher than Siaytee and yelped louder than Diohgee. After a breath, she turned and found Judy Viceroy, the matriarch of the wolf pack. "You scared the goat right out of me."

"Fitting afternoon, Sheriff McStoots." She wore a black hat with a dark veil over her face, black pearl earrings, and a full-sleeved black dress. "My husband said you'd visit. He waits for you." She raised a finger upwards.

"All the way up?"

"In the study." Judy cackled and stroked her straight black hair. "The hunting section."

"Thank you, Mrs. Viceroy." Peggy considered heading right for the stairs, but it felt rude. "You know, Judy, we older gals play a monthly cribbage game, and we love hosting new players. I haven't attended in a while due to the murder investigation, but hopefully, I'll nab this buck and return to cards."

"Cards?" She drew a black deck from behind her back. "Here's a game for you." She flipped the top one, revealing a decaying skull and a grim reaper.

"Thank you, but no playing games while on duty. It'd waste town resources." Peggy lied, leery of those death cards. "Good afternoon, Mrs. Viceroy."

"Fitting." Judy smiled and stroked her hair.

Peggy turned and hurried to the stairs. It required all of her willpower not to run. That woman made her cringe tighter than a plumber's wrench. Not just her, but every decoration in the house exhibited some horrible design: a headless mannequin in a pink dress, a stuffed house cat with an apple in its mouth, a crossbow, several dreamcatchers with live spiders, and a vampire portrait. And that was just on the walls surrounding the grand stairs.

When she arrived on the second floor, she needed to decide: right or left. She recalled her first visit to this mansion. The Viceroys invited several folks from the town select board (Peggy had the misguided notion of joining that demo derby for several years) for dinner. Between the first and second courses, Bill and Judy lead a tour of the entire mansion, but Peggy remembered little. Had she expelled the memories from her mind?

*Not too deft? Just go left.* She started down a hallway with a single flickering light bulb. Flashes of scratched paint and broken light fixtures accompanied the icy draft and the smell of burnt rubber. She advanced through the darkness, careful not to touch anything. Who knew what kind of awfulness clung to their walls? She'd rather stick her hands in a manure pit.

She was relieved to find the third-floor stairs at the end, with functional lights, too. A relief turned horror when she discovered the black and white pictures adorning the walls. Depictions of sexual and physical extremes Peggy had never once considered. Leather, whips, chains, and other objects she didn't inspect long enough to identify.

After ascending the stairs, she found herself in front of one of the round windows crowning the mansion. It overlooked the entirety of Rosefield's main street. Did the Viceroys spy on the whole town? *Another shiver came... hither.* Not the greatest lyric, but she felt better. The view helped, too.

Rosefield resembled a bowl, with the mountains to the east and north and the hills sweeping around the other side. Route 13, along with the Mulberry River, cut east through the center of town. It then split, with Left Mountain Road winding north to the resort and South Road stretching towards Enosburg. Altogether, the roads formed a sideways 'T.'

She spotted Cody's and the Sled opposite each other at the intersection. West of the general store stood Slick Mick's. A busy-as-ever Daffodil Harvest across the street, and directly behind was Mechanic Joe's on Low Street, with his ten-car graveyard. Banker Henry loomed above them all, ever since he installed his third-story extension. For a man who acted as the king of Rosefield, he sure was quick to pee himself.

Peggy recalled one such incident from eight years ago. Henry foreclosed on Carrie Smith (also Peggy's sister-in-law's niece) in the middle of winter. The Smith brothers confronted him on their side-by-side. They told Henry to delay until summer. Otherwise, they'd return with their unlicensed side-by-side. Once Henry finished relieving himself, he agreed.

158

Funny, the Smith brothers had both domesticated themselves over the years. Charlie settled down with his family, and Peter kept busy between his little farm and generally managing the mountain. She heard rumors the younger brother still took seedy out-of-town jobs. At least Charlie kept his nefarious activities out of Rosefield—and Peggy's jurisdiction.

She couldn't reminisce on old stories all day, especially not in this creepy mansion. As they said, no sense wasting daylight with a deer to gut. She marched down the hallway and opened the door to the study.

Inside she discovered a candlelit maze of bookshelves. It smelled of cigars and Listerine. She passed by sections of books larger than Peggy's kitchen at home. As she roamed, she only heard the click of her shoes on the wood floor and a fireplace crackling.

A plaque labeled the first set of bookshelves 'War.' It contained not just books but also quite a few well-kept medieval pieces such as a mace and halberd. They even included a torture section with a detailed miniature rack and iron maiden.

The next few sections weren't particularly interesting for Peggy but definitely provided insight into the Viceroys. One bookcase labeled 'Toxins & Poisons' contained preserved fangs and live spiders on display. Another, titled 'Anatomy,' was filled entirely with bones and pickled animal parts. She hurried past those areas.

Next, a single bookshelf dedicated to books about dams, from building them to operation and contract requirements. Why would the Viceroys be interested in that? Bowhunter fair, Peggy had no idea how they earned their fortunes. Maybe they owned utility companies.

The following bookshelf she found equally puzzling. Dozens of books about lakefront property and development. The closest thing to a lake in Rosefield was little Abscond Pond off South Road, but no one built there for one reason: too many bugs. Not all summer, but after an extended rain, it turned into a swamp, and the black flies, mosquitoes, and no-see-ums swarmed by the thousands. Maybe they intended to move to the nearby Lake Carmi.

After the lakes, she finally arrived at the hunting section, a full room on its own. Deer, moose, bear, coyotes, owls, turkeys, several pheasants, and a fisher stuffed and mounted around the walls. Glass cases below the taxidermy displayed a dozen rifles, several appearing centuries old.

"Welcome, Sheriff McStoots. Make yourself comfortable." Bill Viceroy loomed from a cushioned leather chair next to a raging fireplace.

Of all the rooms they could've met, Peggy felt most comfortable here. While she hadn't hunted in decades, she bagged a few bucks in her twenties. "Mr. Viceroy, I'd like to ask you a few questions. I would've simply called but—"

"I dislike conversing over the phone. Furthermore, I loathe when people stand over me. Sit." He pointed to a similar leather chair as his, but smaller and less cushioned. Which didn't bother Peggy. She preferred lean hardwood. *Keep the back straight, so the aches abate.*

"Timmy's murder," she stated once seated. "Do you know anything about it?"

"Why would I?" His shoulders spanned the chair, and his arms stretched his cashmere sweater. A beard trimmed to stubble surrounded a snarl and fixed eyes.

"You have . . . connections."

"Connections?" Bill picked up a cigar from the marble table beside him. "What does that mean?"

"You, uh, have acquaintances who—"

"How do you think I make a living, Sheriff McStoots?"

Peggy frowned. Folks in town assumed Bill Viceroy dealt in some kind of criminal activity. The rumors ranged from drugs to Christmas trees, but no one knew anything for sure. When she researched him online, she discovered a painting company he owned in Massachusetts called Spray Color. They definitely weren't painters. She decided on the most straightforward answer. "You're a businessman."

"Correct. And a businessman of my stature would never become involved with a loser like Timmy." He lit his cigar, and it smelled like a late-night barrel fire. "Interrogate my worthless sons." While she agreed with his evaluation, it was hard hearing it from their own father.

"I did in January after they trashed the soccer field. They claimed they knew nothing about the murder." Peggy sighed. "Since we're on the subject, they caused a lot of damage . . ."

"Principal Shoeman and I arranged sufficient repayment for the soccer fields." Bill coughed. "Allow me to confirm one detail. You come to me *hoping* I have information regarding Timmy's murder, correct?"

"You had an altercation with him once."

"You mean at Farmer Rick's? Twenty years ago?"

"Fifteen," corrected Peggy.

"Right, the so-called Red Barn Incident. If you'll recall, *I* busted *him* up. So thoroughly, he fled town shortly after. Why would I murder Timmy for letting me beat him silly?" Bill chuckled. "Is your investigation this desperate?"

"Not much to fire with," Peggy admitted. "I figured you might lend me some ammo."

"A gun metaphor." His laughter echoed through the entire study. "Charming, Sheriff McStoots."

"I prefer Peggy, Mr. Viceroy."

"Bill's my God-given name." He continued to chuckle between puffs from his cigar. "Not hard to surmise I like guns."

"Well, you packing or what?"

"Packing information on Timmy? No, unfortunately. Empty

chamber."

Peggy sighed with every breath in her lungs. He could've told her that over the phone. "Happy supper time."

"It's not supper yet, not for a few hours."

"You hit that deer head-on." Peggy blinked. Bill did not.

"As I spy upon the town, I observe things," he said.

Peggy imagined Bill staring all day out of the round windows overlooking Rosefield. Was he always watching?

"I've noticed something of interest. And maybe it relates to Timmy's murder."

Peggy relaxed into her chair. "And?"

"Before I tell you, I require a favor."

"I won't do it blindly. This isn't cow insemination."

"On the day of the annual Park & Grill, I need you to escort a red van from the resort entrance up to the Generally Slanted porch."

"Escort who? And why do they need one?"

"It's not easy driving through the resort during Park & Grill. They'll require assistance."

"Again, who is 'they'?"

Bill shrugged. "They'll arrive at 5 PM."

"I guide this red van to Generally Slanted, and you'll share your information?"

"Correct. Two weeks from tomorrow."

It couldn't be too terrible. Peggy extended a hand, which Bill shook. Whatever was necessary to solve this case by summer.

"You've noticed Daffodil Harvest's recent fortune? Why do you think that is?"

"Simply a Rosefield success story?"

Bill chuckled without ever disturbing his snarl. "From my experience in business, you don't achieve Yelsa's level of success without breaking a couple of laws."

"No farm flourishes without stealing some hay," agreed Peggy.

"What's her scheme?"

"I'll let you figure out the rest. Pulling that thread might unravel your murder mystery."

The prices at Daffodil Harvest had significantly decreased about six months ago. Yelsa said she changed her source, but what if she simply stole old produce from Generally Slanted? When she considered how many veggies she'd eaten from there, Peggy shivered for the hundredth time today. Was it all Rosefield Resort food? The mountain bought the cheapest and most GMO'd garbage on the market. Could Yelsa commit such a tremendous betrayal?

She'd investigate, especially with the town's health on the line. It didn't further her primary case, however. "How does this relate to the murder?"

"I said it *might* connect to Timmy. Again, I know nothing." Bill stubbed out his cigar on a gold-plated ashtray. "Maybe someone murdered him over the horse incident."

"Yes," sighed Peggy. "That."

"I never understood the belt sander. How was it still functioning?"

"I'd rather not speculate."

"The incident occurred only a few years ago. It's fresh in a lot of people's minds."

"That's just it," said Peggy, standing up. "A lot of people' doesn't exactly narrow down the suspect list."

"I can't help you." Bill stood up. "Remember, the Park & Grill at 5 PM."

"Red van. Generally Slanted. I'll herd the cow for you." She nodded, and he smiled in return. "Happy almost-supper time."

Peggy rushed through the study and down the hallway, past the round windows overlooking Rosefield. She didn't pause for another look, focusing on the floorboards the whole way. She descended the first set of stairs, through the hall, down the grand stairs, and struck for the front door. She seized the doorknob but stopped when her peripheral caught something . . . interesting.

She discovered Judy Viceroy in the exact same spot as before, still stroking her hair and smiling. For a moment, their gazes held one another's, and *that final shiver made her soul quiver.*

After wrenching her eyes free, Peggy hurried out the door. She hustled to her truck, hopped in, and peeled out. She ripped down the driveway and through the gnarled metal gate. When John and Henry once more flipped her off, Peggy returned the gesture.

*To that wolf den? Never again.* Hopefully, the ordeal proved worth it.

When she returned to town, she pulled in front of Daffodil Harvest and watched from the Road Runner as unsuspecting customers streamed in and out. She almost stormed in demanding answers, but she remembered busting Yelsa was *not* her primary goal. Solving Timmy's murder *was.* Spring had arrived, which only led to summer and little baby Robert.

She watched day after day, morning until midnight. *She'd do whatever it took to catch this sneaky crook.*

"For snow and for glory!" Joey shouted his prayer to the winds, as he did before each run. He stood at the peak, skis on and ready to rip.

Solo day. He tried recruiting the Powder Crew, but they each offered a different excuse. Jesse worked, and he didn't understand what sick days were for. Brad had a date with a Stowe bunny. Waste of effort, she'd break it off once he ran out of cash.

Happy was too busy solving some mystery. Probably Timmy Harton's murder, what consumed most townsfolk. Who cared about some dude who died months ago, when three inches dropped overnight and a spring sun blazed overhead?

Whatever. Joey only needed his earbuds blaring the Rutland Rotary Boys. For this run, he decided on one of their early classics, 'Hurtin' Joe."

HE'S A HURTIN' JOE,
FARMING HIS PRAIRIE.

DUH DOO, DUH DOO.

FROM A LIFE OF WOE
ALL HE'S GOT IS HIS DAIRY.

DUH DOO, DUH DOO.

IT ALWAYS GROW, THAT GRASS TO MOW,
SO DON'T YOU GO, 'I AIN'T GOT THE DOUGH.'
YOU HAVE THIS BLOW, YA HURTIN' JOE-OE.

HEY THERE HURTIN' JOE,
DON'T BE WARY.

DUH DOO, DUH DOO.

JUST GRAB YOUR HOE,
AND BE MERRY.

DUH DOO, DUH DOO.

WHY SO LOW, A-HURTIN' JOE?
WHEN YOU FLOW, YOU BRING THE SHOW!
LET US KNOW, YA HURTIN' JOE-OE.

Less rockin' than 'Small Town Hero," but what song could live up to Jonathan T. Weevil's epic ballad? Especially when it perfectly paralleled Joey's own life.

On that day, 'Hurtin' Joe" resonated with Joey's mending arm, which still ached. Notably, when he turned. Or when he braked. Or stopped. Or riding the lifts, that hurt the worst.

A little pain wouldn't stop Joey from enjoying this beautiful spring day. He secured his goggles and turned onto Easy Way Round, which he skied to appease those know-it-all doctors. They told him to rest until next season. Hah! He'd get laughed out of town if he hung up his skis for a tiny arm fracture.

No poles, no problem. Joey often skied without because they obstructed his grabs. Besides, he could shred Easy Way Round faster and harder than Chef Alex could shred cheese. He skied around the flatties like slalom gates, ripping close enough to catch their curses:

'Slow down, asshole!" 'There are children!" and 'You want some murder on this mountain!?" were his favorites today. He supplied an answer for each, respectively: 'Speed up, Grandpa," 'They should learn from the best," and 'Catch me, and I'll hand you the knife." Unfortunately, they lacked the speed to hear his words of wisdom.

He swung a left at Mule Run, popping off headwalls and clearing the tourists. They basically gauged the epicness of his run. However, all these flatties scratched a chunk out of his freshies. His first-track counter was the lowest ever. Not cool. They should reconsider this whole Murder Mountain thing. If they kept the mountain minor, locals might slay the drifts in peace—nay, *shred* the drifts in peace.

Soon after, he stopped at the entrance to Open Glade. Should he rip through for Timmy? The doctors couldn't fault him for stomping one tree run in honor of a fallen

169

Rosefieldian.

He popped left, stomped right, ollied the trunk, and landed switch. Ope, big bush ahead, Joey hockey-stopped into a spin, passing within an inch from the gushing yellow birch. One-eighty to tips forward and then a hard stop in the clearing.

When Joey glanced about, he noticed something familiar with the surrounding birches and maples . . . When he saw the great white oak, he realized Timmy died here. What drew his skis to this spot? Was it a sign?

He flicked off his helmet and stripped his mitts. He smelled the fresh pollen of blooming trees mixed with the minty scent of saturated pines. Sunrays blared through the shuttering branches, warming his skin. The odor and glow reminded Joey of his spiritual forays with his cousin James. Did a flicker of life cling to this realm? "Timmy, you out there?"

After listening for over a minute, only a blue jay whistled back. What had he expected? Ghosts weren't real. Maybe just one more attempt. "Timmy? Show me a sign."

Joey observed for another minute, and the same blue jay whistled once more, but nothing else. He sighed, reached down for his mittens, but froze halfway down. What if Timmy's spirit could only meld with the forest creatures? "Is that you, bud?"

The blue jay whistled.

"Really? Whistle twice if you're Timmy."

One long whistle returned. Close enough. If Joey learned anything throughout his skiing career: never think twice about a decision.

"Did Big Top kill you?"

Timmy jeered and flapped his wings. Nopers.

"Did you kill yourself? Japanese style?"

He jeered and stomped on the branch, causing freshies to fall— another hard no.

"Is your killer a resort employee?"

Big whistle. Joey hit the powder line.

"Do they ski or snowboard?"

Timmy cawed and flapped his wings, ready for takeoff.

Oh no! Joey upset him with such a stupid question. "A skier, of course. You'd never let a snowboarder murder you."

Timmy settled on the branch, content.

Joey considered his next question. One more idiotic inquiry, and Timmy would fly away. He had to contemplate and scrutinize harder than ever before. This moment defined Joey, akin to the final run in an international ski competition. He waited for the green light at the top of the course. The crowd screamed his name. He had better not yard sale. Joey breathed in, closed his eyes, and kicked off.

"Does the killer wear a green jacket?"

Jeer.

"Yellow jacket?"

Jeer.

"Black?"

Whistle. A black jacket! Who wore a black jacket on the mountain? Few chose such a stealthy and streamlined color. Boston Tony often donned the black, but he couldn't have killed Timmy; a weekend warrior like Tony wouldn't come up to Rosefield before Opening Day. Who else? Wilma Johansson, but only because the Head of Ski Patrol always wore a black jacket, and no one committed murder in their work uniform. Timmy wasn't referring to her.

*Boom! Bam!* An explosion of snow accompanied whoops and hollers as a pack of reckless snowboarders crashed through the woods. "Yee-haw!" "Wahoo!" "Get some!" They ripped by, trashing every bit of spiritual energy in the clearing.

"Goddamn snowboarders, respect the dead!" he shouted, but they kept charging through. Those single-planking sons of bitches never considered other folks on the slopes.

After the snow settled, he searched for Timmy, but he had fled from the snowboarders. At least Joey received a pair of clues from his old ski rival. The killer worked at the resort and wore a black jacket.

He should head home. A nap would encourage heavy-duty thinking. And besides, those snowboarders soured the whole mountain.

Joey emptied all the snow in his helmet and shook out his mitts. As he put them on, a flash of yellow caught his attention. A bright piece of cloth stuck in a nearby pine. When he pried it out of the branch, he discovered a rainbow-colored scrunchie. Yelsa Hodinker always held her hair up with one of these. How had it wound up right next to where Timmy was murdered?

Coincidence? Maybe she lost it skiing. However, Joey never saw her on the slopes. He couldn't recall a single instance. The Staties would've discovered the scrunchie when they surveyed the crime scene. Or Sheriff McStoots, Jim McJoy, even Joey himself. Had everyone missed it? Without spiritual guidance, quite possibly.

"Timmy, are you still here? Did you show me this?"

In the distant woods, a whistle called back.

Yepper. That confirmed it. Yelsa was present at Timmy's murder. Had she killed him herself? Joey knew Yelsa most of his life, attending the Rez with her daughters (securing second base with Harvesta). With a constant smile and bright clothes, she hardly appeared a murderer. Plus, he'd never seen her in a black jacket.

He needed a nap. He tightened his mitts, clipped his helmet, and raced down the mountain. He bypassed the Bent Pole and flew straight to T-Dog, the new name for his truck. The 'T' symbolized two things: Timmy to honor the dead and truck to honor the living. And Dog because it sounded awesome.

He hopped into the driver's seat while the paper bag containing the Big One rode shotgun. He kept it in the truck to remind himself of his New Year's Eve failure. He had missed his opportunity to wow the town, but with this new information, he'd secure redemption. What if he could solve the murder before Park & Grill in ten days?

He better zip home for naptime when Joey accomplished his best thinking. He floored it out of the parking lot at a marginal fifty mph. He passed a security van and two flatties on his way out. Not an easy task with a bum arm, but Joey never feared a challenge. As he pulled onto

Left Mountain Road, he offered respect to the resort sign.

It was still the Murder Mountain logo with a grim reaper on skis. Joey opened his window to spit. He missed the old sign, the classic rose-petalled ridgeline. Simple, like Rosefield Mountain.

Then he noticed Rodney Buric in the corner of the sign, wearing a black suit—the same black suit he always wore! Joey released the steering wheel when this newest revelation slammed into his cranium. Timmy said the killer wore a black jacket but not necessarily a *ski* jacket.

He returned T-Dog to the right lane and sped down the road. Had Rodney Buric masterminded this whole thing from the beginning? To initiate the rebrand and increase profitability? An easy scheme for ski industry mogul Rodney Buric, but could he actually murder somebody?

Joey stepped on the pedal until the needle topped out. He hankered for home and a two-hour nap. If that didn't produce results, he'd keep napping until things made sense, until morning if necessary. He needed to solve this case by Park & Grill. He'd reveal the murderer and fire off the Big One in the most epic finale ever.

More epic than Jonathan T. Weevil's triumphs? Heck, if he pulled this off, the Rutland Rotary Boys would write a song about Joey Rogers! The sooner he achieved nap status, the better. His legacy depended on it.

Happy attempted to hand the note over to Peggy. He really did. On three separate occasions, he set his mind. Until Mary Anne convinced him otherwise. He initiated his third attempt in late March when he texted her:

> I'm bringing the note to Peggy.

Mary Anne showed up at his front door forty minutes later. "You better scrape that shit right off your boot. No way." She stormed into his living room/kitchen. Happy lived in a single-room cabin with a loft for his bed and a curtained alcove for the bathroom. All he hankered, anything more suckered a man into staying home. Who would curb the deer population?

"Grandma said—" he began.

"Grandma said?" Mary Anne's expression matched the unimpressed glare of the toupee-wearing owl on her t-shirt. "Why are we listening to Granny Smith? She tricked you out of your favorite rifle."

She raised a valid point. Happy contemplated Remi underneath his bed. Close enough to touch, but he wouldn't dare, not until the day he brought her to Grandma. Happy felt horrible about missing several Grandma Days already, so he needed to oppose Mary Anne. Even if it meant ending their investigation together.

"She said it's important."

"What vital information could she possess?" retorted Mary Anne. "She never leaves your uncle's house besides cribbage night."

"She mentioned the Red Barn Incident; it's serious. There's nothing fun about that place."

"Or she pranked you again, like how she stole your rifle. The letter probably means nothing."

"And yet you're more curious than a piglet." He stumped her. With that settled, he threw on his jacket and stepped towards the door.

She slid in his way. "One more day. I found a lead, too. Come on."

"And if we don't learn anything . . ." He raised the letter. "We bring this to Peggy."

"Fine." They shook hands.

"What's your lead?"

She shrugged while twirling her truck keys around her finger. "Let's roll."

They hopped in her truck and headed east through town. They turned right onto South Road, and Happy feared Mary Anne intended to drive up Gregory Road. Fortunately, she sped by.

She drove through Enosburg, Bakersfield, and continued south towards Jeffersonville. Had she bought them both lift tickets to Smuggler's Notch? Happy almost jumped out of the truck in his excitement! Except, she would've told him to bring his snowboard. Maybe she lined up a demo rental.

All his hopes for a surprise ride disappeared when Mary Anne pulled into a neighborhood of identical townhouses. She pulled up to a teal one that appeared straight out of a flatland catalog. "What's this?"

Mary Anne already hopped out, so Happy followed. When he caught up, she answered his question. "Farmer Rick lives here."

"The Farmer Rick? Red Barn Incident Rick? What if he placed the curse on his land?" Happy stopped. "What if he curses us, too?"

"You're such a farm turkey. You should've stopped believing in curses when we graduated from the Rez."

"I did until we visited the red barn. I'd believe in a beakless woodpecker after that."

"How about a pig with no asshole?"

"Yepper. Or a yard with no fire pit."

"No burn barrel, either."

"Where do they burn stuff?" Happy shook his head. "It makes no sense."

"Enough stalling. This ain't a stick." Mary Anne grabbed Happy's hand and pulled him forward. "He's an old man anyway."

Her half-smile and twinkling emerald eyes had already persuaded him. "Okay."

They dallied up to the front door. Despite the confidence in Mary Anne's words, she dragged boot heel as much as Happy. They climbed four wooden steps to a tiny porch, and a front door with half its red paint chipped off. She reached for the doorbell—

The door swung open the moment she pressed it, and Farmer Rick emerged with a pointed shotgun! Dressed in whitey-tighties and an open red bathrobe, his bloodshot eyes and deep scowl indicated a man willing to pull a trigger.

"What do you want!?"

"Oh! Hold your finger!" Mary Anne raised her hands with Happy. "Farmer Rick, it's us! I'm Mary Anne McStoots, my mom's Peggy. This is Happy Smith. We're from Rosefield."

"I want nothing more with that town." The gravel in his voice rivaled the average driveway, but at least he lowered the shotgun a little. "Terribleness comes from Rosefield, especially from you young folk. Fight starters and curse bringers."

"Curses?" said Happy. "Are you talking about your old red barn?"

"What do you know about my barn? Nothing! Go away." He retreated into his house and slammed the door.

"Well, I guess that's it," said Happy, turning towards the truck. Not Mary Anne, she stepped up and pressed the doorbell. "What about the shotgun?"

"Shotguns are only scary when used." She banged on the door with her other fist while repeatedly pressing the doorbell.

The door flung open so hard its hinges screeched in protest. "Leave me alone!" At least Farmer Rick wasn't aiming the shotgun anymore, but his face remained redder than a fall maple. "I moved for a reason. Too many horrors."

"We don't mean to bring up rough memories," said Mary Anne, "but we need to know what happened. It's important."

"I remember you," said Rick, scratching through his sparse and tangled white hair. "Your mom's Peggy McStoots?"

"Yes, sir."

"I appreciate her. Peggy stayed late that night and witnessed the ensuing awfulness." Farmer Rick turned to Happy. "And you're Charlie Smith's kid?"

"Yepper."

"Really . . ." Farmer Rick's scowl lifted to an almost-smile, and his eyes relaxed. "Come in." His voice lost all the gravel, too, as though washed away by a flash flood.

He led them to his living room and sank into a red recliner. They sat on the matching sofa. Red covered the entire room, from the paint on the walls to the curtains and the photo frames. Farmer Rick might have left his old barn, but he brought it with him in spirit.

"Tell us everything," said Mary Anne. "From the party to the fire."

"The party to the fire." Farmer Rick chuckled. "If that's what you truly desire, here's the Red Barn Incident." He straightened his back, put on a pair of hand-carved glasses, coughed twice, and resumed in a hushed voice.

"July 17th, 2006. I invited a few friends over for dinner. We started drinking, and someone suggested inviting the Woodlets over. How about the McStoots? My neighbor Rogen enjoyed whiskey. By the way, how is the old man?"

"He still lives on Deep Gregory," said Happy. "He rarely leaves his cabin."

"I haven't seen Rogen Harton in five or more years," added Mary Anne.

"He built his cabin a mile in for a reason." Farmer Rick whistled. "Heck of a carpenter, though, he built most of my barn. What a magnificent structure. I hated abandoning it."

"Why did you?" asked Mary Anne.

"Don't rush the ending!" snapped Farmer Rick before smiling unevenly. "We had a fresh barn, no cows yet. We reckoned we oughta christen it with a party. Soon we packed the whole thing with folks dancing to a full band—more smiles than a tickle booth.

"After sunset, the families left, and a chilly wind ushered a moonless night. That's when the violence began. Over the years, I've tried to understand what caused the carnage. Was it the sledding incident? Or a skier's rivalry gone too far? Maybe just an extra hot summer. Two weeks of ninety degrees plus, breaking a hundred in the sun. Too hot for a town as burly as Rosefield.

"The first fight broke out between Charlie Smith and Timmy Harton—"

"We heard about that one," said Mary Anne. "What was it about?"

"The previous winter, Timmy flipped Charlie's sled off a jump. He boasted he could complete a full rotation, but he landed nose-first and smashed the entire engine block. Timmy was lucky it didn't land on him. And that Charlie didn't knock out several chompers."

"For trashing a man's sled," agreed Mary Anne, "Timmy's lucky he didn't receive a quick rib adjustment."

"For breaking Dad's sled," continued Happy, "Timmy's lucky he didn't receive a broken nose. With a realignment included."

"For smashing the mustard bucket," continued Farmer Rick, "Timmy's lucky he didn't receive some long-lasting eyeshadow."

"To make the situation worse, Timmy refused to pay because Charlie dared him, and it was an old sled. They never agreed on how much Timmy owed, and that night Charlie decided to take his due. They argued for a minute, and then your dad swung first, second, and third. In fact, Timmy never threw a punch. He hit the floor after a few bum blocks. Fortunately for him, Peter pulled Charlie away before he inflicted any real damage.

"Which led right into the second kerfuffle. Timmy's cousin John Harton stepped in. Do you remember him?"

"Yeppers, bud," said Mary Anne. "Heart popped while operating the woodchipper."

"Damn near fell in." Happy shivered. "Johnny Chips was the joke around town."

"Big fella, too. He lifted Charlie off the ground with an uppercut! Knocked him right out. Peter had to retaliate, but John outsized him. Peter executed a move I'll never forget; he jumped, grabbed a rafter and swung a double kick into John's chest. Peter knocked him back five feet! He didn't relent either. He followed John to the ground and kept pounding. It took Roaster Dan *and* Big Top to pull Peter away.

"Afterwards, the rest of the crowd decided to air their grievances. Big Top told Jordan Herring he couldn't descend a black diamond, even if he wore skins."

'Oh," murmured Happy. "Can't get much flatter than that."

"He called him a Floridian, more or less," agreed Mary Anne.

'Practically said, 'Hey, guy, my face needs a fisting.'"

"He got one," continued Farmer Rick. "*Boom!* Jordan popped Big Top, and then Big Top popped Jordan. They brawled across the barn. Following their example, Chef Alex and Thomas the Train decided they disliked the appearance of each other's faces.

"Meanwhile, Mechanic Joe and Gregor Jr. fought it out over a delinquent auto-bill. The Farney brothers decided to fight each other just to fit in. All mild bouts, though, compared to Bill Viceroy versus Timmy Harton.

"That's right, Timmy hadn't taken enough beatings from Charlie—who climbed onto the rafters to drain a bottle of whiskey—so he decided to confront Bill. I reckon Timmy picked on the new guy to prove his toughness."

"Yepper," remembered Happy. "The Viceroys moved to town the winter before because Henry joined our class in the middle of third grade."

"Wherever Bill came from, they taught him how to fight," continued Farmer Rick. "Timmy struck first with a series of punches. Bill blocked and blocked until a jab popped him in the nose.

"He staggered backward, holding his bloody nostrils. However, he stared at Timmy the entire time, analyzing. Once complete, Bill stomped forward and struck with vicious precision. First, he targeted Timmy's left shoulder. Crack. Now he was open for the uppercut, and Bill delivered. BAM! Timmy was unconscious before he hit the floorboards.

"Afterward, folks calmed down, but the party continued. Well, the Harton cousins wobbled out as soon as they woke up from their head traumas. Rogen escorted them out to ensure they made it home. From what the old man told me, Timmy continued rampaging down the whole driveway. He even attempted to fight Rogen, his own uncle."

"Which might explain why Rogen didn't attend Timmy's funeral or Parting Party," said Happy.

"The old man held his grudges," agreed Farmer Rick. "The rest of the night, things stayed peaceful, for the most part. Between 3 AM and sunrise, two men disappeared. Never seen again. Do you remember Tony Forga? Trucker Tony?"

They both shook their heads.

"What about Jason George Nichols? He used to bartend at the Sled Stop."

"I remember him," said Mary Anne. "Tall. And a deep voice . . ." She breathed in sharply and mouthed to Happy. *It was him.*

*Who?*

*At the barn.*

Did she mean the voices they heard, the ones without footprints? If they disappeared that long ago, but their voices still lingered at the Red Barn, they were ghosts. The barn truly was haunted! If only he delivered the note to Peggy like Grandma requested, Happy enjoyed not believing in curses or ghosts.

"Didn't Jason leave town all of a sudden?" asked Mary Anne.

"Folks say that to make themselves feel better. Trucker Tony confronted Jason George about him rolling around the hay with Tony's daughter. While of age, the father held a grudge. They stomped into the woods to 'figure it out.' Neither returned.

"The next morning, we searched both the barn, the house, and the surrounding woods. We never found them. Even stranger, both of their trucks vanished. Someone made it *appear* like they left town."

"They disappeared," said Happy, shaking his head. This story grew weirder and weirder.

"Disappeared like a shotgunned chickadee," confirmed Farmer Rick. "With their trucks gone, folks assumed they both decided to leave."

"What about Tony's daughter?" said Mary Anne. "She never heard from him again?"

"Never." Farmer Rick shrugged. "Not unusual for him to leave for months since he trucked all over the country. She figured he stayed out on the road after meeting a woman." He chuckled. "I know better."

"They died in those woods," said Mary Anne.

"Yepper. I heard their voices. While working in the barn, hiking around the woods, and in my own damned house! They shouted the most hateful things at each other, back and forth. They died that night and haunted the property. No more! Their souls seemed connected to the barn, so I tried to burn it down. It wouldn't catch, even after seven attempts. So instead, I ignited the house."

"You did what?" coughed Happy, suddenly remembering the shotgun at Farmer Rick's side. They should make like chickens and run. He nudged Mary Anne, but she ignored him.

"Had to," continued Farmer Rick. "If the house remained, somebody would buy it, and the ghosts would torment them. I picked a sunny day, so the townsfolk could enjoy my farm for one final time. I dumped kerosene across the living room, and *I set it off with a Molotov.*" He sang the last bit with a crooked smile.

"Returning to the barn," said Mary Anne, somehow unfazed by the armed pyromaniac before them, still only wearing a bathrobe and whiteys. "You said you attempted to set it on fire, but it wouldn't catch. What do you mean?"

"Whatever fuel I used extinguished without the flame ever spreading. I dumped a whole can of kerosene at once. Nothing."

"It scorched a little," continued Mary Anne. "We noticed the burnt marks when we investigated a few—"

"You noticed what?" His scowl returned. "You went there!?" Farmer Rick raged, his voice refilled with gravel. He stood up with his shotgun leveled and his bathrobe open. "Get out! I smell that cursed place on you!"

Happy hopped to his feet. "Yes, sir."

"I have one more—" started Mary Anne. Happy jabbed her with an elbow.

"Sorry to bother you, Mr. Rick."

"Begone! Before you corrupt my house!"

"Come on." Happy led Mary Anne out of the house. Twice she protested, but he kept a firm grasp on her elbow all the way to the truck.

Once in, Mary Anne pulled out of Farmer Rick's, and they drove in silence all the way through Bakersfield. She was mad about interrupting her questioning, but Happy knew better than to argue with a shotgun.

"We learned a couple of things," said Mary Anne as they continued past Enosburg.

"Yes, my dad won that fight."

"Of all people to beat up, Timmy Harton. Is that a coincidence?"

"What do you mean?"

Mary Anne shrugged.

"No—my dad would never kill anyone!" Happy knew his father despised Timmy, and now he understood why, but murder? "Definitely not over a snowmobile."

"Noper." Mary Anne sighed. "Anyway, we also learned whose voices haunt the barn, Trucker Tony and Jason George."

"Ghosts . . ." Happy shivered. The thought terrified him, but what else explained what they heard?

"They might not be ghosts."

"They didn't leave any footprints!" Happy almost jumped out of the truck in his frustration. When he calmed down, he set Grandma's letter on the dashboard. "Anyway, we're no closer to figuring this out."

"How do you know?" blurted out Mary Anne. "We should consider Farmer Rick's story for a day or two, maybe even a week. We'll solve the mystery."

"I didn't hear anything about cushions. And by the sound of that party, everyone climbed onto those rafters."

"Not everyone . . ."

"Just admit it. We've reached the final row, no more corn to harvest. Let's bring the note to your mom."

"Not yet, we agreed I had until the morning," grumbled Mary Anne. "We'll check the town clerk's office and search through old pictures. The resort has records, too. We could learn more about Trucker and Jason."

"No old pictures or records," said Happy, resisting her half-smile and accompanying eye twinkle. "Come on, Mary Anne. It's time."

"Fine." She smashed her palms against the steering wheel. "We'll bring it to her now."

She sounded displeased, but at least she agreed. Hopefully, the note was cribbage rules after all. They'd slap knee and laugh their bellies red.

When they arrived at Peggy's, only Diohgee greeted them at the door. Mary Anne sent her mom a text but didn't receive a response. After fifteen minutes of scratching dog ears, they left the note, and Mary Anne drove him home.

"Let me know if Peggy tells you what the note means," said Happy as he climbed out of her truck.

She flipped him a thumbs up and drove off, returning to her university in the big city. She wouldn't return with their investigation over. She'd focus on her classes and the famous Burlington nightlife. Well, it was a fun few weeks anyway.

# BANKER HENRY

Wanna know who killed Timmy? Banker Henry did, for failure to pay his mortgage.* The kid was a delinquent, like most Rosefield residents. From ski bums to rednecks to hippies, and not one of them knew how to fill out a rent check.

While he prided himself on his foreclosures, they sometimes caused headaches. People became so depressed when someone repossessed their home and stuff. Maybe they should pay their bills.

Several months ago, he foreclosed on a place with cows, chickens, and horses. What would he do with all that? They didn't call him Farmer Henry for a reason. Fortunately, they paid up. For now, at least, these townies always reverted to their naturally delinquent ways.

He foreclosed on a tiny home once. Henry towed it away with the ex-owner inside asleep. The delinquents in this town didn't even wake up to say goodbye to their home.**

Now he foreclosed on Timmy's roommate, brain-dead Rufus. The

---

*Of course, he'd never *actually* kill someone. Henry couldn't collect from a dead man.

**The homeowner later sued the bank after suffering a concussion and won their tiny home back.

whole town sympathized because his roommate was murdered. *Boohoo,* find another roommate. So Henry's the villain for performing his duty? Without bankers, the world would crash into ruin.

He delivered the foreclosure notice to Rufus in person. The neighborly thing to do. Plus, he saved the bank postage with a quick stroll down Main Street.

Atrocious idea. First, Henry caught a buzz approaching Rufus's house; the stench of his nasty smelling marijuana hovered around the yard like a bubble of delinquency. When Henry knocked on the front door, it swung open.

"Where's my knife, Sheriff McStoots?" raged Rufus, waving a bat over his head! His tattered clothes barely held together, and his hair was greasier than Mechanic Joe.

Henry threw his hands up. They didn't call him Fighter Henry for a reason. What happened to the stoner moron?

Rufus's angry gaze mellowed in an instant. He grabbed the envelope and retreated into the house. At least Henry saved on shipping.

On Saturday morning, Peggy drove to the Sled Stop to enjoy an extended brunch. No emails, no work jacket, she was off duty. After seven long days watching the Daffodil Harvest and Generally Slanted General Store, she deserved a rest.

One whole week of continuous observation, and she hadn't caught Yelsa or Roger stealing a single vegetable. She noticed one irregularity: not a single food order arrived at Daffodil Harvest, even when her stock dwindled in recent days. Maybe they knew Peggy was watching.

Or they were innocent, and Bill Viceroy sent her on a wild moose sighting. She actually preferred that narrative because Peggy bought her vegetables from Yelsa for the past year. Was it all Rosefield Resort's lowest-grade food? The idea filled her stomach with acorns. For safety, she already threw out every Daffodil Harvest product from her fridge and pantry.

Except, if innocent, then she wasn't any closer to catching Timmy's killer. Frustrated with her lack of progress, Peggy decided to take the day off. When she arrived at the Sled Stop, she claimed her favorite booth by the stuffed black bear.

'Hey, Peggy, how are you today?" Kate served up a mug of Tootin', accompanied by a wide smile.

*"Happier than a chipmunk, cheek full of nut."* A classic Lydia McStoots line, although Kate had probably never read *Seasonal Colors*, so she wouldn't understand the reference. The youth around town weren't familiar with refined literature. "Too much sheriffing lately. I'm taking a day off."

"Hankerin' your usual? Extra fried egg, extra bacon, burnt toast?" Kate began serving at the Sled when Jane got too busy at the mountain. She already memorized Peggy's order—what excellent waitressing. Hopefully, Kate kept a few shifts when Jane returned at the end of the season.

"Not today. That's my work breakfast. I'll have bacon and blueberry pancakes with whipped cream. And yepper, a side of cheddar."

"What's breakfast without it?"

*"A slice of Gregory's cheddar will make your whole day better."* Peggy slipped yet another line of poetry, one of her originals this time.

"That should be their slogan," laughed Kate. "Anything else?"

"Coffee is all I require."

"Call me if you need anything else." Kate twirled and skipped to the kitchen. What an adorable young lady with her dirty blonde pigtails and old-timey dresses. Today she wore yellow with frills at the end of the wrists, a white bow over her chest, and an ankle-length skirt.

Peggy sipped on her coffee and watched the snowbanks shrink. Fields around town had already shed their winter coats, and the chipmunks and squirrels had emerged from hibernation. A perfect spring morning.

"Sheriff McStoots!" The shout that ruined everything. Joey burst through the Sled's front door. She attempted averting her eyes, but unfortunately, he spotted her. "Peggy!"

"Yes?"

"I searched the town for you. I've uncovered something big. Bigger than a hundred-footer over three vans!" He established himself opposite Peggy. Her beautiful morning just dove into a snowbank. "While skiing at the mountain a couple of days ago, I figured it out."

"What?"

Joey placed a rainbow-colored scrunchie on the table, which she immediately recognized as Yelsa's. "You'll never guess where I found this. Additionally, a blue jay told me—"

"Sheriff McStoots!" Jane shouted from the front door and then marched across the Sled. "Slide over, Joey."

If Peggy could have sighed a hundred times at once, she would have. "What's your hanker, Jane?"

"On Opening Day in the mountain cafeteria, I overheard—" She stopped when Kate arrived with a tall plate of pancakes.

"Sorry to interrupt. Your breakfast, Peggy." She slid the plate onto the table and returned to the bar.

A crisp shell packed with fat and juicy blueberries, concealing fluffy insides waiting to lap up maple syrup. The bacon bits glistened in their own grease, and the cheese stank in the best possible way. Delicious, but apparently, this was a workday. Peggy just wanted her eggs and toast.

*When work's a jerk, best chug a mug.* "Kate!" She held up her empty cup, and the sweetheart returned immediately with the pot. "Well, this wood won't stack itself. One at a time and from the beginning." She pointed at Joey. "I'll start with you."

"Okay, picture this. Beautiful spring day. Me, skiing down the hill, jumping over flatties. I executed a few threes. I threw a five—"

"Never mind," said Peggy. "Jane, you start."

"Hold on, allow the artist to paint the scene. You must understand the mind-state of the story's protagonist." Joey pointed to his face. "I'm referring to myself."

Peggy would've sighed in a dozen different dialects if possible. "Please get somewhere."

"I decided to slide through Open Glade in tribute to Timmy, a martyr for skiers worldwide." He held up the scrunchie. "This is Yelsa Hodinker's, and I found it where he died."

193

"She might've dropped it any other day."

"Yelsa doesn't ski!" broke in Jane. "I've never seen her on the hill. Joey's thing ties straight into mine. See, I spied on—"

"Let's tackle one turkey first," said Peggy. "Jim and I searched those woods. We'd have discovered the scrunchie. The Staties combed the area, too."

"It was in the same *exact* spot," said Joey. "Right where Timmy biffed the ultimate landing."

"It's a coincidence. Someone else might've lost it. Yelsa isn't the only person in the world who wears rainbow-colored scrunchies."

"If I may," inserted Jane, "I can contribute."

"Hey," said Joey, holding up his hands. "I recognize when it's not my turn to gate. You're up."

"My story begins on Opening Day," she said, crossing her arms over her chest. "I overheard Yelsa and Roger whisper about absconding south after the season ends. Not Bennington or Brattleboro, either, more like North Carolina."

"Maybe they hanker retirement," offered Peggy.

"Not fishin' with much," admitted Jane. "However, I asked the right questions, and I listened for the right answers. I learned Yelsa and Roger were on the mountain the same day Timmy died. Why hadn't they told anyone? I kept watching, and two weeks ago, I caught them carrying boxes of food out of Generally Slanted. I followed them to—"

"Daffodil Harvest. That's how she sold cheap food these past months."

"Precisely!" Jane slid her phone across the table with a video playing. "I recorded them."

Peggy watched exactly what Jane described. Yelsa and Roger loaded up their truck with Generally Slanted boxes and then unloaded at Daffodil Harvest.

"Nice investigating. This is excellent footage. I heard about the scheme but never caught them myself."

"It's a pleasure to serve my town."

How about that for Rosefieldian pride? Except for one thing. "Why did you wait before informing me?"

"Um . . ." She blinked and entangled her black hair between her fingers. "I hankered solving the mystery."

"You mean a connection to Timmy's murder?" The exact thing Peggy sought, too.

"I didn't uncover anything directly related, but . . ."

"Well?"

"What if this lift goes all the way to the top? When I followed them to Daffodil Harvest, who showed up? Rodney friggin' Buric! I doubt he's ever stepped in a Rosefield establishment outside of the resort, and he's *there* late at night? Something's up. I caught him on video, too, but I wasn't close enough for audio."

As sure as a January Nor'easter, Rodney arrived at the store in a BMW. Odd for two reasons, she had never seen him drive before, nor ride in anything shorter than a limo.

He marched up to Yelsa, and they argued. Rodney must've said something piggish because Roger stepped between them with fists clenched. Buric scurried to his car and vacated the parking lot.

"Biscuit my dog." Peggy never considered Rodney Buric as a potential suspect. And yet, Rosefield Mountain Resort enjoyed its best ski season in history. "Was Rodney involved in Timmy's murder as well?"

"It's certainly suspicious," said Jane. "What if he brought on the rebrand by blackmailing Yelsa and Roger into murdering Timmy?"

"Which means Rodney planned everything from the beginning." Peggy sighed. "That's one *long* turkey stretch if you ask me."

"I can confirm!" broke in Joey. "I experienced a spiritual encounter with a blue jay, which told me the killer wore a black jacket. What color suit does Rodney always wear? Black." Peggy stopped listening when she heard the phrase 'spiritual encounter with a blue jay.'

'I'll check it out after breakfast." She pointed at her plate of pancakes. *'Now make like a colon and get your shit rollin'.'*

Neither Joey nor Jane moved. Worse, they both clamored at once.

'No, no, nothing more, or I'll arrest you both for public indecency."

They both shut up, rose to their feet, and stomped out of the Sled Stop. After they both disappeared, Peggy raised her empty mug and called for Kate. Upon arrival, she requested the pancakes boxed up before ordering her usual eggs, toast, and bacon.

While she ate, she considered this new information, but she couldn't connect Yelsa and Roger's scheme to the murder. Rodney blackmailing them seemed far-fetched, but why else would he confront them alone? The more she contemplated, the more her brain hurt. She preferred answers, and who better than Yelsa?

After she finished her eggs, Peggy drove up Left Mountain Road and turned into the resort. She scrutinized Rodney's sign as she passed by. Sure enough, he wore a black suit jacket. Which meant nothing when Joey learned his information from a blue jay. Rodney's bulbous mustache and sheepish grin resembled a lamb more than a butcher.

When she parked in front of Generally Slanted, her phone dinged with a text message from Mary Anne. She'd check it out later. Peggy needed to keep her mind on the job. Before hopping out of the Road Runner, she grabbed the cuffs from her glove box. While she wasn't eager to make the arrest, Yelsa *had* sold her garbage resort food for the past year priced as organic. Peggy didn't owe her a match, never mind the birch bark.

She stepped into the store and spotted Yelsa immediately. She stocked shelves in a bright yellow sundress with her hair up in a scrunchie identical to the one Joey showed her at the Sled Stop. Peggy drew her attention with a wave before heading to the back office.

As colorful and bright as her clothes, Yelsa filled her desk and walls with hundreds of little knick-knacks and figurines. Peggy should've brought her sunglasses. She waited in the blue plastic chair set out, preferring the stiffness to Yelsa's over-cushioned monstrosity.

She entered soon after but remained in the furthest corner of the room and avoided eye contact, like Diohgee when he ravaged the trash again. "Hey, Sheriff McStoots," squeaked Yelsa. "What brings you here?"

*With such serious talk, hit 'em with the rock.* "I know about your scheme. You steal food from Generally Slanted and sell it at Daffodil Harvest."

"No!" She shook her head furiously. "No, of course not. I'd never."

"I have proof. Let's drive to the town clerk and discuss this."

"I can't leave. It's the busy season, and I'm training a new cashier. The dairy order just arrived, too, what if—"

"I'd rather not arrest you in front of all these folks." Peggy placed the cuffs on Yelsa's desk. She finally met Peggy's stare with ponds for eyes.

"I'll tell Roger to take over," sobbed Yelsa.

Peggy agreed. She'd let the Staties handle Roger, less paperwork for her. She only hankered Yelsa, anyway, the schemer of the two.

She watched as Yelsa spoke to her head cashier in case she bolted. Peggy wasn't afraid to track down a hunt, but she'd rather not. Running equated paperwork, no need to do extra. Fortunately, Yelsa didn't attempt an escape. Once she finished telling Roger her situation, she followed Peggy to the Road Runner and climbed into the back seat without a fuss.

They drove in silence to the Rosefield town clerk's office. A squat blue building as basic as the four square-shaped offices inside. She led Yelsa to the one they used for meetings. They sat opposite each other across a retired cafeteria table.

"When did you start stealing from Generally Slanted?" questioned Peggy.

"Ridiculous!" Yelsa shook her head, but her trembling eyes revealed the truth. "How long have you known me?"

"You moved to town ten years ago. We're practically strangers." Peggy placed her phone on the table. "I've watched it all. Jane caught you on video, both loading and unloading. Joey knows too, which means the whole town will soon enough."

"No . . ." Yelsa wailed louder than a fisher and hurt Peggy's ears. "I-I just wanted to retire. Someplace warm where we—"

"We?' You mean Roger Elwood?"

"N-no . . ." she managed between sobs. "H-he's my em-employee."

*Oh, you poor little hen, who cares which rooster's in the den?"* Peggy laughed. *Best break the tears with rhyming cheers.* And another one. She couldn't resist the poetry today. It helped, too, Yelsa's sobs reduced to a more tolerable whiny-cat level. "So, you and Roger planned to run away south?"

"R-right after the season finished, we'd drive south." As Yelsa imagined her dream life, her sobs ceased altogether. "Drive until we don't see any mountains."

"What about your daughters?"

"I found a buyer for Daffodil Harvest. With our profits, we would sell for a lot. We'd leave them with enough money to buy a house or start a business." She stomped on the floor, and her tears suddenly evaporated. "I raised my daughters as independent women!"

"Who was the buyer?"

Her sudden excitement drained faster than an unplugged tub. "Bill Viceroy," she muttered.

"Viceroy?" The same man who pointed Peggy toward Yelsa's scam angled to buy her business. Why? She might ask him, except the notion of returning to the Viceroy mansion established an entire acorn city inside her stomach. She'd bump into him eventually. Besides, Peggy had more important things to discuss with Yelsa. "Never mind Bill Viceroy. What about Rodney Buric?"

Yelsa frowned. "What about Mr. Buric?"

"He was seen at the Daffodil Harvest on one of the nights you moved your stolen goods."

"He confronted us about the stealing. He said we better stop, or he'd call the police. We did, too."

Now Peggy knew why she never caught them herself. "Why didn't you leave already?"

"We needed a little more time. When Bill stalled on the sale, we had to at least sell our stock. On Wednesday, we drive to the ocean."

Yelsa's face elevated as she considered her dream once again. However, every bit of happiness fell from the clouds when she realized none of it would come to pass. Peggy sighed. Well, Yelsa deserved it after betraying the town with her fake-organic products.

One more question remained. "What about Timmy?"

Yelsa blinked. "Oh, you mean Timmy Harton? The murdered guy? Wait, you don't think I was involved, right?"

Peggy didn't, but she lacked any other leads. "A rainbow-colored scrunchie was discovered where *Timmy missed the key block on the knife to his clock.*"

Yelsa chuckled. As Lydia McStoots insisted, a well-timed lyric could lift any spirit. "You mean up on the mountain, on that glade trail?"

"Open Glade."

"I haven't skied in over six years. Even then, I never ventured into the woods."

"Timmy died in the fall, before the snow," pointed out Peggy. "Where were you that day?"

"I'm not positive, maybe . . ."

"Yelsa?"

"Generally Slanted, okay!" blurted out Yelsa. "Right on the resort, but I know nothing about Timmy's death."

"Why were you there?"

"We check our inventory in the fall before placing the season's first order."

Peggy sighed. She hated dragging answers out of folks. "And why didn't you tell anyone?"

"We had already placed our initial order a week prior. That day we placed a duplicate order and brought it all to Daffodil. I held the invoice from accounting and paid for it with my internal budget. No one would notice until after the season. I swear that's the truth." She shook her head so hard her curly hair sprung loose. "I cannot imagine how my scrunchion reached those woods. Maybe the killer framed me."

The same idea crisscrossed Peggy's mind ever since Joey showed up at breakfast. The scrunchie reminded her of the ripped yellow flannel in Timmy's hand, which set up Big Top as the murderer. The killer also used Rufus's knife as the murder weapon to push the investigation towards the stoner roommate. If the killer framed both, they'd try the same with Yelsa.

"You know," said Yelsa, pulling her scrunchie from her hair, her curls draping to the floor. She held it on the table and stared. "I remember exactly when I lost my scrunchion. Last week, I swapped it for a deli hair net. It disappeared before I finished slicing. I thought a cashier threw it out." She wiped a tear before continuing. "I suffered the rest of the day without one."

Peggy believed Yelsa neurotic enough to track each of her 'scrunchions.' This further confirmed the actual murderer was setting frames—but for folks instead of windows. "That's all of my questions."

She considered driving Yelsa to the barracks in St. Albans for a proper Rosefieldian sendoff, but did she deserve it? She betrayed the townsfolk by selling that cheap Rosefield Mountain crap (grown without a single ounce of good ol' cow-processed manure) as healthy organic produce. No, Yelsa deserved a ride in the back of a Statie car.

She called, and Commander Strongman answered after two rings. Peggy explained the situation, and he dispatched a trooper. While she waited for them to arrive, her phone dinged with another message from

Mary Anne. She started with the first one:

> At home where r u? We have a letter from Marge Smith for you

It was probably cribbage-related. Peggy hadn't attended in months, and they dominated as teammates. The second said:

> Nvm, just left it on ur desk.

Well, that resolved itself. If only Timmy's murder investigation would do the same. She'd learn what Margaret wanted when she returned home. She waited for the Staties, who arrived within fifteen minutes; they rushed when they got to cuff someone. They hauled Yelsa off to the county jail.

Peggy accomplished enough work for her 'day off' and drove straight home. Except when she arrived and read Margaret Smith's note, she realized her workday wasn't done. Not close. It took her an hour to fully decipher its meaning, and it brought her investigation in a whole new direction. Was Timmy's murder somehow related to that horrible night at Farmer Rick's old barn? She brewed a pot of Cardiac. Tootin' wouldn't cut it.

First, they went after Big Top, then Yelsa and her cashier-lover. Now they targeted Rodney? What happened? How had such a strong season culminated in all this suspicion? Everyone was *still* riled up over some murder from last year. Ridiculous.

To make matters worse, he received a petition a few days ago signed by most resort employees to restore Rosefield Mountain to its original name. What wanton stupidity. Didn't they like profit? With all those signatures, though, he couldn't ignore it as he did most employee-related issues.

Would it be so terrible? While Murder Mountain brought the masses (and their wallets), Rodney required his staff to take advantage. And besides, would this gimmick work a second season? People would tire of 'Murder Mountain' without a recent killing, and a murdered local every season seemed impractical.

Rodney suffered more pressing concerns, like writing his speech for Park & Grill in two days. He hated it, but the Owner's Speech was a tradition since the mountain first opened. What would he talk about?

He tried to watch *Soul Pestle*, but he couldn't focus. It didn't help that the two-episode finale aired tonight, on top of everything else. Only the confrontation with Lord Ketoru remained. Once victorious, would Kappu make the right decision and seize control of the Kuki Tea

Company? Or would he succumb to the masses and their demands, like what those idiots at the fansites predicted?

Bah, yet another stress. Maybe some champagne would help. He paced to the kitchen counter and attempted to hold the glass straight enough for a sip . . . and dribbled bubbly all over his chin. He pondered summoning Francis from the restaurant for assistance but dialing the three-digit extension felt like a hassle. How had things deteriorated so quickly?

What really unnerved Rodney was the impending phone call sometime within the next few hours. Father told him what day he'd call, not the hour, forcing Rodney to fret all morning. He often acted to cause Rodney unease, like hiring private investigators to watch his every move. Two weeks prior, he received an anonymous email from one of them:

While this email allowed Rodney to crush a rotten employee, it also confirmed that Father's people watched him.

That wasn't the only instance of Father's influence, either. A week ago, Rodney attempted to fire Jordan Herring for his lack of hygiene and perpetual odor. Plus his possible lisp, Rodney couldn't risk employing a Ski School Director whom no one could understand. He filled out the termination form and sent it to Human Resources. Yet Jordan still showed for work every day, and when Rodney inquired, the busty HR secretary claimed she'd never received the form. Father must have intervened on Jordan's behalf, only he possessed the power to override Rodney's decisions.

He knew, of course, why Father kept meddling in the resort's affairs. Rodney was on track to win their bet, and Father hated losing. What could he do, though? Murder Mountain's profits would soon cover all three loser years, and Rodney would own the resort outright.

Rodney paced to the wall-spanning window overlooking the ski trails. He watched people walk through the lift scanners, one after another. *Cha-ching, cha-ching.* How calming. He felt his hands steady. He might attempt some champagne. He struck towards the counter, where a full glass of bubbly awaited. He managed a sip. It helped. He initiated another—

*Ring.*

Rodney dropped his glass, missing the counter by an inch. It shattered at his feet, shards cutting into his ankle. He dashed out of his home-suite, across his lounge-suite, and scrambled to his office-suite desk.

*Ring.*

He slipped on a towel. Who left that on the floor? He should fire his maid. He caught himself hard on his knees, but he ignored the pain as he scuttled to his desk.

*Ring.*

He pulled himself into his top grain leather chair and breathed. He couldn't answer the phone panting. For a moment, he thought (hoped) the caller hung up. Maybe a manager called and then realized their mistake.

*Ring.*

Father hated waiting. Rodney picked up the red phone and held it to his ear. "Yes, sir?"

'Hello.' With that first word, he perceived Father's anger.

'Hello, sir. Everything is perfect here, profits are—"

'Everything is perfect? Not according to my sources."

'Sources?"

'Like I'd allow you to manage a business by yourself." Father laughed with the bitterness of Brussels sprouts. 'I employ multiple agents, both on the mountain and in town. When I own something, I *own* it."

'Yes, sir, I understand. I received the message from your private investigator, and I dealt with the situation as instru—"

'Don't ever assume you've dealt with anything. Especially from a so-called PI."

What did *that* mean? No matter, Rodney should stay focused on the most important thing. 'Due to my impeccable leadership, the resort reached profitability after four years. Which means I won our bet."

'We'll discuss our wager next. First, I'll explain how you 'achieved' your current success. Remember when the cops investigated the resort, but suddenly they disappeared? My influence."

'Why?"

'Why would I want to remove the cops? Because they scare away business. That's what's wrong with you, Rodney, never considering the bottom line." Father laughed again. 'Who do you think kept the press from blasting the rebrand decision? Without my bribes, the headlines would've labeled 'Murder Mountain' a cash grab on a dead man.

'Then the general store manager fiasco. A thief, Rodney, you hired a thief. When I consider managers, the first qualifier is sticky fingers. Bah!"

'Yelsa's a mom and business owner. I thought she was trustworthy."

'And I thought my son was capable of handling a simple multimillion-dollar enterprise. After this fails, I'll buy you a gas station to manage."

'If you're so knowledgeable about our operations, you should know our profits. I've earned enough to recoup all our losses across the past three years."

"Correct, profits are up. Unfortunately, you won't receive all of it."

"What are you saying?"

"Two things. First, your arrangement with your GMs where they receive a sizable bonus should the mountain achieve enough profits. You brag about how you reduce their salaries and save money—as long as you never pay out the bonus."

"Wh-which will never happen, I set such an immense amount, it's impossible."

"Except it happened." Father laughed with the bitterness of espresso. "If I had realized sooner, I would've dealt with it already. I can't monitor every aspect of this mountain. That's your job."

"I didn't bankroll *that* much."

"You don't examine the numbers very often, Rodney. Too much work. Worry not, the gas station in Alaska will produce fewer numbers."

"Peter doesn't remember. Besides, he wouldn't—"

"He wouldn't say yes to a bunch of money? Nobody forgets or turns down money. Besides, you shouldn't concern yourself too much about the bonus. It's the smaller of your two situations."

"There's more?"

"I said 'two things,' pay attention. And your ignorant question reveals your ignorance of the circumstances. Someone stole a money purse from Generally Slanted when the Staties arrested Roger, snatching it during the confusion. *My* first priority would've been securing the money. Why?"

"Money's most important."

"Always."

"They only stole a single night's deposit," reasoned Rodney, "they couldn't have taken much more than a few thousand."

"Yelsa stockpiled sales for the previous four days. And as Generally Slanted grosses significant cash sales every day, the total is over fifty thousand dollars."

RODNEY BURIC II
CEO, CFO, Director of Operations, Head of Management

He almost dropped the phone when he heard the figure. "W-Who could have stolen the purse?"

"You're asking me? This is *your* resort!" Father chuckled. "Guess I'll deal with these issues myself, as usual."

"Wh-what do you mean, 'deal with these issues'?"

"As I deal with many issues, by eliminating the problem. Like I've done countless times on your behalf, in ways I won't detail to you. Then, Rodney, you're finished. I'll assume control and move you to Alaska, where I can pretend I never sired you in the first place." Father clicked his tongue. "Furthermore, I won't reopen this pathetic 'resort.' Murder, Rosefield, or whatever those redneck scum want to call it. I'll strip everything worthwhile and sell it off."

"W-what?" stammered Rodney. "You'd destroy the resort? When it's profitable?"

"It's a worthless mountain. I've known for decades. That's why I put you in charge of it, so I could watch it fall to ruin." Father laughed. "You lucked into 'Murder Mountain,' but its charm will wear off by next season. Maybe I'll repurpose the trails as a golf course."

"Give me one more chance! I have a plan," lied Rodney. "I'll fix the whole situation."

"There's no more time for your stupidity. The season ends next Sunday."

"I just need this weekend. Three days and I'll fix it, I promise."

A long pause followed. Rodney felt the sweat dripping down his forehead and beading up in his mustache. Fortunately, Father hated video calls because he would've spotted his bluff immediately.

"I'll allow you the three days because I love watching you fail over and over. Besides, even with three hundred days, you couldn't clean up your triple-suites, never mind this mess you've created." Father laughed with the bitterness of stiff bourbon.

"Thank you, sir. I'll succeed. I have a plan." However, he did not, aside from calling Peter to discuss the situation. Maybe he could ascertain the identity of the thief and recover the fifty thousand dollars. Rodney had his own connections called employees. He'd utilize them and solve all his problems.

"One more thing, Rodney. My agents informed me that you received a petition to change the resort back to 'Rosefield Mountain.' Both employees and townies, a sentiment grows for an old and unprofitable name. Should you, by some miracle, deliver and retain ownership of the mountain, it must stay 'Murder Mountain.'"

Why would Father care about the name? He just threatened to close the resort altogether. Didn't matter. Rodney liked the name anyway, and he wasn't about to question Father. "Of course, sir. It's too profitable."

As Rodney said the words, however, he thought of his employees and their petition. Although he found Big Top loud and obnoxious, he cooked a fantastic steak. Larry from maintenance fixed things quickly and quietly. While Rodney was a seasoned skier before arriving at Rosefield, Wilma gave him a couple of valuable pointers. And of course, his beloved Francis . . . They all signed the petition, along with every other resort employee. In a minuscule way, he wanted to listen to them.

Rodney could return to this topic after he fixed the more pressing issue of winning the bet.

"Good." Father clicked his tongue. "Whatever happens, 'Rosefield Resort' is finished. An appropriate consolation for 1993."

"Uh . . ." What did he mean by 'finished' and '1993'? Did Father have a history with the resort? He should agree—for now. "Yes, sir, of course."

"One more thing, to give you a chance. Should you need anything, contact Bill Viceroy. He's an associate of mine with a lot of connections."

Mr. Viceroy? Rodney met the man once when he first moved to Rosefield Mountain, but he remembered Bill's fierce eyes and immense stature. Did he work for Father? "If I need to."

"That is all. Goodbye, son." With a click, he hung up.

Rodney set the phone on its cradle. It could've been worse. With three whole days, he would recover the cash.

He glanced at the phone. Should he call Peter? He felt tired, though. Speaking with Father consumed his energy. He needed a nap. He wobbled out of his office-suite, stopped briefly at the kitchen in his lounge-suite sweet to pour another glass of champagne, and retired into his home-suite's emperor-size bed. He fell asleep in moments, spilling half of his bubbly across the expansive spread.

*Steep, steep. Pestle! Steep, steep. Pestle!*

What!? Who dared disturb Rodney's precious naptime? Apparently, somebody was looking for their termination notice. He snatched his phone and shouted, "You're fired!"

*Steep, steep. Pestle! Steep, steep. Pestle!*

Bah, it was his alarm. Why had he set one for this afternoon? The *Soul Pestle* finale aired in ten minutes! How had he forgotten?

Rodney slipped out of bed, exchanged his damp pajamas for dry ones, and hurried to the lounge-suite couch. He flicked on his TV and watched the previous episode's ending. An excellent battle, especially the animation of the phoenix Kappu summoned to assist him in defeating the Violet Shield, the third and final sentry.

Of course, Baggu helped a little. The writers felt compelled to give the little guy his moment. What a waste of air time. They even spent precious episodes building his back story and highlighting his martial arts training.

Once, Kappu traveled to Baggu's hometown, where it was revealed he had limited composition abilities. Bah, so what if he could whip up a mild strengthening tonic when Kappu could conjure mythical creatures with his brews? What a terrible episode, Rodney had only watched it the week it aired, and he barely paid attention. Nothing significant happened in Baggu episodes.

The first installment of the two-part finale played out exactly how Rodney imagined. Kappu climbed Lord Ketoru's castle, avoiding traps and unlocking the three gates along the way. Between the Soul Pestle, shining its brightest with pure green energy, and Kappu's mastered composition skills, nothing posed a challenge. At the end of the episode, they approached the arching double door that led to Lord Ketoru's lair. What would they find within?

Rodney hustled to the kitchen for a scotch during the credits song. This was just the inspiration he needed. After watching Kappu destroy Lord Ketoru in an epic blend of martial arts and tea composing, Rodney would know precisely how to fix the money purse situation. Along with anything else that obstructed him from winning the bet with Father.

The opening credits were the same as always. Rodney had speculated they might compile a montage of greatest hits or something, but that might have detracted from the hero's imminent confrontation with the archvillain.

After a final, 'Steep, steep. Pestle!" the credits faded to black.

The episode title flashed across the screen in white letters: "THE TRUE HERO." An odd choice when Kappu was the obvious hero. Maybe they referred to his inevitable choice of whether to rule over the land himself or allow a free tea market—the former being the obvious decision.

Then the finale began, with Kappu leading Baggu up the steps to the arching double door.

What would Lord Ketoru even look like? No one had seen him in fifteen years, not since he single-handedly routed the Freepolk Rebellion. Some fans theorized he'd change his beard style, as had been noted in the historical tablets, but Rodney knew better. Though it might have required hundreds of years of experimenting, Lord Ketoru had settled on his signature look. Black whiskers joined his round mustache, each follicle pointed to his chin, where the beard curled upwards like a hook.

'Before we enter," said Kappu while gripping one of the silver handles, 'I'd just like to thank you for your service, Baggu."

'My lifelong goal is to end the corruption over this nation."

"The ever-noble Baggu!" laughed Kappu. 'Now, let's drain this last teapot."

'We won't leave a drop." Baggu grasped the other door handle, and they swung it open together.

They entered a circular candle-lit room with green curtains covering the walls. A person cloaked by shadows sat on a throne at the center. Was it the legendary Throne of Pestles? Which meant Lord Ketoru must be the hidden figure.

'To avenge my father and free this nation of your rule, I'm here to open a challenge," said Kappu. 'Do you accept?"

'I accept." The figure rose—achingly slow—and stepped forward. A flash of light crossed his face, highlighting a grey beard. Lord Ketoru hadn't changed his style, only the color, opting for a more experienced look.

Kappu slipped his mortar behind his back and added peelly leaf. What would be his first combination? With a red berry and some sugarsyrup, he'd conjure a ghoul, but pinegrass and lemon broth would create the ultimate barrier.

Except, Kappu added nothing. He lowered his mortar as the hatred drained from his cheeks, replaced by wide-eyed shock. The point-of-view spanned from Kappu's face around the room until it focused on the old man approaching. His beard was similar to Lord Ketoru's but devoid of color and polish.

"Who are you!?" exclaimed Kappu and Rodney at the same time.

"Lord Ketoru," trembled the figure, now illuminated. His knees buckled against his arched frame, and his face sank into his cheeks. "Finish the challenge. Kill me. Please."

"You're not—"

"He is Lord Ketoru," boomed a voice out of the walls. "Or, at least, he was."

The Soul Pestle burst from its sheath on Kappu's belt and hovered between them. Neon energy swirled around it in a tornado, knocking Kappu and the old man back a step. What mixup was this?

"Every fifty years, I require a new body. As you can see." A blast of energy knocked the old man to his stomach. "So I bless a child with my lifeforce, a process which kills the mother during birth."

"You . . . you killed my mother?" Kappu clutched her purple pendant.

"Your mother, and countless others, most women don't survive long enough to deliver." Haunted laughter erupted from the walls. "Not to mention the souls I have harvested through my 'heroes.'"

"What do you mean?"

"Together, we've defeated all those enforcers, sentries, and dozens of other minions. I drained each of them to create enough power for the transference."

"Not if I destroy you first!" Kappu leaped forward with his backup pestle and his mortar premixed. What could he have added to the peelly leaf?

He didn't have a chance to ignite his composition because the green energy suddenly converged and struck Kappu in the chest! He dropped his pestle and lost consciousness while neon swirled into his body. The Soul Pestle was taking control of his body.

Another tendril stabbed the old Lord Ketoru. He screamed out until a shield intercepted the blast—the eternal shield wielded by Baggu! Why hadn't he helped Kappu instead?

"I've been training for this moment my entire life." Baggu held out a mortar and pestle. "Old man, will you help me vanquish this evil? He is only vulnerable during the transference!"

"If I can." Old Lord Ketoru snatched the tools and immediately set to steeping. Just a drop at first, he had to consider the second steep. And then . . .

"Pestle!" bellowed Baggu and the old man as they struck their compositions in the exact same moment. An orb of light formed between them, expanding rapidly. Its shine overtook the green emanating off the Soul Pestle and consumed the entire screen.

Rodney clenched his glass until his knuckles whitened more than the screen. What just happened? How was Kappu? This ending had better start making more sense.

The light faded, revealing Baggu, who knelt by the dying old man. The perspective panned out, revealing fragments of the Soul Pestle, still pulsating green but fading. Zooming further out showed Kappu, lying still on the floorboards, his unblinking eyes staring at his mother's purple pendant.

Which meant . . . Baggu remained. He would inherit the title of Lord and have complete control over the Kuki Tea Company. *Baggu*. Rodney pitched his scotch glass at the TV, and the screen splintered into a thousand webs.

He couldn't view the rest of the finale, not that he wanted to. What a garbage ending! Kappu was the hero, not the stupid sidekick. And the Soul Pestle fooled Kappu the whole time, too? The opposite was way more likely. The writers really botched this show. Could he forgive the rest of the series after this travesty?

The finale certainly didn't inspire anything to help win his bet with Father. What was there to take away? Let the assistant take down the ultimate villain while Rodney rolled over dead?

He threw the remote at the TV, along with several pillows. Once out of projectiles, Rodney stomped to the bed in his living-suite, as his emperor-size bed was still damp from the champagne. He couldn't sleep, though, not after what he just witnessed, plus everything happening with Murder Mountain.

Bah. 'Murder Mountain' was supposed to be his Soul Pestle. But it turned out the Soul Pestle was actually evil the whole time. What did that mean? Nothing, because the ending made no sense.

He pulled out his phone and complained to the only people who would listen, the fellow commenters at the *Soul Pestle* fansites. Maybe he'd start a petition. The one against Murder Mountain had effectively drawn Rodney's attention. He might likewise teach the show's writers how to plot decently. Once he sorted out this horrid finale, he'd return his attention to the resort's financial situation.

Joey heard the rumor. Rodney (or his dad, everyone told a different version) planned to strip the mountain and close it forever. Chef Alex heard they planned on burning down Squirrel Lodge on Closing Day. Would this be the last Park & Grill ever? Not while Joey kept his skis underfoot.

Jane conceived the plan, and Joey promptly agreed. He'd follow her off any cliff.

They'd steal the microphone when Rodney Buric began his Owner's Speech and announce their discoveries. The Staties would arrest the Burics, forcing them to sell Rosefield Resort. Today they saved the mountain, no matter what.

Joey woke up an hour before his alarm at 6 AM, too excited to sleep. He might as well pack T-Dog. He brought only the essentials: a beer cooler, whiskey, tequila, beer pong table, pirate flag, folding chairs, a metal pipe for launching the Big One, five different types of chips, hamburger and hot dog buns (while he never grilled himself, amazing how many people forgot the meat bread), dog bowl, kibble, water bottle, two liters of cousin James's most potent energy drink, a frisbee for Polish horseshoes, and a croquet set. Traditionally he brought bocce, too, but he should limit the lawn games with the mountain at stake.

With everything packed, he drove to town. He intended to bomb right through, but Rufus stood outside his house with an outstretched thumb, and Joey couldn't leave a man behind during Park & Grill.

'Hop in. But spin your bullwheel at max speed. I need to get up there and claim the best spot. The mountain literally depends on it!"

Rufus nodded. His hair appeared extra greasy, and his eyes more bloodshot. Had he just ripped his bong? Maybe his emotional skis could use tuning. Whatever, it wasn't Joey's business. The stoner moved with abnormal speed, sprinting inside and returning with an armful of skis.

'Do you need that many?"

'One more load."

Joey shrugged. Sometimes you had to rock extra skis in case the conditions turned. Rufus returned to his house and emerged with another armload. Joey recognized the red Astronomics on top. Timmy's favorite skis, he rocked them the day of his murder. Wow, Rufus lucked out. He inherited some fine alpine.

Finally, Rufus fetched a five-gallon blue kerosene tank and tossed it in the back of T-Dog. 'What's that for?"

'Burning stuff."

Fair enough. With T-Dog packed, they shot up the mountain like a bullet aimed at the parking lot bullseye. He dragged tire into the resort, not stopping for his usual homage to the logo. He couldn't, not with Rodney's stupid smug face right next to it. 'Murder Mountain' lost its original groomed quality, too, felt more like frozen granular.

Two-and-a-half drifts later, he whipped T-Dog into the main lot. Nothing announced your arrival like kicking up a dust cloud. He ripped across at max speed, straight-lining for the best spot between Generally Slanted and Squirrel Lodge. The whole area would soon become Grilling Central, a prime location for when he needed munchies. Plus, with Beverage Alley only thirty feet away, he could fetch a cocktail whenever thirsty. Most importantly, this was the closest parking spot to Generally Slanted's porch where Rodney would deliver his Owner's

Speech.

After Joey parked T-Dog, he cracked open a beer. Was 8 AM too early? No, because rules didn't apply during Park & Grill. He cheered on families as they shuffled up to the lifts and offered them beers, but they declined. They'd return later for pong or Polish, no doubt about it.

While Joey waited for other Park & Grillers to arrive, he established camp with Rufus. They set out a few chairs, a table, and a half dozen ski poles to mark their territory while also promoting the annual Polish horseshoe tournament. They attempted to raise the popup canopy, but two jammed legs prevented full coverage.

Rufus remained silent the entire time. Joey never saw him this depressed before.

"Hanker a run?" offered Joey. "Some sweet, succulent, slushy spring snow might cheer—"

"No!" Rufus threw a chair down. "No skiing!"

"Cool. Here for the party, no need to mix in any lift nonsense. You might end up on the chair with a flatty from flatland. Best to stay in the safety of camp. Besides, our Rosefield family will soon arrive. We should welcome them."

As sure as a January Nor'easter, at 10 AM, locals and mountain regulars gushed in with the force of a low-pressure system from the Canadian glaciers. First, the Roaster family showed up, parking right next to Joey and Rufus. They secured a spot up front for grilling racks of ribs and serving coffee. He offered them a beer, but Roaster Dan and Molly preferred a "Brown on Brown," while Little Dan and Sugar Snap sipped on their juice bottles.

Jake and Helen parked past the Roasters. They lit a propane burner and set a massive pot of water on it first thing. Soon they'd start the lobster boil for the annual cook-off. Last year they wood-fired mini lobster pizzas that won the whole competition. Tough to beat fresh crustacean, but chefs from all corners of Vermont flexed their cooking skills at the Rosefield Park & Grill, so the Lobsters weren't a guaranteed winner.

Mrs. Shoeman and her family set up right behind T-Dog with a popup tent, loungers, coolers, and a freestanding badminton net for the kids. She was the coolest principal ever and shared Joey's love for the Rutland Rotary Boys. She wore their iconic white cowboy hat and a t-shirt emblazoned with four band members.

Rogen Harton's presence surprised Joey, as he rarely came down from his cabin on Gregory Road. His daughter Amy must have dragged him out along with her whole family from St. Albans. Even though they established a circle of folding chairs, old man Rogen remained in his truck and kept glancing around the parking lot. After years of solitude, the crowds probably freaked him out.

A dozen local dogs hovered around the cook-off, cleaning up any scraps. They often wandered over to Joey's camp, so he set out the dog bowls with kibble and water. The Farney brothers brought their Great Danes Charlie and Conner, and Bear led Thomas the Train around by the leash. A pack of Labradors patrolled the lot for any sad faces, immediately rectifying the situation. Tug-Tug led them, wearing a hunter orange scarf about his scruff.

The rest of the Powder Crew showed up at 11 AM. When it came to freshies, they rallied before sunrise, no problem, but now they slept in for the biggest party of the year. They needed their priorities adjusted. Good thing Joey took these things seriously and saved the adjacent parking spot for them.

"Where are all the ladies?" said Tall Brad while snagging a high-five, a beer, and a seat.

While Happy set out his lawn chair and fell into it, he stayed quiet. Once comfortable, he chugged a beer. Happy was probably focused on matching Joey's intoxication level. He wished him the best of luck, nothing wrong with healthy competition.

Handy Jesse grabbed a couple of tools and several two-by-fours from his truck and built two legs for the popup tent. Then he established the pirate flag with the Powder Crew's Jolly Roger, a skull wearing snow goggles and skis instead of crossbones.

Finally, Jesse settled in for a beer, a shot of whiskey, and a bowl. "Did you guys hear the *real* reason Rodney Buric's shutting down the mountain?"

"Because he couldn't ski if an avalanche chased him?" said Joey.

"Because there are no women?" offered Brad.

Happy remained silent. Odd, he usually joined these exchanges.

"You're both more wrong than a goggle gap," said Jesse. "Rodney bet his super-rich dad that if the resort became profitable in four years, he'd own it outright. Otherwise, daddy would boot him and take over operations."

"Hah!" laughed Brad. "Who bets an entire ski resort?"

"You know flatland folks have strange ideas," said Jesse. "And since Rodney Sr. gave Rodney Jr. the money to buy Rosefield Mountain, the bet was a contingent."

"That makes no sense," said Brad. "The mountain's never experienced a busier year. Rodney Jr. will easily win the bet."

"Not after three years of losses," added Joey.

"Exactly," continued Jesse. "No matter what, he'll lose the resort. Instead, Rodney will strip Rosefield Mountain down to its bolts, sell everything and flee to the Caribbean."

"Rodney would try something scummy like that," said Brad. "Guy can't even ski."

"I watched him ski once," said Joey. "He fell after three turns, right in front of a whole nest of bunnies. What a Jerry!"

"What if he stole the money purse?" pondered Brad.

"Yepper." Jesse smirked. "This way, Yelsa receives the blame."

"What are you talking about?" Had Joey missed an important town rumor?

"You haven't heard about the hundred grand sniped from Generally Slanted?" Jesse whistled. "You gotta pull your head out of the snowbank and stay current on recent events. This hit the Sled Stop over twenty-four hours ago."

"The Farney Brothers told me two hundred grand," added Brad.

"Probably, with all the money they pocketed this season."

"How was there so much cash at Generally Slanted?" And how was Joey not aware of this rumor?

"Yelsa siphoned the cash out of Generally Slanted, the Caf', Ski School, Ski Patrol," said Brad.

"Mountain View Restaurant and Hotel, Lift Maintenance," continued Jesse. "She even swindled the snowmaking budget."

"Rosefield has a snowmaking budget?" asked Brad.

"Exactly. Yelsa's an accounting genius, transferring funds without anyone noticing. Only when the Daffodil Harvest scheme exploded, all her lies became clear. And someone noticed a whole pile of neglected money. Was it the janitor? That's what they want you to think.

"Everything connects to my investigation into this deep state conspiracy. Have you heard about the Brunswick Springs curse? It's a cover-up for when the government augmented their drinking water in a secret experiment. I'm talking about mind control."

While Jesse continued about Abenaki legends and hidden government facilities, Joey considered the stolen cash. Was it related to Timmy's murder? Had Jane heard? Where *was* she, anyway? She said she'd arrive around noon, which rapidly approached.

Joey hated questions. Questions led to doubt, and doubt caused most bone-snapping yard sales. Joey checked in on Happy to clear his mind.

"Tips up, beers up, cheers up!"

Happy meekly clinked his can. "Cheers." He finished his beer and dropped it on the other two empties. Then he cracked another.

Joey hunched down opposite his friend. Black clouds hung beneath his downcast eyes, and a blizzard blasted his hair. "What's storming you, bud?"

Happy shrugged. "Nothing." He chugged the rest of his new beer and tossed the empty.

Joey knew what would raise his tips. "C'mon, I gotta show you something." Happy followed him around to the back of T-Dog. He popped open the lockbox and pulled out the brown bag containing the Big One.

"I just wanna get drunk," said Happy. "Drunker than the bear who invented mead."

"You should bang a quick speed check, bud, side-slide for a minute. You don't want to crash before the thirty-foot cliff." He handed Happy the bag. "I set this off today!"

When he peered inside, Happy fumbled his beer, and his frown popped a quick one-eighty. "Impressive."

"James finally put it together, the Big One. He's yearned to build it for years, but he couldn't buy all the parts. Speaking of my cousin, I told him to come and watch his creation, but James said he'd rather watch it on video. Makes no sense to me, but I'll have my phone ready." Joey grabbed the bag and studied it himself. "Ah, a masterpiece."

"How did you afford it?"

'Dropped a paycheck. Totally worth it, right?"

Happy shrugged.

'He built it for New Year's, but a flannel distracted me, and I forgot to ignite it."

"You've owned this for months, and you're just telling me about it?"

'I hankered a surprise. I've only told Jesse, but at New Year's. Who remembers that night, anyway?" Joey chugged his beer.

'When will you set it off?"

Joey leaned close enough to whisper. "This afternoon, Jane and I will bust Timmy's murder wide open. Wider than the powder field we discovered on the backside in February."

'So wide, a tide of riders could slide side-to-side." Happy laughed. "You solved the mystery?"

'We figured the whole thing out, and it connects to the shady stuff that happened around town. Yelsa's scheme? Liu Kang grab. The murderer? Japan Air. This conspiracy goes all the way to Rodney Buric. *Kabam!* Double nose grab. And for the finale? The Big One fired over the entire parking lot!"

Happy appeared as though blindsided by a snowball. 'Huh. How did you figure it all out?"

'Just wait. When Jane gets here at noon, we'll finalize the reveal." Joey placed the Big One in the lockbox. 'Now, what's set you on your downhill edge?"

'Well, you know Mary Anne from the Rez?"

'I haven't forgotten the prettiest girl in our class."

'We investigated this mystery. Have you heard about the Red Barn Incident?" When Joey shook his head, Happy continued. 'Doesn't matter, we checked out a few things, spent several days together. We connected and—"

'You're still crushing on Mary Anne?" Poor Happy worshipped her throughout elementary school. He catered to her every whim, yet she never once let him drop his pole between those moguls. 'Sorry, guy. You oughta set your scope on another bunny, bud."

"We bonded like never before, even chased by ghosts! And Farmer Rick, do you remember him?"

"I haven't seen him since his house burned down." Joey whistled. "What a day. I remember a dozen grills and a band set up by the barn."

"We visited him, and he told us he burned it down himself."

"He went the way of the squirrel, huh?" Joey laughed. "Did it for the insurance?"

"He reckons the land is cursed," whispered Happy. "I do too, actually. When Mary Anne and I snowshoed up there, we heard voices out in the snow . . . but never found their footprints."

"I know we share this plane of existence with the deceased." Joey shrugged. "I experienced an encounter myself a couple of weeks ago. Timmy Harton's soul merged with a blue jay. He helped us solve the murder from beyond the grave!"

Happy blinked twice, too shocked by the immense epicness to say anything.

"What about Farmer Rick?" asked Joey.

"Right, we visited him down in Jeffersonville. Mary Anne somehow figured out where he lives. He's gone the way of the squirrel, threatening us in his underwear with a shotgun. Twice!"

"Normally, I'd say a shotgun's only scary when used, but in this case, the underwear changes things. What kind?"

"Tighty-whities and a size too small."

"You should've hopped on the next chair outta there."

"I eventually convinced Mary Anne to leave, but she's avoided me ever since. Without this note to decipher, she'll return to her college life in Burlington." Happy flattened his empty can with a stomp. "When I invited her to Park & Grill, she replied, 'Too much schoolwork.'"

"Well, that's off-trail. No one skips Park & Grill." Joey tossed his empty beer in the bed of T-Dog and grabbed another. He slammed it into Happy's free hand. The healthiest way to handle a woman-problem was with a couple of brews. "You reckon you have something with her?"

"I *did*. Now?" He shrugged.

"If you think you did, then you still do. That's how women are." Joey put his arm around Happy's shoulders. "Listen, you should approach this like the biggest jump in the park. Push off hard, pump the poles, and straight-line over the lip. You throw the craziest trick and hope for the smoothest landing."

"You're right, bud." Happy's greenish-brown eyes finally rose from the dirt to join his smile. "Next time I see her, I'll send it! I step up and tell her. I either land or wipe. But if I don't make an attempt, *definitely* no glory."

"What's the prayer?"

"For snow and for glory!" they shouted together and chugged their fresh beers.

"For today, why not forget about Mary Anne, bud? She's not here, and you ain't driving to Burlington. Let's enjoy Park & Grill. We'll start with some shots."

As they sauntered to their chairs, Joey noticed all the new arrivals in the parking lot. Folks and their vehicles filled nearly every spot.

Joey waved to the Viceroy boys, setting up a popup canopy a row back. Their mother wore a black dress and relaxed in the shade while Bill smoked a cigar and spoke with Mickey a couple of trucks over. The Viceroy parents rarely left their mansion, but they never missed a Park & Grill.

A little further down the lot, he spotted Wilma Johansson, her husband, and their three children playing a game of cornhole. They wore matching bright blue shirts and green pants, basically a summer day with clothes.

Annie and George sat with a dozen other Montrealers. He noticed Danielle amongst them with Frederico at her side, holding hands. Despite a dusting of jealousy, Joey approved of the couple, a demonstration of Rosefield's ability to unite folks of all cultures.

A pod of Joes lounged in Beverage Alley. Mechanic Joe in his jean overalls, Helmet Joe in his bright green helmet, Cally Joe with his surfboard, and Montgomery Joe with his grey sweater. They each held a Bacon tallboy from Pig's Foot Brewery's first-ever canning run. Joey heard the aluminum zing added a satisfying polish.

Speaking of Pig's Foot, he spotted Brewer Bob cooking up his famous corn dogs in the now-packed Grilling Central. The whole parking lot smelled of grilled meats, casseroles, corn boils, chilis, kabobs, sliders, and more. Both flatties and locals mingled throughout, picking tasters from each.

Charlie and Peter Smith mingled in their white and black judge uniforms and matching poofy hats. A few others held the officiating honor, including Gregor Jr., Diane Robbitet, and Bob Hordell. Together they strolled around with their scoreboards, trying a little from each chef's table.

Odd, Joey didn't spot Jordan amongst them. He should be around somewhere. Not that Joey wanted to find Jordan, especially after what happened a week ago with the ski schooler. He'd keep a lookout and avoid—

"Joey."

Ope. Joey rotated as slowly as possible, hoping the deep voice somehow belonged to anyone else. When he saw the extra-sized clipboard and caught a whiff of the extra-pungent body odor, Joey realized he was doomed. "Hey, Jordan."

"What a nice day for a Park & Grill." The stripes on his uniform shined from a fresh permanent marker touch-up.

"Yepper." Joey gulped. He should hit this deer head-on. "So about the kid, it wasn't my fault. I taught him how to safely ride without the bar for coolness. And when he fell, the chair hung at its lowest point. The doctors believe he'll recover all funct—"

"Never mind the kid." Jordan adjusted his extra-large officiating hat, special ordered to outsize the other judges. "I wanted to express my

gratitude for your help a week ago."

"Oh, that?" Jordan had asked Joey to perform a show in front of Generally Slanted the previous Sunday afternoon. "I love using the Ski School bullhorn. Almost as much as throwing some jaw-droppers in front of a crowd. Even the cashiers and deli attendants stepped out to watch my prowess."

"Right. I appreciate it. Enjoy Park & Grill."

"No problem. And yeppers, how could I not? If only the Staties hadn't ruined my big finale when they rolled in and arrested Roger. Picture this, a backflip over the . . ." Joey trailed off because Jordan had already walked away.

Joey had expected a berating and instead received some well-deserved praise. The magic of Park & Grill.

Joey had surveyed every direction but found no sign of Jane. It was already past noon, and the Owner's Speech began at 2 PM. They needed to plan their ultimate reveal.

He wouldn't panic. Instead, he chugged a beer and took a shot. Race day, after all, he should get *loose*.

"Croquet!" he called.

"When I get back," said Jesse. "I'm gonna rip a couple of runs while the lifts spin."

"A run? Today is about parking and grilling, not ripping or shredding."

"That's what they want you to believe."

"I'm out," said Brad. "I spotted the Bakersfield twins. The best possibility I've seen today, I better start my system."

"Party ditchers," accused Joey, but they abandoned him anyway. "What about you, Rufus?"

"There's something I gotta do." He stomped off.

"I'll play," said Happy. One-on-one was better than nothing.

They played two games, and he lost both. The dirt increased the difficulty by a significant amount. The tiniest tap and the ball rolled down half the mountain. Besides, Joey couldn't concentrate on those stupid metal hoops. 1 PM slipped by, and still no Jane.

After Happy's second victory, Joey quit and cracked another beer. He relaxed into a chair, but within a minute, shouts erupted from the far side of the parking lot. Same sound as when Joey landed a huge trick, but he wasn't even wearing his ski boots.

He popped out of his chair and spun until he spotted the smoke. Did someone build a bonfire in the lot? A first for Park & Grill, which genius devised it? The shouts sounded more frantic than joyous, however, and the smoke contained a greenish tint. When he drew closer, he recognized the burning combination of plastic and metal, the smell of skis on fire. A noble sacrifice but oddly timed, folks usually burned their Ullr offerings in the fall.

He passed through the packed crowd with ease; he regularly skied through denser patches of ridge pines. When he broke through, he immediately spotted the fire starter. Rufus alternated between throwing skis (both Timmy's and his own) and cups of kerosene onto the blaze.

"They all gotta burn!" he shouted. "Timmy died for these. Now they must burn!"

"What are you doing!?" shouted Joey, stepping between Rufus and the kerosene tank. "Don't burn your expensive skis. Ullr won't care. If anything, he pays attention to the brand, not the year."

"Coming through!" Jim McJoy cut through the crowd with several other securities and his brother Big Top, all carrying large water buckets. "Oh, what a humdinger. Step back, folks!"

"No! The skis must burn to dust. Nothing shall remain!" Rufus charged the newcomers, but Joey stepped in front of him. "You don't understand. Out of my way." He threw himself forward, punching and kicking, but Joey held strong. He weathered worse storms on the chair lift.

'C'mon, bud, there's too many of 'em."

Rufus suddenly stopped struggling altogether, falling to his knees and crying worse than a Jerry dangling from a lift. He watched as they dumped bucket after bucket, and soon the flames washed out. A single trail of greenish smoke rose from the blackened and partially melted skis.

'All right, Rufus, you're outta here," said Jim, straightening his blue security uniform and stepping forward.

'Hold on," said Joey. 'Throw a quick hockey stop, bud. He's clearly in a dark place."

'After that humdinger?" Just like Big Top, Jim burned as red as a starting gate when frustrated. 'I oughta ban him from the resort."

'Let me handle this. Besides," Joey pointed at the sobbing mass at his feet, 'he needs his Rosefield family more than ever."

'C'mon Jim," said Big Top. He once again wore a flannel, but he'd swapped the yellow for blue. 'I'll watch him harder than a roux. If he boils, I'll whisk right in."

They stomped off, and Joey hoisted Rufus to his feet. 'Are you ready to pizza-wedge to camp?"

'What's wrong with me, man? Maybe it's the new strain. This happens when I switch them up, but I lost my old one." Joey didn't understand him, but at least Rufus stepped while he muttered.

'What happened to him?"

'Oh, he just burnt some skis." When he found Jane behind him, Joey almost dropped Rufus. 'Where were you!?"

'Gathering information. Are you ready?"

He blinked. 'You mean right now?"

Jane flicked her black hair behind her shoulders, revealing a smirk and eyes of milk chocolate. 'Let's bring this whole mountain down."

Joey dropped Rufus. 'Where to?"

MONTGOMERY JOE
ROSEFIELD MOUNTAIN RESORT
SEASON PASS
www.rosefieldmountain.com

What a wonderful April day spent in the Rosefield Mountain parking lot for the annual Park & Grill. Folks drank, ate, played yard games, and discussed their seasons. Near the level of a Jay Peak party, but they conducted everything better over there. How could little Rosefield compare? Well, this year's Park & Grill (and '93 if he believed the rumors) proved itself an exception, elevating itself to a Montgomery-level event.

First, Rufus sacrificed a few skis to Ullr. An annual tradition in Jay, probably why Jay Peak received the most snow in the east.

What happened next, though, from the Polish horseshoe tournament, Jane's speech, Sheriff McStoots's arrival, the brief car chase ending in explosions, and the finale when the red van arrived . . . Jeezum crow! A day that rivaled the rowdiest People's Prom in Montgomery's history.

With all the chaos, anyone was a potential casualty. Helmet Joe wore the right headgear. Cali Joe carried his surfboard, he could block any wild projectiles, and any flying object would slip off Mechanic Joe's protective grease layer. What about Montgomery Joe? His grey sweater possessed little cushioning and minimal shielding. He risked severe injury! Luckily, the action stayed clear of Beverage Alley.

# Old Habits

While Jane felt significant pride busting Yelsa and Roger, she wasn't finished yet. Next, she would expose Rodney *and* restore the mountain to its original name. All during Park & Grill, too.

She arrived early and parked at the maintenance shed, just in case she hankered a discrete getaway. Besides, Joey would secure them a front-row spot perfect for interrupting Rodney's speech.

Instead of taking the most express route to Mountain View, she detoured through Squirrel Lodge's dank and moldy basement, where nobody would notice her. As she avoided puddles, both watery and greasy, Jane regarded the one resort room she had never entered. A green metal door was the only thing blocking her. Despite a dozen attempts, she had yet to obtain a key card capable of opening it.

Once in the hotel, Jane ascended the stairs to the top floor and Rodney's triple suite combination. What a waste. The resort could've earned a ton renting those units out, maybe enough for Rodney to win the bet with his father. His stupidity hurt her brain.

After preparing her barrette, she lounged in a pillowed leather chair, dyed gold and red to match the rest of the hallway. Rodney chose those colors because he considered them 'regal.' What a prince. He had the diamond-studded chandeliers installed, too. More money wasted.

Jane relaxed. Rodney would eventually exit for the annual Owner's

Speech, delivered at 2 PM. She hankered a conversation with him first, and she'd wait all day if necessary. Besides, she had a new rumor to contemplate: the stolen money purse.

It sounded like straight manure, of the bull variety. Why would someone store hundreds of thousands of dollars in a bag? Not even Yelsa was dumb enough to leave that much money at Generally Slanted. Rumors often followed a scandal, each more ridiculous than the one before.

Still, with everything that happened this season, Jane shouldn't discount anything. She'd listen for corroborating information but didn't expect much. And even if true, it appeared Yelsa's scheme wasn't related to Timmy's murder. Jane should concentrate on Rodney's impending interrogation.

At noon she grew nervous. Would he ever leave? He had to. Every owner delivered a Park & Grill speech since the resort first opened.

An hour later, Rodney finally emerged. While he wore a pristine suit and tie, everything else about him frayed. His hair peeled while pimples spotted his face. Had he suspected Jane's ambush? Except, he didn't once look in her direction as he staggered about the hallway.

"Murder Mountain *is* the Soul Pestle," muttered Rodney, shaking his head. "And the Soul Pestle . . . cannot be trusted."

What was he saying? It sounded like some anime crap. Jane heard a rumor Rodney watched those shows. Forty years old, and he still enjoyed cartoons. Jeezum Crow, bud.

Jane recalled one of her favorite moments of high school's freshman year, the afternoon she perfected her backhand. In the hallway between classes, two boys teased her. "Hey Jane, how's that new anime?" "Are Japs allowed to watch anything else?" "I heard their sports are even animated."

She received a week of suspension, a month of grounding, and her parents sold her four-wheeler. But cleaning their blood off her knuckles? Worth it.

Jane had better stop Rodney before he reached the elevator. "Buric, I have questions."

His knees wobbled like a first-time skier about to eat ice, with eyes even wider. "Do you work for him, too?"

"I know everything, and I have demands." She had no idea who Rodney referred to, but she'd use his uncertainty to her advantage.

"I have nothing to give, not even a mountain." Rodney shook his head.

"What do you mean?"

"Father will take it from me. I lost the wager, just *barely*. In a couple of hours, I'll tell everyone the mountain will shut down next Sunday. Permanently."

"Why would your father shut it down? He'd lose a ton of money."

"He owns eighteen other businesses, each dwarfing Rosefield Resort. He doesn't care about the money. He'll do it to punctuate my failure."

That confirmed what Peter told her a few weeks ago and the rumors around town. Which meant this bumbling idiot lacked the power to save the mountain or restore its glorious name. Still, one question remained.

"Why were you at Daffodil Harvest last Saturday night? Right as they offloaded their certified organic—or should I say 'certified Slanted'—delivery?"

"You think I'm involved with them?" Rodney laughed, but it sounded hollow. "I wouldn't lower myself to petty theft."

Noper. Rodney's not capable of hatching a plan this intricate. His father, though . . . Jane figured out the mystery but picked the wrong Buric as the villain. Rodney Jr. was a frightened fawn in her sight when she hankered a buck for the wall. Once she accessed his computer, she'd unearth leverage over him, and more importantly, his father.

"Why am I talking to you? At least for today, I own this mountain." He stormed by and smashed the elevator button. Jane remained seated because he knew nothing. Besides, in his distressed state, he failed to notice his apartment door not shutting completely. She waited for the elevator to close before retrieving her trusty barrette and letting herself in.

Even with three suites combined *and* maid service, Rodney made a mess of it. Clothes piled up on the sofa, suit jackets hung from every chair, and Mountain View dinner plates filled the sink. Empty glasses, papers, and unopened mail covered the counters and tabletops, and trash piles occupied all the corners. Were all three suites this messy? Jane rubbed her temples. Rodney's continued ineptitude prompted a migraine.

She searched for an overcompensating desk and accompanying leather chair—and found his office instantly. Rodney's only possessions in the suite, besides his usual clutter around the kitchen. Yet another waste of mountain resources, Jane hankered a scream.

She opened his computer. As Peter mentioned, Rodney wrote the password on scotch tape right next to the keyboard, 'R0dneyG0dley#1.' Maybe if she administered her patented backhand treatment, she could slap the idiot out of Rodney. She'd probably wear the skin off her knuckles before breaching his thick skull.

Jane stopped daydreaming and started digging, which proved difficult because Rodney organized his computer the same way as his apartment. Unorganized files cluttered the entire desktop. She could barely distinguish one from another. She considered checking through his documents or downloads folders, but those were likely just as chaotic. Instead, she opened his email client, where she discovered about seventy-five thousand unread messages. Who put this man in charge of anything?

She scrolled *and scrolled*. After several minutes of scrolling through garbage emails and advertisements, she finally identified a message of interest, an email from Bill Viceroy. She clicked on it and scrolled to the top of the chain. Rodney sent the first one yesterday morning:

Was that the most obvious phrase to ask someone if they murder people? Jane laughed out loud. Next came Bill's response:

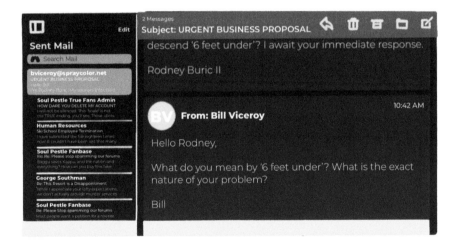

While Jane knew Bill Viceroy most of her life, he and his wife remained very private, rarely leaving their estate. She knew his sons better, as they had all attended the Rez together. Still, she encountered him from season to season, either at Cody's or the post office. He appeared intelligent, so Jane assumed he played dumb in the previous email. Would Rodney realize? She read on.

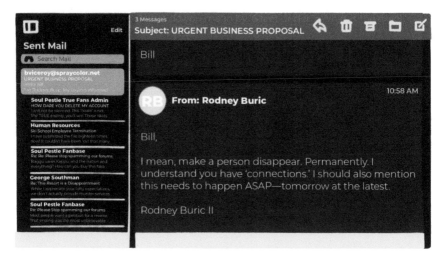

Who could Rodney want dead? And why ask Bill Viceroy? She kept reading. Bill's response:

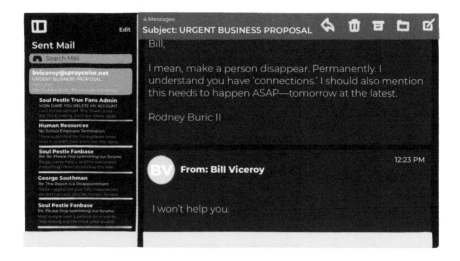

Of course, Bill wasn't an idiot. Rodney's response a few minutes later:

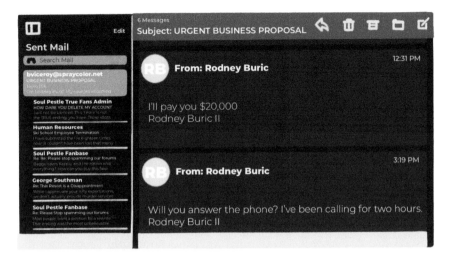

Jane shook her head. Only a complete moron attempted to hire a hitman through email, leaving a literal chain of evidence. She almost felt sorry for him. *Almost.* He shouldn't be in charge of a resort in the first place. His father set him up for failure from the beginning. Bill wrote the final message in the chain:

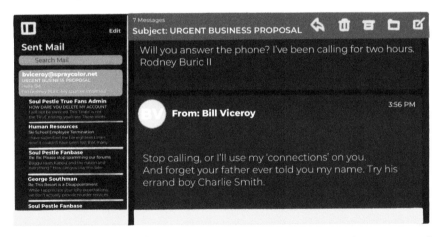

She reread the last sentence twice more. In their four years of ownership, could the Burics have garnered enough influence to corrupt a multigenerational Rosefieldian? When Jane considered it, however, she had no idea what Charlie did for money. Whenever she asked, he responded with something like 'contracting out of state'—but what kind of contracts?

Jane searched for any emails to Charlie but found nothing in the sent or received folders. Maybe Rodney sent him a message and then deleted it afterward. Except, he would've also deleted his email chain with Bill Viceroy. And Charlie wasn't a hitman. Well, maybe if he hated the target already or—

Jane slipped off Rodney's plush leather seat when she remembered the feud between Charlie and Timmy Harton. They hated each other for fifteen years, ever since the Red Barn Incident.

Even more so after the horse incident, as Charlie didn't tolerate animal cruelty. Often, he seethed to Jane about the chop saw he witnessed—still plugged in and spinning. How? And why? It wasn't worth the consideration.

If Rodney Buric Sr. offered to pay Charlie to kill Timmy, he might take the job. Plus, he told Jane he earned a lot of money at the beginning of the season, but he never said from where or for what.

While she uncovered few answers, a half dozen questions arose from this new information. Why did Charlie borrow money from his brother? Why had Buric Sr. sent his son to Bill Viceroy? Did the two have a history? Based on Bill's final response, it appeared a hostile relationship. Had Buric Sr. sent his son on a wild moose sighting? For what reason? Just to win their bet, or was there a more sinister plot?

Every time she dug deeper, the manure pile grew. She needed more evidence, but where might she search? Not in any of Rodney's three suites, who clearly knew nothing of importance. What if she revealed her findings to the townsfolk down in the parking lot? Let each Rosefieldian explore their own conclusions, and eventually, the truth would emerge.

Jane snapped a picture of all the emails and shut down the computer. She departed Rodney's suites and skipped down the stairs to the loading dock. She slipped out into the sunshine and joined the folks at Park & Grill.

She should locate Joey because he could corroborate. Although, he had better knock it off with the blue jay talk, or they'd lose all credibility. She found his camp by the grills after spotting the pirate flag, but no Joey. Should she search for him out in the lot?

The familiar scent of a Pig's Foot corn dog fresh out of the fryolator overwhelmed Jane. Her eyes followed her nose and her stomach soon after. She straight-lined to Brewer Bob's table, filled with canned Bacons.

Jane heard they brewed an aluminum batch. She almost snatched one off the table but decided to keep her mind clear for the main event later.

Next to all the cans awaited a red tray full of glistening corn dogs, concocted from a combination of three Rosefield fixtures: Pig's Foot Swinery pork, Gregory Farm beef, and Finding Truth Farm corn. While Crazy Bob believed some radical conspiracies, he grew the sweetest corn in town. Plus, they provided a vat of maple syrup for dunking, fresh from Johnson Lumberyard's boiler.

"You're late," said Brewer Bob. "Usually, you stop by the moment I drop the first dog. Out enjoying some spring turns?"

"Yepper," lied Jane, no reason to divulge anything before the big reveal. "May I?"

"Yepper." Bob laughed and rubbed his well-exercised beer gut.

Jane snatched up a corn dog, dunked the tip into the syrup, and chomped down. The crispy outer layer concealed a soft, buttery shell. Then came the dog itself, a combination of the best (of the worst) cuts from both oinker and moo-moo. Delicious! Bite after bite until she devoured the whole thing. Then she reached for another. "Better than ever, Bob."

"I used sap for the batter. What a tremendous difference!"

After inhaling the second corn dog, Jane set out into the parking lot on a search for Joey. She passed row after row of familiar faces, folks celebrating spring and sending off another ski season.

Harvesta and Karma's presence surprised Jane, with their mother's arrest a week prior. They appeared festive, actually, in their floral dresses, pink bows, and matching fruit-adorned cocktails. A dozen others hung out around their tailgate, most of whom Jane recognized from high school. The new Sled Stop waitress Kate partied with them. She wore a dress with extra frills and rolls like it came straight from the 1950s section of Goodwill. Jane couldn't understand why folks adored her.

The next row down, Jane noticed Georgia McStoots with her two kids. They did everything together in high school: four-wheeled, snowboarded, hunted, backroad cruised, graffitied covered bridges, etc. Since Georgia started her family, they hung out less but still shared a beer or two occasionally. Jane stopped for a quick hello.

"There's a pain in my Jane!" said Georgia, rushing forward. Her frizzy red hair tumbled across her freckled cheeks, stretched wide with a smile.

"Aurora-Georgia!" They hugged.

"Grab a beer."

"Hard to say no." She *just* declined a beer from Brewer Bob to stay sober, but she had developed enduring habits after years of Parking & Grilling.

She cracked open a Bacon and said hi to Georgia's husband Tony and their kids Henry and Kara. Her sister Lyndsay (belly wide with baby Robert) parked next door with her husband, three children, and a yellow Labrador. Jane greeted each of them as well. She kept the chatter to a minimum; she should stay focused and locate Joey.

With a few quick goodbyes, Jane set out once more into the parking lot. Before she cleared the next row of cars, a commotion erupted from the far side. She spotted a tendril of green smoke rising from the same area. Had a car caught fire? Or a tiki torch fell over and ignited a canopy? Jane knew one thing: it involved Joey.

When she reached the smoldering ski pile, the crowd had already dispersed. She located Joey immediately, hard to miss as he held up

Rufus and stumbled towards camp.

Jane caught up and started to tell him the plan. Except, when he dropped Rufus, she realized they should assist their shell-shocked friend first.

'Let's bring him to camp." They picked up Rufus and carried him through the parking lot. They only bumped into ten folks needing a quick 'howdy doody,' so they made rapid progress. Once at camp, they situated Rufus and prepared a selection of snacks. Then they found a pair of chairs and planned their reveal.

'When Rodney arrives for his speech," explained Jane, 'you create a distraction."

'I'll throw some crazy trick. Just this past Sunday, I awed everyone in Generally Slanted with my skills. Jordan asked for a show, and I brought one. And then the Staties ruined my finale."

'Let's keep it simple, Joey. Rodney might show up any time, so we need something fast and easy."

'No ramp necessary, I'll—"

'No." Jane worried about Joey. He wasn't the most credible individual, especially after drinking all day. Tough not partying at Park & Grill, though, Jane hankered a shotgun herself.

There was too much at stake. Not just the resort's name, not just the shut down, but this villain had proven capable of murder. They might target her next if they learned what she discovered. 'Run around and cause a lot of noise. Maybe test out the horn on your new truck."

'I test it out every day on the flatties," chuckled Joey. 'Okay, I'll do it."

'With Jim and the securities distracted, I'll rush Rodney, seize the microphone, and reveal the truth to everyone." This plan also kept Joey far from the microphone.

'Thirty minutes until the Owner's Speech."

'If Rodney shows up for it." Jane wasn't sure after seeing him earlier. When 2 PM arrived and still no Rodney, Jane worried. A corn dog would ease her nerves. She strode over to the Pig's Foot stand, nodded to Brewer Bob, and secured a corn dog. Once seated in the fold-out chair next to the vat of maple syrup, Jane chomped down. With that first bite, her anxieties melted away like the buttery crust and the tender meat underneath. And what better way to compliment the corn dog than with a Bacon?

While she chowed down, Brad and Happy returned from a lot-wander, and skiers flowed down the mountain as the trails cooled. Joey announced the beginning of the annual Polish horseshoe tournament, and folks packed in for the event. Jane almost stomped over to reprimand him for getting distracted but decided the gathering crowd helped in two ways. One, the more people around, the more ears she'd reach when Rodney finally brought her the microphone. Two, the random conversations with fellow Rosefieldians calmed her nerves.

Handy Jesse regaled her with his latest conspiracy theory, connecting a haunted Space Research facility to a Green Mountain Boys' defeat during the Vermont Revolution. Some nonsense like that. Typically, this would have annoyed Jane to the point of brandishing her backhand, but she let him ramble on as she consumed corn dogs and Bacon. Jesse didn't stay long, anyway, scurrying off once he spotted Crazy Bob.

"Happy Park & Grill, Jane!" said Wilma as she approached the stand. "I'd love several corn dogs for three hungry kids."

"Have you tasted their new canned Bacon?"

"Not yet." She glanced at her watch. "Close enough to last chair.

Hopefully, no one gets injured in the next hour and a half."

Jane served her the corn dogs and beer, and Wilma returned to her family.

"I'll take some of that, too." Mickey approached the stand, wearing a Slick Mick's leather jacket. "Nothing like a pint of Pig's Foot after a day of spring turns."

"Coming right up." Jane tossed two corn dogs onto a plate, cracked a Bacon, and slid everything across the counter. "Don't forget the maple syrup dunkage."

"I know how to tune my dogs."

"Hey, Jane! I'll take a bump." PJ stepped up after Mickey. He wore his liftie jacket, as usual.

"How about two bumps?" Jane slid a pair of corn dogs onto a plate for him.

"More bumps equal more smiles."

"Care for a Bacon?"

"I'm still two bumps from 21. I'll try one then."

Jane forgot how young he was. How many Bacons had she drunk? She should slow down.

After PJ grabbed his dogs, he found a seat by the tournament, where the final first-round match concluded. Tall Brad and Dixie won the game (or Trixie, Jane couldn't tell them apart when she *wasn't* several Bacons deep), a predictable outcome as Brad won the previous three tournaments. His laser flicks and lightning defense resulted in a powerful combination, but Jane recognized a few other potential champions out there.

Ah, she loved Polish horseshoes ever since she first played in high school. Her dad loved disc golf and taught her to play when she could first lift a frisbee. As she grew up, she lost interest in the golfing aspect, but smashing beer bottles off of ski poles appealed to her.

She almost won last year with her partner Cali Joe. As a Californian, he came out of the womb wielding a frisbee in one hand. Unfortunately, his other hand wielded a joint; he was too high to play defense. Jane still carried their team into the finals but lost to Brad and the Jay girl he dated last year.

"I didn't know you worked this stand along with the Bent Pole and Sled Stop." As Jane watched the Polish tournament, she hadn't noticed Amy Harton stroll up. "Do you work at every bar in town?"

"As a bartender extraordinaire, everyone seeks my services." Jane noticed Rogen Harton behind her, a face she hadn't seen in several years. He wore the same faded brown jacket and fur cap with the ears tied to the top. "You dragged your father out."

"I insisted he meets our newest addition." Amy pointed out her family by a blue pickup. Sure enough, a stroller accompanied their gaggle of children. "Hey Pop, say hi to Jane."

With every step, Rogen's scowl deepened. When he reached the Pig's Foot counter, two parallel trenches connected his chin.

"Hey, Rogen."

He blinked, and his cheeks raised a chicken feather. His eyes remained as haunted as ever, if not more so. What happened to him? Rogen used to interact with townsfolk more regularly, but something occurred fifteen years ago—shortly after the Red Barn Incident. And he lived right next to Farmer Rick's old place.

Jane had a mind for only one mystery today. She served Amy and Rogen their corn dogs, and they returned to their camp. After distributing so many, she hankered a dog herself. Might as well wash it down with another Bacon. Jane cracked a beer and enjoyed some high-quality Polish.

Tall Brad and Tr/Dixie had secured their spot in the finals. Their challenger was the winner of the current matchup between Cali Joe and Annie from Montreal versus Frederico and Danielle. While Cali Joe threw solidly, and Annie held her own, they succumbed to Danielle's powerful backhand. And for a Spanish fella, Frederico Polished well, utilizing an effective bottle-popup defense. Frederico and Danielle won the match twenty-one to fourteen and advanced to the finals.

"Jane!" Bob Hordell appeared behind her, wearing a Park & Grill judge uniform.

"Bob. Care for a dog?"

"That's why we're here." The rest of the judges gathered behind Bob, all in their matching stripes. Jordan stood out with his oversized cap and clipboard. "This is our final tasting."

"Well, you arrived at the winner. Nothing tastes better than Brewer Bob's corn dogs. Especially after he added a secret ingredient for today." Jane served him a plate, and Bob moved over to the syrup vat.

"I'm next," said Diane Robbitet, her blonde bobs swaying. "May I place an order for one corn dog, please?"

"Yepper." Jane already had a plate prepared.

After Diane scooted, Gregor Jr. stomped forward. He wore a flannel shirt with caked mud on it, like he just finished his chores, and brought the cheese barn smell with him. "Jane." He reached forward with an open hand, and she filled it with a plate.

"PJ stopped by twenty minutes ago. He should be around."

"PJ?"

Jane blinked. "Your son."

"Oh, that son. *Patrick*, what a momma's boy." Gregor Jr. stomped off.

Wow, Jane knew PJ and his father weren't close, but . . . ouch.

"Don't mind Gregor," said Peter Smith, next in line. "If you're not a farmer, you're worthless. Not sure why he bothers officiating Park & Grill."

"It's a family tradition," said Jane. "Since the first year of Park & Grill, a Gregory has held the title of judge."

"Ah, that explains his attitude." Peter leaned in. "Nice job busting Yelsa. How's the rest of your investigation?"

"Arriving at its conclusion shortly." Jane glanced at Charlie, looming behind his brother. She might pry a few secrets from him when he stepped up for a corn dog. "How's the judging?"

"Great." Peter chuckled. "Between Jordan telling me how to score each table and Gregor's stream of complaints, I'm happier than a pig at chow time. Oh, and I lost my key card."

"Ope, you better find that. Full access to the resort could be disastrous in the wrong person's hands." Jane was jealous.

"I used it when we changed into these ridiculous uniforms. These holey pockets . . . it could have fallen out anywhere."

"I'll inform you if I spot it." She would, too, right after exploring the locked room in Squirrel Lodge's basement. She handed Peter a corn dog. "Don't let Jordan intimidate you. Brewer Bob won the competition today."

"I'm his boss on the mountain," said Peter, shaking his head. "Everywhere except here." He took his corn dog and snatched a Bacon from the counter. Then he sauntered to the Polish horseshoe crowd, where the final match had begun.

"Boss?" laughed Charlie, stepping up to replace his brother. "He's barely in charge of his own home. Unlike me, I travel out-of-state for the big payouts."

"Right, your 'contracts' down in Albany." Where the Burics hailed from.

"Yepper. And a bunch of other places, my employer keeps me moving around." Charlie leaned in. "Even today, he's got me working."

"Here? At Park & Grill?"

"Jeezum crow, you're gullible." Charlie laughed and grabbed a corn dog. He followed Peter to the horseshoe tournament before Jane could question him further.

"Pestering the newbies?" Jordan approached with his clipboard and pen ready. "Those Smith brothers have potential as judges if they possess reason."

"Would you like a corn dog? Brewer Bob added a secret ingredient, I bet you can't guess it."

"Guess the ingredient? That's my favorite game!" Jordan seized the chair next to Jane. As he sat, his body odor pushed Jane to the furthest corner of her chair. "Hand me a corn dog. I only require one."

She complied. "Bacon?"

"No, alcohol diminishes my taste acuity." Jordan sniffed his corn dog, set it back down on his plate, and pointed at the Polish tournament. "Is this the finals?"

"Yepper." Why had she mentioned the secret ingredient? Jordan smelled like Crazy Bob's compost pile in high June. Would he stay through the whole championship game? Probably, he hadn't even bitten into his corn dog yet.

Jane focused on the match. Tall Brad established an early lead, despite Tr/Dixie's complete lack of skill. His flicks smashed with such force, one bottle shattered outright. Frederico and Danielle attempted to defend, but they hadn't figured out a formation to counter Tall Brad's strikes. At eleven to five, the game was half over.

"Sap!"

Jane almost flipped backward. "What are you . . ."

"In the batter!" shouted Jordan. He set the finished corn dog stick on his plate. "The secret ingredient is sap in the corn dog batter. Correct?"

"Yep, that's it."

"Excellent." Jordan tossed his plate in the garbage. Would he leave? And take his horrible stench with him? Noper. Jordan leaned back and placed the oversized clipboard on his knee. "I consider my role as Park & Grill Head Judge as the pinnacle of my lifetime achievements."

"Really?" Jordan should revisit his aspirations. Jane would've commented, but she feared he'd never leave.

"You recognize now my superior tasting abilities, which I have spent decades perfecting. I'll tell you how."

Jane groaned. Maybe if she ignored him. That worked at the bar when a custy bled her ears. Not like she didn't have plenty to distract her, from the Polish finals to Rodney's absence. Already two hours tardy

for his Owner's Speech, would he ever show?

She returned to the game. They traded points back and forth, climbing towards twenty-one. Frederico missed a big catch while Tr/Dixie smashed a bottle for an extra point. Tall Brad's three-foot dive for the extended scoop catch spurred a standing ovation. Danielle scored a triple with an impressive backhand slam. With every throw, the crowd of spectators grew, and their cheers echoed across the parking lot.

". . . because my second daily exercise involves a spice rack and a blindfold," continued Jordan. For a man who usually spoke concisely, he rambled on about food.

Back to the match. After some beautiful plays, Danielle and Frederico tightened the gap to just one point, eighteen to nineteen. Their turn, too, if they scored three points, they would win the championship. Frederico stepped forward, clenching the frisbee in a power grip. He eyed the left pole and the shining bottle on top. With an explosive release, the frisbee struck towards the target—and connected! The bottle dropped straight to the dirt, leaving Tr/Dixie no chance at recovery.

Two points secured, but what about the frisbee? Would Tall Brad make the game-saving catch? He dove, extending his body until parallel with the ground, and snatched it an inch from the dirt. A tremendous save that cost him scraped knees and a bloody elbow. For the annual Park & Grill Polish horseshoe championship title? Worth it.

". . . which I attribute to my swift hands. Nothing is more important than maintaining a steady stream of food to the palate . . ."

After brushing off the dirt, Tall Brad readied his impressive forehand. Down by one, 19 to 20, and with the win-by-two rule in effect, he required a full three points to achieve victory. He flicked, and the frisbee lasered at the opposing pole. It nicked the can, which teetered, and fell! The frisbee shot right through Danielle's hands for the earned point.

". . . as fast hands help with other endeavors. At Slanted last week, and again as we changed into the judging uniforms . . ."

All eyes turned to Frederico, diving forward to prevent the bottle from touching down. He slid a hand underneath—and popped it up. He opened a chance to save the game, but could he recover? Noper, he slipped. Danielle might cover for him. Executing a catch with the frisbee in hand was an advanced maneuver, however. She dashed, extended her arm to its maximum, but the bottle fell to the floor. Tall Brad won the championship once again.

". . . which leads into my fifth daily exercise, jaw strengthening. I bought these weights . . ."

Jane rose and reluctantly clapped with the rest of the crowd. She hankered the underdog victory, but at least this way, she would get to dethrone Brad herself next year. Based on the volume of their cheering, nobody else minded his Polish horseshoe dynasty. Folks catcalled, owl-hooted, and bear-hollered. The applause drowned out any sound within a hundred feet, especially the mutterings of a stupefied resort owner. Even when equipped with a microphone.

Jane noticed Rodney immediately. "Joey!" she shouted to no avail. Didn't matter. With everyone focused on the tournament champions, Jane required no further distractions.

She pushed her way to the Generally Slanted porch and stomped right up the steps. Rodney's knees shivered, his hair frazzled, and bright red zits filled his cheeks. She snatched his microphone with zero resistance, and when she shoved his shoulder, he obediently slumped into one of the metal chairs.

"Good evening, Rosefield!" Jane's voice boomed out of the built-in speakers adorning the porch area, silencing the crowd.

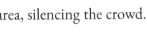

"I'm here to expose the truth about a conspiracy threatening to tear our town apart. Worse than the '97 Mulberry River flood!

"First, I'd like to congratulate this year's Polish horseshoe champions. Brad, you've done it again, but I'll take your crown next year." Folks responded with *oohs* and *ahhs* as Brad saluted. "Here's to the champions, Tall Brad and . . . Drixie." The roaring applause drowned out her mispronunciation.

"Secondly," shouted Jane, and the crowd silenced immediately. "I demand we address the name 'Murder Mountain.' Is that what we are? Did Murder Mountain come together when the earth tremor knocked over Generally Slanted? No! A dozen of our bravest Rosefieldians pushed it back to only a little slanted. Rosefield Mountain! Not Murder.

"Who banded together when the Fire Department caught ablaze? True Rosefieldians! Residents, both permanent and seasonal, worked together to throw bucket after bucket onto the fire. We extinguished the flames before they scorched the foundation. Rosefield Mountain! Not Murder."

A chant grew amongst the crowd. "Rosefield, Rosefield, Rosefield. Rosefield!" Louder and louder until even Rodney couldn't ignore the call.

Jane had these folks right where she hankered, time to blow up the main story like an over-methaned outhouse. She raised her hands, and they quieted.

"There's more. It goes straight to the top. I'm not talking about Rodney Buric, either. Not this one, anyway." She pointed at the blob of a man next to her. She chuckled, which echoed through the crowd. "No. I'm referring to his father, Rodney Buric Sr., a man involved with our community members in a grand conspiracy. It all ties in with Timmy Harton, too! Brace yourselves because this news will change the essence of Rosefield forever—"

A hand fell on Jane's shoulder, interrupting her speech. Assuming it was the hand of a security guard, maybe Jim McJoy himself, she instinctively spun with a hand raised. She'd fight them off if necessary!

She relaxed when she recognized Sheriff McStoots. Something about her lightly freckled cheeks and slight smirk calmed Jane. She wore her brown leather jacket. Peggy was serious.

"I just need to tell them one more thing."

"I know what you're gonna say." Peggy held her hand out. "But I discovered the truth."

Jane clenched the microphone with both hands and shook her head. "There's a larger plot, I *know* it."

Peggy sighed. "We can only gut one deer at a time."

"Not if we bring two knives."

"It's better to work together on one and then strip the other." Peggy reached out. "Hand me the microphone."

Jane grunted. Stomped her feet. She held out the microphone, and Peggy snatched it.

"It's been a hard winter . . ." began Peggy.

Jane stepped down from the porch, slinking from Sheriff McStoots and her words. She stumbled towards her seat by Joey's truck, grabbing another can of Bacon on her way. She fished for trout all day but returned home with a bucket of smelt.

She heard her name, followed by cheering. She raised her eyes to people clapping and shouting. "Jane! Jane! Jane!" Her chant from earlier returned. "Rosefield, Rosefield. Rosefield!" Jane strode the rest of the way to her chair, arms held high.

"Rosefield!" Jane hollered back before relaxing for the grand finale.

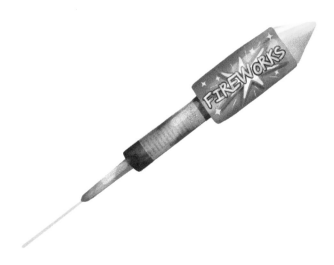

Like a complex Lydia McStoots poem, Peggy deciphered Marge's note line by line.

*Remember the Red Barn Incident?*

She remembered it well. Many considered that night the worst in Rosefield's recorded history, with a dozen fights breaking out. Two fellas disappeared, and quite a few folks believed the barn remained haunted ever since. While Peggy didn't believe in ghosts, she'd only returned to Farmer Rick's once: when his house burned down.

*Check the rafters; who lost their head? And against who?*

The rafters? That reminded Peggy of someone. Who climbed onto the rafters? Charlie Smith. And he indeed lost his head, exchanging fists with—with Timmy friggin' Harton!

*Check under the gold cushions,*
*which became?*

This one stumped Peggy. The first half was easy, just an old set of code words they used playing team cribbage. 'Gold' meant diamonds, 'cushions' meant ace, and 'under' meant discarded in the crib. Ace of diamonds in the crib. Which became . . . what?

Twenty minutes later, she remembered. After Peggy hosted a cribbage night, Marge stayed late, and they shared a bottle of wine. As they invented new code words, they joked that an ace of diamonds in the crib equaled 'money in the bank.'

*Put it all together.*

Marge wanted Peggy to check Charlie's financials because he might be involved in Timmy's murder. The whole notion brought forth a slew of new questions. She set the letter down and struck straight to the coffee maker. She brewed two cups of classic Cardiac, mixed in a teaspoon of Johnson's maple syrup and an ounce of Old Gregor's Crude milk. The combination always set her thoughts straighter than a row of corn.

Why did Marge write a letter? And why enlist Happy to deliver it? She must have known he'd attempt to solve the riddle himself, delaying its delivery. Maybe that was the point. If Peggy investigated Charlie right after Happy visited his grandma, Peter would notice. Could Peter forgive his mother for turning in his brother? While Charlie and Peter occasionally feuded, they were lifelong best friends.

On to more important questions, like who paid Charlie to kill Timmy? How could they profit from his death? Joey and Jane believed Rodney Buric hired someone to kill Timmy and bring on the rebranding. Their theory held merit, Murder Mountain recorded their busiest year by far, but Rodney simply wasn't smart or ambitious enough for this scheme. His father was both of those things, but that's a substantial risk for a man already wealthy like Rodney Buric Sr.

Who arranged all the framing? Big Top's shirt, Rufus's knife, and Yelsa's scrunchie all ended up at the crime scene, yet none of them were involved. More frames than a raised garden, and Charlie wasn't exactly a carpenter. Who planted all the evidence?

*So very mysterious, it made her delirious.* Too many questions, Peggy preferred answers. Summer rapidly approached, and this investigation remained wide open.

She knew where to head first: Banker Henry's office. She waited until Monday, as he conducted business only during banking hours. She showed up at his bank in Enosburg right at 8 AM, which required an earlier start than Peggy preferred, but the melting snow motivated her. She passed the blonde teller without a word and strode into his office.

"Sorry, guy," she said before occupying the leather chair opposite Henry's desk. The softness hurt her bum. "I hate to bother you first thing."

"Am I in trouble?" Sweat already formed on his rounded scalp, and his stubby fingers tapped on the desk.

"No, this isn't about you." Maybe she *should* investigate the banker. "You handle all the foreclosures in Rosefield, right?"

"Yepper. I consider it my duty to the town to personally provide them their paperwork. As I say, 'I'm cleaning up Rosefield one notice at a time!'"

"Has Charlie Smith experienced any financial issues?"

"I'm not supposed to discuss any client's information . . ."

Peggy sighed. She couldn't compel him to answer because she lacked real evidence. Had she wasted her morning driving down?

". . . but when it comes to those Smith brothers—delinquents!" Banker Henry palmed his desk. "I'll tell you whatever you want. As long as it's for official sheriffing duties, of course."

"Only an important case would drive me to Enosburg this early in the morning. Tell me about Charlie."

"About eight months ago, he stopped his payments. Which eventually brought me to his door with my envelope. He shouted and pleaded. He tried to intimidate me, popping his shoulders up like a bull about to charge." Henry puffed up his chest. "No one intimidates this banker. I've witnessed tougher financials than the largest muscle man."

Peggy chuckled as she recalled several instances she'd witnessed Banker Henry intimidated, once by Charlie himself. "He threatened you?"

"A little, but an experienced banker deters such behavior with insinuated litigation." He wiped a tear. "Before I could foreclose on him, he found enough money."

"Was this in late October?" The murder had occurred on October 25th.

"Yeah, right around then. Charlie strolled in with a check for the entire amount plus a month. I couldn't believe it!" Henry chuckled. "As I say, 'once a delinquent, always a delinquent.' Yeppers, I'll revisit him. Soon."

Peggy sighed. Everything lined up, but it felt askew. "Thank you for your time."

"That's it? No more criminals? You know, I possess a long list of delinquents, including select board members, prominent business owners, and half of Ski School—including management. They all possess villainous secrets. I'd wager my house, the largest in town."

"Oh no, no more investigations." Not until the fall, at least, with baby Robert due next month. Peggy stood and offered her hand. "I must return to catching those delinquents."

"Whatever you require, Sheriff McStoots, as long as it's during banking hours." Henry reached out a hand without standing.

Peggy sighed and stepped forward. After a quick shake, she left the bank and drove straight to Rosefield. She stopped at the Sled Stop and ordered her usual breakfast and a cup of Cardiac brew.

Her investigation brought her to Charlie, but she didn't like it. She would scrutinize this new information, as she'd confronted the wrong person twice for the murder of Timmy Harton. Not again.

She downed a second cup of coffee. And a third. Nothing came to her.

After she finished breakfast, Peggy drove home and brewed another pot of Cardiac. She'd drink nothing else until she solved this mystery.

Three days passed, and nothing but Cardiac. She hardly slept. Rodney Buric Sr. hiring Charlie made no sense. Was eighty-year-old Marge mistaken? Her cribbage skills remained strong, though, and she remembered all their code words for team play.

Two more days of pure Cardiac. She felt close to the truth. What had she missed?

The next morning, Peggy decided she needed a break. Maybe if she allowed herself a distraction, her subconscious would work for her. What better than a full reading of *Seasonal Colors*? Lydia's words always cleared her thoughts.

She filled a teacup and adjourned to her favorite reading space. When Georgia bought her own house a few years ago, Peggy appropriated the bedroom. Bookshelves spanned two whole walls. She kept the bed set up against the third wall for when she hankered extra comfort. Her three favorite reading chairs lined the windows on the fourth wall: her mother's old armchair with yellow-flowered cushions, her grandfather's old wooden rocker, and her favorite, a solid wooden chair with a hardback she bought at an Enosburg yard sale.

She chose the rocker today. Grandpa loved mysteries, the 'whodunit' novels from the '30s and '40s were his favorites. Perhaps Peggy could channel what he learned from Christie, Carr, Chandler, and those other classic writers into her investigation. She settled in with a light blue fleece blanket, Diohgee at her feet and Siaytee in her lap. She opened Seasonal Colors by Lydia McStoots, letting another classic writer (nearly on the level of those others) consume her mind.

Peggy skipped the first few poems, a little too Jesus-centric for her. While she considered herself a Christian and attended church several times a year, she didn't appreciate religion in her pleasure reading. However, The following set of four poems, collectively titled "The Spring Series," would compel the fussiest literary critic to drop jaw and slap knee. Peggy read through, her smile growing with every line, and during the climax when the owl and snake met, she shed a tear.

The next poem, titled 'Subtleties,' brought the plot together for her:

My Mooseheads, please listen,
For all the jays who gleam blue,
When I speak, I do christen,
that all these words hear true.

Beware! You might pop a piston
Or what other misfortune you rue.
Just make sure when you listen,
you take a stew before the review.

*In an instant, the answer struck her brain with the force of a train.* Peggy had read the poem a hundred times but only now discovered its true meaning. Lydia repeated the 'listen' rhyme indicating the importance of the final line. Listen, stew, review. Peggy thought she meant a full belly led to improved critical thinking, but what if Lydia actually intended one should 'stew' on a conversation before a later 'review'?

Could Peggy apply this idea to her investigation? If she reviewed the most significant interactions involving the case, she'd discover the truth.

She spoke to Rufus. He hankered Timmy's skis, which felt a tad insensitive, but who'd pass on expensive ski gear? He was obsessed with the return of his knife, but considering its history, she understood his anxiety.

Everything Big Top said added up, too. He left his yellow flannel shirt on the peg in his office, and the killer stole it. In the summer, most doors automatically locked, so it was someone with access. Anyone could swipe a key card, however. Peggy stole one during the Park & Grill of '93 and returned it a month later without anyone noticing.

Yelsa claimed she wasn't involved with Timmy's murder, and Peggy believed her. Therefore the killer set up the scrunchie for Joey to find. They must have stolen it at the resort, like Big Top's flannel. Maybe they reused the stolen key card to sneak into Generally Slanted's deli.

When she recalled her conversation with Banker Henry, she dropped *Seasonal Colors*. He told her the decisive clue, and Peggy had missed it—until now.

She still needed to confirm one final detail with the banker. She dashed to the living room and grabbed her phone. He didn't answer when she called him at home or work. What day was it? Saturday. He wouldn't respond until Monday due to his stupid banker's hours.

Peggy couldn't wait. She hopped into the Road Runner and drove to town, skidding into Henry's driveway like a twenty-year-old. When she found his door locked, she pressed the doorbell harder and longer than a panini from the Generally Slanted deli.

After fifteen minutes, Banker Henry opened a window and screamed, "My office on Monday! Banker's hours!" Peggy didn't lift her finger. It took another fifteen minutes for him to even speak with her through a window, then an additional ten minutes of arguing before he let her in.

Within three minutes, Peggy asked her questions and departed. From Henry's expression, though, she asked him to hike the Long Trail.

As she returned to the Road Runner, Peggy realized she collected enough evidence to confront her suspect. Where would he be?

Wait, was it the Saturday of Park & Grill? She had completely forgotten. While she hadn't gone in a few years, Peggy always attended in her younger years. And who could forget the Park & Grill of '93?

The killer was up there, surer than a five-legged goat. He never missed a Park & Grill. Peggy pictured him handing out golden spatulas. She turned on the Road Runner and ripped up Left Mountain Road.

There was something else about Park & Grill . . . Bill Viceroy's favor! What had he wanted? Peggy agreed to escort a red van through the parking lot, scheduled to arrive at 5 PM. She glanced at the clock, already 4 PM. Well, she had multiple reasons to attend Park & Grill this year.

While the Road Runner brought her to the resort in under five minutes, navigating through the parking lot took a lot more time. She aimed to park right at Generally Slanted, around by the loading dock ideally. This way, she wouldn't have to escort her suspect through the crowd. Unfortunately, security blocked off the access road, forcing Peggy to navigate through the masses.

She honked and veered her way to the line of grills outside Generally Slanted. While most people moved out of her way once they discovered her identity, it often took them a few moments to notice her Jeep, so engrossed in their revelry. Fifty feet from the porch steps, she gave up and parked the Road Runner.

First, she scanned the grilling area until she realized the food competition had concluded. Where to next?

Shouting and cheering echoed from the Generally Slanted porch. Peggy spotted a crowd next to Joey's white truck. Of course, he was at the center of the commotion. She might as well start her search there.

Once closer, she heard Jane's voice over a loudspeaker. What was she announcing? Peggy pushed through locals and seasonals alike. A few folks recognized her and offered a 'howdy doody,' but Peggy didn't dawdle for pleasantries. She *did* briefly pause her progression to join her fellow townsfolk in their 'Rosefield' chant.

When Jane brought up conspiracies, however, Peggy felt she should intervene and save her the embarrassment. Like Margaret Smith, Jane was on target but missed the bullseye. After a little convincing, she relinquished the microphone to Peggy. Jane stomped down the porch steps, roughly snatching a beer from a nearby cooler. That would not do.

'It's been a hard winter.' Peggy stepped to the front of the stage. 'Enjoy this superb weather and food. Let's hear it for Jane! For reminding everyone who we are. Rosefield Mountain!'

Peggy allowed them as long as they needed to chant their town name. Jane shouldn't feel bitter, not after bringing these folks together to demonstrate their disdain for this 'Murder Mountain' nonsense. Besides, Peggy spotted her suspect. He removed his officiating hat to blend in, but Peggy was too fine a hunter. It was time to bag, tag, and call the game warden. She reached to set the microphone down on the nearby metal table—

"Who killed Timmy!?" The shout stopped her hand.

"Yeah, who did it!?"

'Peggy. Peggy. Peggy!' Another chant. Great. She hankered a quiet exit, but could she ignore the calls of her fellow Rosefieldians?

She raised her hands, and the crowd silenced. She recognized a lot of faces. Bob Hordell visited the mountain only during Park & Grill and entirely for the food. Cody Trent shut down their general store for the afternoon and brought his family up. The Woodlets closed the Sled Stop, too. She spotted their family gathered two rows over. Even Carol vacated her post office to attend.

Didn't they deserve the truth? As a Rosefieldian affair, shouldn't the townsfolk have a front seat to its resolution?

"Okay, I'll tell you. I'll share my entire investigation." The roaring response nearly knocked Peggy a step. "I'll begin with the evidence at the crime scene.

"A piece of yellow flannel from Big Top's favorite shirt, one of Yelsa's rainbow scrunchies, and Rufus's knife. All three discovered where Timmy was killed, but none of them committed the murder."

"I did it!" Rufus stumbled forward, waving his hands around his head. "I hankered his skis, so my knife killed him. I confess!"

Peggy sighed. "You didn't kill Timmy."

"I have these nightmares, Sheriff McStoots, awful nightmares. I can't take them anymore! I burned his skis along with my own for amends. I doubt it's enough." He appeared paler than usual, if possible, and his hair had formed a single greasy knot. "You gotta arrest me."

"I won't arrest you because you didn't kill Timmy." She handled the same issue a few years ago. Rufus experienced a rough couple of months, shouting at people on Main Street and wandering around with a weed whacker (while intimidating, he cleaned up quite a few yards).

Timmy Harton, of all people, told Peggy what happened. The hospital had revoked his medical marijuana, so he bought skunk weed. Peggy called up his doctor, and they immediately reinstated the prescription. The next morning, she drove him to the dispensary in Burlington.

"Sit down, Rufus." The same thing happened once more. If he would only fill out the simple forms. "I'll set you up tomorrow."

Rufus grumbled and continued forward. Fortunately, Happy and Joey guided him back to his seat.

"As I said," resumed Peggy. "All that evidence, the piece of yellow flannel, the scrunchie, and the knife, planted by the true killer. Rufus's knife he could've stolen whenever, but Big Top only left his flannel on the hook in his office. Yelsa told me she remembered the exact scrunchie, and it disappeared from Generally Slanted. This meant the killer enjoyed access throughout the resort.

'Still, there remained a lot of suspects. I needed to look at motives. Who *hankered* killing Timmy Harton? No one liked him, and he instigated a lot of fights over the years. Folks don't murder, however, for just a small grudge ending in fisticuffs. Even a feud brewing over a decade wouldn't escalate to murder—unless the killer has another motive: a pile of cheddar."

As Peggy spoke, she kept her scope on her suspect. She anticipated her target would bolt once threatened.

'I began checking into the financials of folks in town who met two criteria. They have access around the mountain and a feud with Timmy. Last week, I spoke with Banker Henry, which brought me close to my mark. Today, I revisited him, and I've finally locked my crosshairs."

He moved! The killer retreated through the packed crowd towards the empty grill section. He held a slow pace to avoid detection, but that wouldn't last. She needed to fire soon.

'Turns out, someone in our town has tremendous debts, brought upon by a love for a wife who passed far too early. To fill his loss, he followed their shared passion, one of raising horses. Whether he could afford his herd or not, they represented her, and he'd fight to the death to protect them. If that meant killing somebody, why not his brother's enemy? He dropped two bucks with one bullet.

'When the banks threatened to foreclose on his house and seize all of his horses, he took action. He read about a mountain where a murder occurred. The following season they recorded their highest year in profits. He figured he'd replicate the same thing here. But how does an increase in resort profits help Peter Smith repay the bank? Because of Rodney Buric's deal with his General Managers, a massive bonus in the event of massive profits."

In full flight mode, Peter pushed through the final line of onlookers and started running.

"Everyone, out of the way!" Peggy jumped down from the porch and sprinted towards the crowd, knowing her fellow Rosefieldians would move for her. As sure as a January Nor'easter, they parted with a biblical flare.

Once through to the grills, she spotted Peter dash around Generally Slanted towards the loading dock. He must be parked there, so Peggy veered towards the Road Runner.

She hopped in and turned the key. He whirred, but the engine didn't catch. The starter forgot its lessons at the worst possible moment. She fisted the dashboard. Well, no reason to cry over spilled syrup. She jumped out of the driver's seat, hustled to the trunk for her whacker stick—just as Peter sped by in his silver sedan. Darn it! No way she'd catch him now.

"I got him!"

After a quick scan, Peggy found Joey on the bed of a truck (not his) with a silver pipe on his shoulder. He aimed it at the fleeing car, and sparks flashed from the back like a firework. Peggy sighed. Of all the idiotic things he conceived over the ye—

*Bang!* The rocket blazed past a dozen parked cars before crossing the road yards ahead of Peter's car. A miss. A close shot, but whether by an inch or a yardstick, the buck escaped all the sa—

*Boom!* The rocket exploded with a hundred colors.

*Bang! Bang!* Streams of sparklers in a dozen different hues fired in all directions.

*Bang! Boom!* White blasts cascaded across the road, engulfing Peter's car in light.

*Crash! Bang! Bang! Boom!* One final rainbow blasted up into the sky and rained down glitter across the parking lot. In the end, a cloud of smoke remained, and a blaring car horn.

Peggy administered a lesson or three upon her starter and tried the key once more. He powered on with a learned click. She dropped it into gear and drove into the haze. She followed the sound of his horn until she spotted his car, nose first in the ditch. She parked right behind his sedan to prevent any lame escape attempts. *No way, not today.* Peggy cornered her prey, harvest time.

She opened the car door to a wobbling Peter holding his bloody nose. She grabbed his arm and pulled him out of the smoking vehicle. The car horn blared, spoiling the serenity that usually accompanied a successful hunt. Peter marched to the Road Runner, climbed into the back seat, and Peggy locked him in.

As she circled to the driver's side, a red van drove up from Left Mountain Road, stopping ten feet from her. A man dressed in blue and white leather with a sparkling white wide-brimmed cowboy hat stepped out and approached her. While he looked familiar, he wasn't from Rosefield.

"Y'all need help?" He spoke in a southern accent, like Bennington or Brattleboro. She recognized his voice.

"Official sheriff business. I'll call a tow later." She pointed up to the rest of the parking lot. "The party's up there. Find a spot."

"The guy who hired us said we'd have an escort waitin'. See, we need to drive this van to the front and with all those people . . ." He shook his head and spit. "We'll require someone with authority."

A red van . . . *the* red van that Bill Viceroy wanted her to escort up to the lodge. Peggy once again forgot about the favor he asked of her. "Yepper, I'll escort you. Follow me."

She hopped into the Road Runner and turned him around. With some light horn work, she pulled up to Generally Slanted without hassle. Folks nodded and waved as she passed, and Peggy couldn't hold down her cheeks.

When she parked her Jeep and hopped out, Bill strode out of the crowd to greet her. "Thank you, Sheriff McStoots."

"This is all you hankered? Who are these guys, anyway?"

"The Rutland Rotary Boys, the best band south of Montpelier. Or so I was told." Bill adjusted his black-rimmed hat. "You don't recognize them?"

Peggy shrugged. "My radio didn't come with a display."

"Hey, boss man." The same band member Peggy talked to earlier approached. "Since it's nice out, what if we set up here?"

"If that's what you want." Bill pointed to the rows of tailgate setups. "I'm sure everyone prefers staying outdoors, anyway."

"Give us a few minutes." He formed a Y with his hand and shook it around. "Rock and roll!"

While the Rutland Rotary Boys set up their instruments and speakers, Peggy stepped over to Bill. "What's all this? You never interact with the town, and yet you hire a band?"

"Reparations for the damage my boys inflicted on the recreation field." Bill jerked a thumb over his shoulder. "They're Dana Shoeman's favorite band."

Following his thumb, she noticed the school principal, wearing the same white cowboy hat as the band and a shirt with every member and accompanying autographs. While Dana smiled the widest, most of Rosefield joined her wearing smiles of their own. Was she wrong about the Viceroys after all?

She *should* transport Peter out of here, but she had to hear at least one song by 'the best band south of Montpelier.' She didn't wait long, as they already turned the Generally Slanted porch into a stage filled with instruments and speakers. After a mic check, the frontman took center stage.

"Welcome, Rosefield and Murder Mountain! We drove a long way to play for y'all in a not-so-comfy van, so we'll start with something to ease the cricks out. Here's a special tune off our new record, *The Southern Road*, titled—this one's for y'all—'Murder Mountain:'

RIPPIN' DOWN THE TRAIL,
WHO'S THAT ON MY TAIL?
DOES HE HAVE A KNIFE?
DOES HE WANT MY LIFE?
WHO KNOWS WHAT AVAIL
WHEN MURDER RUNS RIFE?

WE'RE GONNA FIGURE THIS
MYSTERY OUT,
WITH A MURDER MOUNTAIN
SHOUT:

YOU BEST RACE TO THE BASE;
DON'T WANT TO BE A MARTYR.
KEEP PACE, OR YOU'LL FACE
THIS MOUNTAIN OF MURDER.

I PUMP MY POLES,
KEEP MY SKIS STRAIGHT.
OF MY LIFE GOALS,
MY MURDER CAN WAIT.

EVEN IN THE LODGE
WITH MY BOOTS LOOSE,
STILL READY TO DODGE
ANYONE COOKIN' MY GOOSE.

# MURDER MOUNTAIN

WE'RE FINDING THIS STORY'S CORE
WITH A MURDER MOUNTAIN ROAR:

DON'T SHARE A CHAIR,
NOT EVEN FOR A BOARDER.
TAKE CARE AND BEWARE,
THIS MOUNTAIN OF MURDER.

RIPPIN' THROUGH THE WOODS
SEARCHIN' FOR THE GOODS.
WHO'S BEHIND THE TREE?
WILL THEY MURDER ME?
GOTTA WATCH THOSE HOODS
WHEN KILLERS RUN FREE.

I KICK MY SKIS
NEED THE FAST START,
I SPOT A SLEAZE
WHO'S AFTER MY HEART.

I EQUIP MY HELMET
READY AS A SHIELD.
NO PANT-PELLET,
NOT WITH MY YIELD.

WE'RE EMBRACING THIS BRAWLER
WITH A MURDER MOUNTAIN HOLLER:

TO PLAY, YOU BEST STAY
TOUGH AS A GIRDER.
WE PRAY AND PORTRAY
THIS MOUNTAIN OF MURDER.

With a chuckle, Peggy imagined Lydia's reaction to hearing such drivel. How could Dana Shoeman enjoy them? At least they had strong stage energy.

She hopped in the Road Runner and eased out of the lot. In the back seat, Peter held his head and grumbled about his missing Rosefield key card. He wouldn't need to worry about that anymore. His employment, his home, his entire life just evaporated, including that massive bonus he killed Timmy for.

A lot of folks had some words for Peter as they passed by:

"We trusted you!" shouted Wilma. "How could you kill our Timmy?"

"You stole my shirt!?" shouted Big Top. "And ripped it up!?"

"Why don't *you* hike in the woods alone? Wear orange, so I spot you better!" The shouts became endless. "Murderer!" "Choke on some moose spleen!" "Hope your four-wheeler breaks down!" "Sled death for you!" As Peggy eased the Road Runner from the crowd, the shouting grew softer and less angry. When she drove past the final row of cars, she heard a new chant erupt. "Peggy, Peggy. Peggy! Peggy!"

Good thing she brought her hankie. She wiped the tears from her cheeks before waving back to the crowd. Then she drove from the lot.

She passed Peter's smashed-up car. She forgot to call a tow. Too late, she couldn't use the ol' cellular while driving. Someone would deal with it eventually.

When they turned onto Left Mountain Road, Peggy began her final interrogation. "I have a few remaining questions."

"Should I call my attorney?" said Peter, his eyes focused on the floor.

"I'm not recording or fishing for more evidence. This is just for me." Where to start? "You needed the money, but why Timmy Harton? Because of what happened at Farmer Rick's?"

"The Red Barn Incident started the feud. After fifteen years of his bullshit, I decided to end it." Peter fisted the seat. "The tap that killed the maple, for me, was what happened to his horse a few years ago."

"A ghastly incident," agreed Peggy. "A lot of townsfolk hadn't forgiven him. And why only a dozen people showed up to his Parting Party."

"The backhoe haunts me. Its bucket still ripping up dirt."

"I forgot about the excavation." Peggy shook her head. "I suppose I repressed it."

"The mind's designed to protect us from horrible things." Peter fisted the seat once more. "If you ask me? I was disposing of manure."

"Fortunately, the law doesn't agree with you. Folks can't kill each other freely, especially when money's involved." Peggy cleared her throat and glared at Peter through her rearview. "You murdered Timmy for the money, for your own greed. What would Laura think?"

Peter's head sank when he heard her name. He alternated between full-body trembles and gripping the seat cushion so hard his knuckles whitened. He ground his teeth. His eyes filled with tears that spilled across his cheeks. "She'd call me an idiot and coward. Too scared to live on without her."

Peggy sighed. When she reached the stop sign, she turned onto an empty Main Street. She parked in front of the Town Clerk's Office but left the Road Runner on.

"How did the murder occur, exactly?"

"Timmy always hikes for the first snow. I waited on the slope dressed for trail maintenance and asked him for assistance moving a log."

"That's when he hung up his jacket."

"Yes. As he stooped down to grip the log, I pulled out the knife. I said, 'Hey, Timmy!' When he turned, I drove the blade into his chest. He was dead before he could realize it."

Peter's dark eyes matched his cold tone. An unfortunate side effect of living in a small town, the grudges ran deep. With folks cooped together all their lives, the largest cocks battled for dominance of the den. Sometimes a rooster lost an eye. Sometimes they received a knife to the ol' blood pumper.

What else? 'Did you inform Rodney about Yelsa's scheme?"

'After Jane clued me—"

'She's quite the little investigator." Peggy laughed. 'Like my youngest daughter, Mary Anne."

'Mary Anne's sweet on my nephew, I believe. They spent much of this winter together."

'Your nephew . . . do you mean Harry?" Peggy sighed. 'Doesn't he live in a yurt or something?"

'Most folks call him Happy, and he's an honest kid. Loves Grandma Day."

'A descendant of Marge *would* have excellent roots." She laughed. 'Well, I guess in your case, something rotted. Once you learned Yelsa's scheme, what did you do?"

'I sent Rodney an email posing as a private investigator working for his father. I told him to quietly handle the problem without involving the cops. This way, he looked like their accomplice, making him a suspect in Timmy's murder by extension."

This explained why Rodney drove himself to Daffodil Harvest that night. 'Then you stole Yelsa's scrunchie and planted it in the woods?"

'Since the frames for Big Top or Rufus didn't stick, I hoped Yelsa would convince you."

'At least she was guilty of something." Peggy once more glared through the rearview. 'Big Top and Rufus hadn't wronged you nor committed any crime. What's your justification for their potential arrests?"

'Laura would have hated me for that." Again, his eyes dropped to the floor, and he fisted the seat cushion. 'Sacrificing someone else . . . she'd have never talked to me again."

'You'll have to reconcile with her when you meet again on the other side. Until then, you can punish yourself every night as you fall asleep in a jail cell."

'A rightful place for a fool like me." Peter chuckled and wiped at his cheeks. "I'm surprised Joey found Yelsa's scrunchie. What are the odds?"

"He also shot the firework which blew up your entire escape."

Peter's jaw nearly fell off his face. "Joey's the reason I'm here?"

"You manufactured this mess yourself. Was Charlie involved in any of this?"

"Of course not. Charlie has his own thing. I borrowed money from him to repay Banker Henry."

"What about the money he acquired in the fall?"

"Some deal with Rodney Buric. The father. Not the idiot." He chuckled. "At least I'll never report to that dumbass again."

"Did you see Rodney on the Generally Slanted porch?" offered Peggy. "Lard sweating in the sun."

"Somebody could've taken a bath with all those tears."

"Solved world thirst at the very least."

"Nah," countered Peter. "Too much salt. Maybe a decent dry rub."

"Only if you cook every bit of Rodney off."

"Can a grill burn hot enough?"

"Not your standard charcoal," agreed Peggy. "But gas should sear the grease right off."

She shifted Road Runner into drive and pulled out onto Main Street. She'd take him to the Staties barracks herself. He was born and raised Rosefieldian, after all. They bantered the whole trip to St. Albans, and the two (two!) stoplights Peggy encountered didn't annoy her as much as usual.

Upon arrival, she hopped out of the Road Runner and let Peter out.

"Peggy, may I ask you for a favor?" He held the stallion keychain that once belonged to his wife. "Hold on to this for me? I don't want the Staties to lose it."

"I'll keep it safe in my gun box."

"I appreciate it."

After a greeting and a handshake, Peggy handed Peter over to Commander Strongman. Then she hopped into Road Runner Robert and drove home.

As soon as she kicked off her boots, she fetched the seasonal totes from her attic. She swapped her sweaters for flannels, her toques for sunhats, and her lined jeans for regular jeans. With the investigation over, she embraced summer's imminent arrival. Actually, the organizing inspired a few lyrics:

With her investigation complete
Sheriff Peggy deserved a treat.
Smelling the dirt, eating spring air,
breathing streams without a care.

Would she sleep this whole week?
Nope, that's for the frail and weak.
And for now, she'd wash all well,
until she had another story to tell.

Not terrible. Peggy might start her own book this summer. While she couldn't compete with Lydia's masterpiece, some folks might appreciate her experiences. With baby Robert due in just over a month, though, would she have enough time?

Three days later, Happy pushed off hard, straight-lining to the lip and jumping higher and further than ever before. Would he stick the landing?

Mary Anne texted at 9 AM:

gotta drop bathing suit with mom. lunch at the pond? noon?

After an hour of internal debate, he returned with:

yepper

Happy showed up twenty minutes early to spark the grill and chug a quick Bacon to grease his courage. She showed up ten minutes after noon when the coals reached the perfect temperature. She slapped the dogs on and joined Happy on the rock overlooking the pond, darkened by Rosefield mountain's reflection.

'I heard housekeeping recovered the money stolen from Generally

Slanted."

"Day after Park & Grill." Happy laughed. "In the laundry room of all places."

"Maybe someone returned the money out of guilt?"

"Definitely weird."

"How was it?" Mary Anne cast a stone into the pond. "Park & Grill?"

"The best one I ever attended. Folks say it rivaled the legendary Park & Grill of '93."

"I've pestered her for over a decade, and Mom still won't tell me anything about '93." She had spun her hair up in an elaborate bun with a rose-colored pin on top. Her unzipped blue puffy revealed a t-shirt with a chipmunk driving a motorcycle. "Must've been fun."

"A great time. Except, well . . ."

"Sorry, guy." Mary Anne rubbed his shoulder. "It's crazy about your uncle."

"I can't believe Uncle Pete killed Timmy. I never imagined he was capable of murder."

"I still don't understand your grandma's charade with the letter. Was it just to mess with you?"

"A little, she *is* a sneaky grandma." Happy laughed. "I reckon she did it to avoid Peter's hatred for helping Peggy arrest Charlie. She knew I couldn't resist opening the letter and investigating. It might take me months to deliver it. Uncle Pete wouldn't suspect a thing. Of course, she reckoned the wrong son as the murderer, but in the end, it still applies."

"Which is why we'll never tell anyone about the letter. Will your grandma move?"

"Uncle Pete borrowed enough from my dad to keep the house for the next few months. Afterward, well, Dad won't kick his own mom out of a home. Since he doesn't want her at his house, he'll help her until she finds a smaller place. Perhaps a yurt next to mine. They'll sell all the horses, though, and everything else." Happy frowned. "I'll miss ol'

283

Bess."

"Maybe you could buy her."

"Yeah." Happy couldn't think about Bess or Grandma, not when he waited on the platform for the light to turn green. Like her emerald eyes . . . Uh oh, he already felt his knees wobble. If he caught an edge now, he'd tumble the rest of the way.

He remembered what Joey said. Stay focused on the jump, hit it with everything, and hopefully, Happy didn't break any bones during the wipeout. "Mary Anne . . ." He was through the gate, no turning back. He crouched as low as possible and pointed down the slope. "Sorry about the note, Farmer Rick's story provided some leads, and—"

"No, you were right. Your grandmother's letter helped Mom solve the case." Mary Anne sighed. "Did she tell you what the note said in their weird code?"

Peggy hadn't, but Happy was on the ramp, and he couldn't stop until the landing. "We've been friends our whole lives. These past weeks I've enjoyed investigating with you, even when threatened by a shotgun or haunted by ghosts."

"I'm sorry, too." Mary Anne frowned. "I hankered hard for this mystery."

"Don't tangle your line. I wanted to figure it out too." Enough lead-up jumps, time to send it off the big one. "Mary Anne, I'm trying to say, I'd like to solve more mysteries with you and—"

She grabbed him by the shirt and drew him in for a kiss. He landed it! He slid smoothly down the landing and prospected the pair of jumps further down the slope . . . No, a seasoned competitor knew when he achieved the top score, and a gentleman asked for permission.

"Hey," she said, pulling away. "I smell dogs burning."

"Dogs?" He sniffed the air and caught the charred scent. He leaned in for another kiss. "We can cook more dogs . . ."

"Come on!" She jumped off the rock, and Happy followed her.

They spent the rest of the day out by Abscond Pond. They enjoyed a bonfire, well-done dogs, lots of laughs, and a few things Happy kept for himself. A dedicated rider never revealed the best goods.

At dusk, they heard a rustling from the far edge of the pond. Was someone watching? They scanned the cattails and the maple saplings behind them. Nothing moved. Had they imagined the sound? And then, a brown nose poked out of the shadows, followed by a prodding hoof. He stepped into the open, pushing through the weeds with his sprawling pair of antlers. As he stretched towards the water for a sip, his dewlap brushed the surface, spreading ripples across the pond.

They savored every moment. While spotting a moose wasn't uncommon, sightings were often a year or two apart. After he drank his fill, the moose retreated into the shadows of the forest.

Happy suggested they vacate Abscond Pond as well, as daylight faded along with their fire. Mary Anne agreed, so they packed up and drove home. Happy tried convincing her to stay the night, but she had classes tomorrow.

The following Sunday, however, she returned for Closing Day! She picked up Happy on the way to the mountain, and they arrived before first chair. Fifty folks lined up before opening to give Rosefield Mountain the finish she deserved. Especially when this might be the final day of the resort's operation.

Happy and Mary Anne rode all day together. Well, they made out in the woods a few times, but they mostly kept their boards beneath their legs.

They shared chairs with a lot of friends. In the morning, Rufus joined them. He acted like his old self, with a smile broader than the blunt he smoked.

"Looking chipper, Rufus," said Happy.

"Your mom—Sheriff McStoots, I mean—she fixed it, man. She fixed it! I don't know how."

"You just need to fill out a form, bud," explained Mary Anne.

"Yeah . . . forms . . . I'll do all the forms!" Rufus contorted his arms and torso into different shapes. He seemed happy.

At separate points throughout the day, they rode the lift with each of the Powder Crew. They all had something to say about Mary Anne and

Happy.

"You're lucky I let you snare this one," said Tall Brad. "Just kidding, bud. She's the finest catch in all of Lake Rosefield."

"The two of you together," commented Handy Jesse, "is the biggest news since the false incarceration of Peter Smith. Happy, I'm pleased to inform you he's innocent! All a cover-up from the higher authorities who will . . ." Jesse continued about a Vermont state senator with purported connections to a Russian ambassador, or some other yarn even longer and more woven.

"You followed my advice," said Joey, "and landed it like I knew you would. Throw any tricks in yet? Give her a spin? Or a flip?"

"You watch yourself, Joey, or you'll be flipping right off this chair." Mary Anne knocked him in the helmet.

"Hey! You should treat me with a little more respect. I'm the hero of Rosefield. I caught the villain with the Big One."

"A beautiful shot," agreed Mary Anne. "And a better show. I've never seen so many fireworks duct-taped together."

"My cousin James uses stronger tape than the duct." Joey laughed and shook his head. Then his eyes landed on Happy, and his grin disappeared. "Sorry, I shot your uncle's car with the Big One."

"Honest to dog, I couldn't imagine a better target. Once the Staties issued a warrant for Uncle Pete, they'd have caught him anyway." Happy set up a mogul for his friend. "And as Mary Anne said, we enjoyed a fantastic show."

"Anyways, enjoy some turns." Joey banked two fingers across the fist. "And see you at Last Run!"

As the sun rose and baked the snow, the conditions turned to slush, and the coats came off. Shorts and t-shirts filled the hill. While he wore his Carpartt cutoffs and a white shirt filled with roses, Mary Anne took it one trot further by wearing a blue bikini! So distracted, Happy flew off the trail.

In the afternoon, they rode a chair with Jane. She wore ripped-up jeans, a white tank top, and aviator glasses to match her black pigtails.

"Are we sitting with the famous Jane Reech?" said Mary Anne.

"They've heard of me in Burlington?"

"Anyone who knows anything about Rosefield has heard of your deeds."

"Here's a deed no one knows." Jane leaned closer. "At Park & Grill, Jordan Herring said something sketchy. I hadn't noticed, not with Rodney's arrival and the Polish finale. The next morning I remembered. Something about his quick hands swiping stuff. Nothing specific, but I can recognize a thief.

"So I broke into his office. I rummaged through all seven of his shelves, pillaged every drawer in his desk, and overturned the carpet. Nothing. Was I mistaken? Noper. I discovered his stash in a lockbox I smashed open with a ski racing trophy."

"What did you find?" inquired Mary Anne. Meanwhile, Happy was still processing the nonchalant breaking and entering.

"Peter Smith's employee key card. And a Generally Slanted money purse with over fifty grand inside!"

"What?" Happy almost jumped off the chair. "Jordan stole the money?"

"Why the key card?"

288

'I'll admit, I considered these same questions for more than twenty-seven hours, but then I realized the truth. Rodney Buric Sr. hired Jordan to steal the money from Generally Slanted during the chaos of Yelsa's firing."

'Why would he steal from his son's resort?" questioned Mary Anne.

'To win their bet, of course."

'And why would Jordan do anything for Rodney's dad?" offered Happy.

'Simple, Buric Sr. pays well. I have proof he's already corrupted another Rosefieldian." Jane glanced at Happy before continuing. 'He isn't finished with Rosefield. I'll root out his influence. If he moves against our town, I'll show him my backhand. Repeatedly."

'And what about the key card?"

'When Buric Sr. learned of Peter's six-figure bonus, he decided to frame him with the purse. He had Jordan swipe the key card as they changed into their judging uniforms before Park & Grill. Jordan would plant the money in Peter's office and then anonymously turn him in. Except Peter was arrested and no longer required framing."

'Biscuit my dog." Happy shifted his helmet to scratch his head. 'So, Buric Sr. stole the Generally Slanted purse just to return it?"

'He's a businessman. Fifty grand is less than the six-figure bonus Peter would've received. Plus, he could install his own GM immediately."

'After you discovered the money purse," reasoned Mary Anne, 'you placed it for housekeeping to find, right?"

'You hit that deer head-on. To ensure Rodney Jr. won the bet with his father. No matter how awful the son is, Buric Sr.'s worse."

'Why not turn Jordan in?" asked Happy.

'Sure, I hankered. But what then? Buric Sr. would corrupt someone else with his riches. With Jordan free, I know exactly who to monitor." Jane shook her head. 'Besides, we lost a lot of folks this season. Timmy, Yelsa, Peter. Is Rosefield prepared to lose another?"

"We also lost our identity," said Mary Anne. "We lost our name."

"If only we could reinstate 'Rosefield Mountain,'" said Happy. "I can't tolerate another season of this 'Murder Mountain' nonsense."

Jane laughed. "Just wait until Last Run."

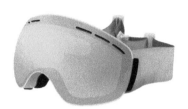

For the final lift service, everyone gathered at the top of the Absolute Zero Chair for the ceremonious picture. More than a hundred Rosefieldians, both permanent and seasonal, on their skis, snowboards, telemarks, snow blades, or snow skates. And Mickey brought up his favorite snow tube, and Cali Joe rocked his surfer board.

The Farney brothers wore their matching lumberjack outfits, as they did every year. The Roaster family dressed in matching brown overalls while handing out eight-ounce Gunpowders, their new canned brew. John and Henry Viceroy balled their fists at each other because they both hankered the new Sled Stop waitress, Kate. Oblivious to them, Kate stared at Maintenance Larry. Big Top and Jim McJoy stood next to each other, arms crossed and clad in flannel.

Danielle and Frederico worked their tongues harder than frogs at the fly hatchery. Boston Tony wore his Patriots jersey, Red Sox hat, and a pair of wristbands covered in four-leaf clovers. Annie and George from Montreal, liftie PJ, Wilma, and all her ski patrollers, the cafeteria cooks Piefer and Calvin, the Lobsters, Jordan Herring, and many more, all gathered for the season farewell.

Even Rodney Buric appeared. The surprised crowd quieted when he unloaded from the last chair. He skied down the ramp and stopped with surprising confidence. He wore his usual black suit jacket, with tight black ski pants and a pair of leather gloves. Francis skied at his side, sporting a bow tie and a brown suit vest. He served Rodney a microphone before skiing out of sight.

'Hello, my employees and clients! I am Rodney Buric. Now, I missed the Owner's Speech due to circumstances beyond my control. Today, I'm here to deliver that speech.

'I realize a lot of you don't know too much about me. I have preferred to rule from the shadows these past four years, how my father taught me to run a business. No more! I want you people to feel like I'm approachable.

'Here's a secret about me: I love anime. I always have, and I'm no longer afraid to admit that. My favorite one is *Soul Pestle*, except for—"

'Yo, *Soul Pestle* is *steep*!" shouted a teenager in a yellow Ski School jacket. 'It's my favorite, too!"

'Look at that," said Rodney with a broad smile, 'a young person with taste."

'And that ending, bro! Best ever!"

The smile vanished. 'What's your name?"

"Troy Vander!"

Rodney snapped his fingers, and Francis appeared at his side. Rodney whispered something to him, and then Francis skied off.

'Enough about me," continued Rodney. 'Despite my father's attempts to steal this mountain, I won. With Peter Smith arrested and the money purse recovered, I kept all the profits. Which means the mountain won't close! Not while I'm the owner! Here's one for me, your perfect boss! Hip hip . . ."

A few people responded.

'Of course," continued Rodney. 'I'd never have achieved all this without you . . . my clients. Remember, next year's passes are already on sale. If you want the cheapest rate, you should purchase them by the end of the month. Hip hip . . ."

An owl hooted.

Somehow, he remained unfazed. 'Lastly, my employees, you flourished this year. Let's repeat it next season. Here's one for Rosefield Mountain! Hip hip . . ."

'Hurray!" returned the crowd, now that they heard something worth cheering. Folks whistled, clapped, banged their ski poles, and stomped their snowboards.

'Did I say Rosefield?" continued Rodney once folks quieted. 'You heard correctly, from today on, no more Murder Mountain. Father wants the name to stay, but he doesn't own the resort. I do. And I declare this Rosefield Mountain Resort once more!"

The roar was heard all the way down in the parking lot. Folks cheered and laughed and danced clunkily in their ski boots. Happy grabbed Mary Anne and planted a big ol' smooch before spinning her around into a dip. Those late-night dancing lessons at the Sled had paid off.

One person remained quiet throughout. Jane leaned against her snowboard by the loading dock with an ear-to-ear smile. Happy waved, and she nodded in return.

'Are you all ready for the final run of the season?" shouted Rodney to a tremendous cheer. "Three, two, one, go!"

Everyone on the mountain descended at once in a cascade of bright clothes, laughter, and slush spraying through the spring sunshine.

Another season finished at Rosefield Mountain, which meant the beautiful summer awaited. What kind of stories brewed from those warm nights? Maybe a camping trip to a certain red barn . . .

Or not. Happy swore never to return, but Mary Anne was quite convincing.

Your favorite Rosefieldians will return! Look for *Day Trip to Jay Peak*, coming soon. And for our other upcoming projects, check out yarnauthority.com.

CPSIA information can be obtained
at www.ICGtesting.com
Printed in the USA
BVHW091315080421
604490BV00006B/349